Also By Sarah Dawson Powell

The Fragile Line Series

Beautiful.

Damaged.

Falling.

Pieces.

Changes.

Karma.

Invincible.

Breakable.

Dreams.

Nightmares.

Burn the Past.

Fireproof.

Bury the Ashes.

Stand-Alone Coming of Age Novels

The Truth About Gracie

In the Moonbeams

THIS IS
WHAT YOU
wanted

Sarah Dawson Powell

On The Rocks Publishing

Published by On The Rocks Publishing

1st edition 2025

ISBN 979-8-9997157-0-8

This book is for the ones who saw stepcousins to lovers
and said, "Sonofabitch, I'm in."

Trigger Warnings

THIS IS WHAT YOU WANTED

Strangulation (not of main character)

Murder (not of main character)

Crude language

Role-playing

Cheating (in the past)

Death of a parent in a flashback

Childhood abuse and neglect (in the past, does not occur on page)

Domestic abuse resulting in death (in the past)

Child sexual assault alluded to (FMC hears about children being trafficked & assaulted. There are no details & no children in the book are victims. FMC decides to make a career change based on what she learns.)

Suicidal ideation mentioned briefly as a feeling (in the past)

Mention of a possible drug overdose (not of a character, no drug use on page)

Sex/sex acts in public places

Fully described sex scenes with explicit descriptions including rough sex, begging, anal play, spitting, oral sex, masturbating, video recording of sex acts, bondage (of arms only), breath play.

THIS IS
WHAT YOU
wanted

PLAYLIST

scan the above code to listen on Spotify!

I Can Fix Him (No Really I Can)- Taylor Swift

logical- Olivia Rodrigo

I Hate Everything About You- Three Days Grace

illicit affairs- Taylor Swift

Don't Speak- No Doubt

Crazy In Love- Eminem

willow- Taylor Swift

Bipolar- Kiiara

Let You Down- NF

august- Taylor Swift

Iris- The Goo Goo Dolls

Sweet Child O' Mine- Guns N' Roses

All You Had To Do Was Stay (TV)- Taylor Swift

When I'm Gone- 3 Doors Down

Pushing Me Away- Linkin Park

King Of My Heart- Taylor Swift

Prologue

I easily spotted Emma's car in the parking lot of Burgandy; a high-end restaurant I've never taken her to. For a second, I consider that maybe if I had, I wouldn't be faced with the possibility of losing her.

I make a mental note to plan a date night somewhere even better.

A month or so ago, she sent the dreaded text while I was at work: *We need to talk*. Then of course she was sound asleep when I got home, making me wait until morning for her to tell me the same thing she'd told me a hundred times before.

"We have to stop, River," she said with tears in her eyes. "We're getting older, and we need to think about the future."

I shook my head, reminded her that she was my future. She remained adamant for a good thirty minutes until she got out of bed saying she needed a shower. I watched her walk away, letting out a sigh, thinking *here we go again*.

It's a cycle with us. One of us panics and tries to end things, insisting what we have isn't real, that we need to move on, but we never do.

After her shower, she returned to her bedroom where I was still sitting in her bed. Annoyance shot daggers from her eyes straight to my heart.

Ignoring her petulance, I got out of bed and approached her as she hunched over an open dresser drawer, a towel held loosely around her perfect body.

It took no effort to pull the towel away, revealing her smooth nakedness to me. My intention was to do things for her to remind her how good I can make her feel, but her frustration was too palpable. She pulled her towel from me, giving a rough shove to my shoulder as she turned away.

"Stop, River. Don't make this harder than it needs to be."

The rejection still stings my soul all these weeks later.

I can see her and her date, Daniel, through the window of the restaurant. They're sitting across from one another in a booth, twin martini glasses between them on the table. Daniel is talking animatedly, and Emma appears to be faking interest.

Daniel is a physical therapist. He enjoys spending time on his boat, hiking, and traveling. He volunteers at an animal shelter. His conversation skills are mid, telling of someone who was raised by parents who made him believe appearances are everything. Daniel doesn't waste his time with girls he wouldn't feel comfortable bringing home to meet the family.

This is the information I've gathered from the conversation he and Emma have had over Facebook Dating. But as I further stalked his social media profiles, I found that my assessment was right. He comes from an affluent family who is into philanthropy. He had a serious girlfriend in college, but her existence sort of vanished with their relationship, so I couldn't learn anything about her or why they called it quits.

The other thing I learned is that Daniel drives a black Mercedes S 500, which is parked way back in the parking lot with hopes it won't be damaged by errant car doors.

I watch Emma nod and force a smile at Dr. Dan, knowing he'd be a great catch for her. He'd probably treat her well, spoil her with luxurious gifts, and take her on exotic vacations. Their wedding would be no expenses spared, everything her little girl heart had ever dreamed of. I would be invited, of course, and I would attend. Then, mid-ceremony, right before they say I do, I would stand and casually walk to the front, pull out a gun and put a single bullet through Daniel's temple. Nice and clean.

I'd go to prison for life and Emma would find a new Daniel.

No point in letting it go that far.

My hand grips the cool metal of the pocketknife, pulling it from my jeans. The click of it popping open is drowned out by the sound of cars passing on the adjacent highway. I crouch down and quickly stab the driver's side front tire of Emma's car, the hiss of the air escaping louder than I expected, before rounding the car and repeating the quick motion on the other three wheels.

She'll know it was me and I don't even give a shit. I've had enough of her thinking she can leave me. It's exhausting having to constantly check her dating apps and track her location. My brain is a clouded mess, and I constantly feel like I'm on the verge of a breakdown. I need her and she needs me. Once she accepts this, we can move forward.

But we can't do that when assholes like Dr. Dan want to fuck shit up.

I walked through the parking lot back to where I parked several blocks away. It's an afterthought when I veer to the left toward the black Mercedes. At this point, Daniel is innocent in this game she and I are playing, but I don't like the threat he poses. He needs to understand that Emma will never be his.

I don't pop his tires. That would be too obvious. Something police would see as related to Emma's tires being slashed. Instead, I run the blade of my knife along the length of the passenger side of the sleek car, betting with myself that he won't even see the damage for a few days.

CHAPTER ONE

Emma

There are few things worse than doing the walk of shame through an apartment building parking lot in a bubblegum-pink mini-skirt and three-inch heels at eight o'clock on a Sunday morning, while do-gooder moms usher their kids into minivans on their way to Sunday school. When I spotted my car parked on the street, I stopped walking, realizing what one of those few worse things are.

"Mother fucker," I mutter under my breath.

The word WHORE is spraypainted in black along both sides of my white Toyota, across the trunk, the hood, and the windshield.

I stare at it for a moment, not surprised, and definitely not amused.

I'm not sure what I feel.

I fished my cell phone from my tiny purse, thrilled that my battery is still at ten percent. After snapping a pic of the vandalism, I unlock the driver's side door and get in. After I start the car and put my phone on the charger, I call my stepmom, Christy.

"Hey, hon," she answers on the second ring, sounding as chipper as the birds I wish would shut the fuck up. "You're up early."

Resting my head on my steering wheel, I let out a sigh and send the picture of my car to her. "Yeah. I stayed over at a friend's house last night." I pause, waiting for the picture to be delivered to her phone. When it does, I say, "I sent you a pic."

A moment later, she draws in a sharp breath. "Oh."

"I can't drive it like this, obviously," I tell her. "But I don't know who to call."

"No, of course not," she says quickly. "You're gonna have to call the police and file a report for insurance to cover it. The police can arrange a tow for you too."

"Okay."

"Who keeps doing this stuff?"

I swallowed the truth. "I don't know."

"Looks like you're somewhere there might be cameras. Maybe the cops can get the footage."

Nearly two hours later, after the police took their report and assured me a tow truck would take my car to a body shop, my friend Makenna picked me up.

She's eyeing the artwork on my car with amusement. "Whose damn apartment is this?"

I toss my purse in the back seat and unlock my phone, which is now at a whole thirty percent battery. "Tom? Ted? Something with a T."

"Was it Tucker? The one with the messy hair?"

Nodding, I say, "Sounds right. Tuck."

Makenna looks at me for the first time since I got into her car. "Was it worth it?"

"Was what worth it?" I open Snapchat as I'm talking. "Was the sex worth getting my car tagged? No. Was pissing River off so bad that he felt he needed to hunt me down and write 'whore' on my car worth it? Yes."

She laughs. "I will never understand you guys."

"Yeah, me either. But he'll be paying my deductible. Don't worry about that."

I'm checking my Snapchat story to see what I posted while I was drunk last night. Nothing overly incriminating, so I leave it all up. Then I cycle back through them all to make sure River saw every single story I posted. He did.

"Do you still share your location with him?"

I shake my head. "No, but he always figures it out anyway."

"Where am I taking you?"

"Home." I open a Snap from River. It's literally him spraying a big black W on my driver's side door. It wasn't like I didn't know he did it. I just wished he hadn't. That maybe Tad or Tim or whoever it was that fucked me with his half-limp dick a few hours ago had a psychotic, jealous ex who saw me going into his apartment.

Makenna is going on about how River probably has a GPS on my car and that I should hide out at her house just to fuck with him some more, but I'm not listening because I'm watching River write WHORE on my car.

Then he flips the camera to show himself. He's wearing a black hoodie, a tuft of his blond hair sticking out from underneath. A shit-eating grin is wide on his face. "Someone's been a bad girl," he says.

I roll my eyes, close out the app, and toss my phone onto Makenna's dash so hard she jumps in her seat beside me.

"Calm down," she says.

"I am calm. I'm just hungover and want to go home."

Makenna is one of the few people who seem to even remotely understand the relationship between me and River. It's why I called her. She has relationship issues that she sometimes talks with me about, but she also has boundaries with Jack. Boundaries I'm not sure I want with River.

When I get home, anticipation tingles inside me with the wonder of what I'll find when I enter our apartment. River's black Jeep is sitting in the parking lot, so I know he's home. When I left Theo's house at just before eight, I had been hoping to get home before River was awake so I could just crawl into bed unscathed. Now it was after ten and he was most likely out of bed. Probably sitting at his desk in the living room playing some asinine video game on the computer.

Sure enough, when I walk in, he's doing exactly what I expected. He's shirtless with his headphones on his head, talking to someone on his mic. He doesn't even look in my direction.

I toss my purse in his general vicinity. Much to my satisfaction, it lands on his keyboard. Before he can react, I duck into the kitchen.

"What the fuck, Emma?" he yells from behind me.

I open the dishwasher and pull out my favorite yellow insulated tumbler. As I start filling it with ice from the dispenser on the fridge, River comes into the room. His cheeks are red and that makes me smile. I love it when he gets flustered. "What's the matter? Did I fuck up your game?"

He cocks his head and paints a smile on his perfect face. "Did I fuck up yours?"

I switch from filling my cup with ice to filling it with water. "Nope, just my car." Shrugging, I add, "Police are gonna pull the surveillance footage from that apartment complex."

He tries to intimidate me with a hard glare. It's a lie, about the police, but let him sweat about it. "Good thing I'm smart enough not to take my

Jeep there. Good thing I'm smart enough to know not to park anywhere near where you are." He moves closer to me. "I'm really sad I didn't ruin your night."

I laugh, pulling my cup from the dispenser. "By the time I saw it, the night was over. Dude was probably balls deep inside me while you were out there with your art supplies thinking you're ruining my good time."

River knocks the cup out of my hand. It falls to the floor with a metallic thud. Water and ice spill onto the laminate floor at our feet. Neither of us look down.

"I'm really fucking thirsty, asshole. Kinda hungover too and not in the mood for your shit."

He pops his neck and sucks in a quick breath. "You're fucking thirsty alright."

I bend to pick up my cup and start the process over, anxious to be done with this bullshit, take a shower and sleep until work tomorrow. When I stand back up, I can tell he's waiting for me to say something back, but I'm not going to. I don't even look at him. Ice falls into my cup and then I switch to the water.

River McIntyre does not scare me. I'd be lying if I said he never had, but those times are rare now. Nearly nine years of whatever the hell this is has allowed me to see every shade he has to offer and there is only one that scares me anymore.

This one wasn't it.

He backs away a few inches. "Did he use a condom?"

I roll my eyes. Of fucking course he did. I'm not stupid.

When I pull my cup from the dispenser this time, I turn to get the lid and straw in the dishwasher, but River is already holding them in his hand for me. I take them and secure the lid before putting the straw between my lips and pulling in a long drink. The cold water feels so good on my palate before flowing down my parched throat.

He knows I'm dismissing this conversation, dismissing him. That's why when I turn around, River is hovering over me with is six-foot-two height, making me press my back against the kitchen counter to create a mirage of distance between us.

"I'm gonna go shower," I say casually, as if his proximity isn't making my pulse race.

"Did he use a condom?" His voice is lower when he asks a second time.

I screw up my face. "Why do you care? It's not like we're fucking."

His eyes go dark. He tugs on my lower lip with his thumb. "Maybe not today, but you know it'll happen again."

My breath catches and I hope he doesn't notice. There's a flutter in my gut yearning for what's supposed to come next.

River's hand runs down my left hip and pulls up the edge of my bubblegum pink skirt. He rubs his thumb slowly across the thin fabric of my underwear as he keeps his sapphire blue eyes locked with mine. He tugs roughly at the fabric, pulling it away from my body like he's debating ripping them off me. My body tingles and I swear I can feel my pussy crying for his touch. I fucking hate that he has this power over my body.

"Was it good?" he whispers. "Did he make you come?"

No and no.

"Did you have to beg him to stop after your fifth orgasm?"

Considering there wasn't even one orgasm, no.

"Were you wishing he was me?"

I was.

I turned my face to the side, his thumb falling away.

River crouches down in front of me, lifting my skirt with both hands. I wiggle some, trying half-heartedly to deter him. His eyes locked on my face, not my underwear or what's hidden behind them.

"Is it going to smell like a rubber or some asshole's sweaty balls?"

I don't give him the pleasure of an answer. He's going to check for himself regardless of anything I say. I'm not even sure he can actually detect whether or not a condom was used just by smell.

I'll have to Google that later.

He pushes my thighs apart with no resistance on my part. I'm anxious, feeling the burn inside me for him. For this half-evil, half-god man that I cannot get enough of. There's a throb at the apex of my legs, crying out for his mouth to possess it.

The tickle of his finger over the fabric of my lace underwear causes me to draw in a breath. He flashes a satisfied smirk before pushing my underwear to the side and taking an exaggerated whiff of my heated flesh.

I fucking want him. I want him every damn day and he knows it. But I have to play coy, as if my heart and body aren't his. I'm never going to be able to move on. I will never love anyone the way I love River.

Some things aren't as easy as they seem.

"What's it smell like?" I take a sip of my water, hopefully giving the impression that what he's doing has zero effect on me.

He sniffs again. "Smells like me."

I furrow my brow and pull my neck back. "Like you?"

Quickly, he nods. "Smells like me because it's mine."

Before I can even attempt to come up with a response, his tongue darts out and his face pushes against my center as he licks the length of my folds, sucking my clit between his lips for nowhere near long enough.

My head falls back. One of my knees gives out. I groan, pushing my hips forward into his face, ready and desperate for more.

But he stands in front of me, amused by the control he has over my body. Amused by how weak he can make me.

It's fine. As long as I stand my ground overall, some rules can be bent. Pretty sure we stopped caring about rules in high school anyway.

I need his face between my legs again. And while I briefly debate being the weak little bitch that I am and begging him, giving him the power he loves to have, I need to be strong. That's way more important than an orgasm.

He backs away, laughing at my obvious plight. "I licked it. It's mine."

My jaw drops, my desire shriveling into nothing. "What are you, twelve?"

He laughs as he leaves the kitchen.

I follow him.

"Imagine if we got to be twelve again." Spinning his desk chair around, he falls into it and looks at me. "Would you do it all again?"

I swallow. River is such a big part of me. Erase what we've shared for the last eighteen years, or even just the eleven he's referring to, and I'm not sure I'd want that life. But there was something I would change.

"If I was six, I would tell my dad that I don't want to go to your stupid birthday party."

Frowning, he looks away. I've said it a million times before. It's nothing new. We were clueless then, but that day, our whole future changed while we held hands jumping in an inflatable bounce house with our classmates, and it had nothing to do with us.

"I don't know, Emma. I probably still wouldn't be good enough for you."

Chapter Two

River

Emma stands in front of her closet staring at her clothes so long that I wonder if she's fallen back asleep standing up. The light is always dim in her bedroom, making it feel cozy no matter the time of day, but it can also make it hard to see her face if she's not beside me.

I wish I had a more normal work schedule like her, but I knew what I was getting into when I chose criminal justice as my college major. Now I'm destined for years of working odd hours before I climb my way up the seniority ladder into something better.

With a short-sleeved yellow dress in her hand, Emma turns around. I closed my eyes, pretending to still be asleep. I call it self-preservation. By avoiding conversation with her, I am protecting myself and my feelings.

I have more feelings than I know what to do with sometimes.

Emma Novak is my soul mate, no question about it. She knows it as well as I do. She just needs time to accept it.

Or something.

It's complicated. But when I tell her that, she argues that there's nothing complex about our relationship and that the reality of who we are is as plain as the nose on my face.

"River." Her voice pulls me from my thoughts. My eyes pop open just in time to see the yellow dress fall into place over her lower half. Fuck, I love yellow on her. It makes her skin look tanner, which makes her beautiful sienna eyes stand out. "Will you have time to do any laundry today?"

"Maybe." I sit up. "What do you need done?"

She gestures toward her laundry basket in the corner. Then she bends down and pulls a few things out, tosses them on the foot of the bed. "Actually, just these. If you're doing your own stuff, you could just add this in."

I washed my laundry over the weekend, not that I would tell her that. "I can wash all of it if you want me to."

Our eyes meet briefly before she looks away. "Just this." She leaves the room, and I lie down again. "Thanks."

I don't have to work until three in the afternoon. By the time I get home from work, she will be asleep. Unlike me, she sleeps like a log. She rarely wakes when I get home, and lately, when she does, it's to glare at me.

She used to text me before she fell asleep, asking to be woken up when I got home. Telling me what she wanted me to do to her body.

And then I would break multiple traffic laws, my dick already hard, as I hurried home to the girl who *is* my home.

Now, after I leave work shortly after midnight, I take my time, knowing I won't be doing anything except sit at my desk and game like the loser she sees me as. It's honestly the only thing that takes my mind off reality.

Reality is that she's right, but only to a point. Our relationship was doomed from the start. But fuck what people think. If we're happy and love each other, then whose business is it anyway?

Fuck our families. They'll get over it.

Remembering that she doesn't have a car, thanks to me and my 'art supplies,' as she so eloquently put it, I offer her a ride.

"I already requested an Uber, but thanks anyway, asshole."

Yep, I'm definitely the asshole.

This time.

When she leaves for work thirty minutes later, I get up and go to the bathroom. Then I return to her room and make her bed, complete with the useless throw pillows. Then I gather her laundry and bring it to the living room. After pulling my favorite Illini South University hoodie over my head, I tuck my feet into my slides, gather Emma's laundry into one arm, and leave the apartment, heading for the laundry room with a pocket full of quarters and the jug of detergent.

It's only when I'm putting her clothes into the washer that I take note of what she gave me to wash. The cheeky, pink lace underwear she was wearing yesterday morning are included.

I narrow my eyes at the sexy undergarment, anger ticking inside me.

What the hell does she need these washed immediately for? Does she have a date? With the shaggy haired dude that she went home from Club W with on Saturday night?

Fuck. I should've gone through her phone while she was sleeping.

I pull the underwear to my nose, breathing in her musk, recalling the sweet taste of her I was briefly blessed with yesterday morning.

When I hear footsteps in the hallway, I drop the underwear into the washer with the other items.

"Hey, River," Lillian from apartment two says as she walks in.

"Hey," I say casually, as if I haven't fucked the shit out of her a handful of times.

"Laundry day?"

I shake my head. "Just some of Emma's things."

Her basket thuds loudly on the table behind me. She leans against the washer adjacent to mine. Her arms are crossed over her chest as she looks up at me. "I just saw her leave in some dude's car."

I place the quarters into their slots in the coin slide. "It was an Uber. Her car's in the shop."

"All I'm hearing is that she's not home." Lillian is short, standing just over five feet tall. She's also very thin with a small chest. Her blonde hair is in two braids on either side of her head. It's not abnormal to see her wearing clothes that look like they were intended for children, like the shirt she has on now with a unicorn and rainbow pattern.

I fight against rolling my eyes at what she implies. "I'm good."

"I know you are."

My smirk is involuntary. Lillian is twenty-eight. She has a five-year-old son named Paxton. Which means she had him when she was twenty-three, the same age as Emma and I are now. "I have a lot to do before work." It's a lie. All I need to do is jack off once or twice, eat, and waste the morning playing Fortnite.

She pushes her slight body off the washer. "You know where to find me."

There are other weird things about Lillian besides the way she dresses. It was pretty creepy when she told me her bedroom was directly below Emma's and that when she heard us fucking above her, it turned her on. I wondered if she could hear the things we said to each other. When Emma begged me to fuck her harder, commanding that I don't fucking stop. Or when her throat made gagging sounds while I plowed my dick into her face. Could she hear us scream each other's names, Emma begging for more, as we came? Or did she just hear the creak of the bed and the thump of it hitting the wall?

Did she notice when those noises stopped two months ago after Emma declared that we had no future and needed to stop what we had been doing for the past eight years and start thinking about the future?

A future where she thought it was even remotely possible for us to move on to other people and find happiness apart.

Yesterday, after I licked her pussy in the kitchen, she showered, got in bed, and turned on the TV. When I looked in at her midafternoon, she was asleep, her lips parted just slightly.

I did nothing but sit on my computer the whole fucking day.

When she got up to go to the bathroom early in the evening, I told her I was going to DoorDash some Mexican food from our favorite place.

"Just get me what I always get," she said when she came out of the bathroom.

She stood near her bedroom door staring at me for a long moment. I stared back. Then she sighed, turned, and went back into her bedroom.

By the time the food came, she was asleep again.

While she showered, I had gone into my bedroom and jacked off, hoping she was doing the same in the shower.

Emma and I were born on the same day, in the same hospital. Eight hours and twelve minutes apart. Then we landed in the same pre-kindergarten class two years in a row. In kindergarten, we had different teachers, but in first grade we were in the same class once again. We attended the same after school program at the YMCA.

There is nothing that will ever convince me our fate wasn't written in the stars.

Our families didn't know each other back then, so it's not like they had a hand in bringing us together. If anything, they're what keeps us apart. They're the reason we chose the same college four hours away from home.

The reason we have lived in lies for eight fucking years.

After I ate my Mexican food last night, I showered, brushed my teeth and climbed into bed beside her. She detected my presence even in her slumber and rolled to me, resting her head on my shoulder. I slid my arm around her, pulling her tight before kissing her caramel-colored hair.

It's so much easier to sleep when she's beside me.

And she thinks I can just move the fuck on.

Back in the apartment, I have about thirty minutes before I need to switch the clothes to the dryer. I sit at the desk and pick up my phone, ignoring the notifications, and choose my photo app. After face ID activates and allows me access to my hidden photos, I scroll to my favorite video. The one from our freshman year of college. Back when nothing seemed impossible. When we were on top of the world thinking we had fooled everyone.

Turns out we were only fooling ourselves.

We're in Emma's dorm room. Her roommate was rarely there, spending all her time at her older boyfriend's apartment off campus.

In the video, I'm sitting on Emma's tiny twin-sized bed, my back against the wall. She's lying across the length of the bed, her legs over mine, only wearing her underwear and a bralette.

"Are you taking a picture?" she asked me as I spanned the length of her body with the phone.

"Video."

"Stop," she says with a laugh.

I focus the camera on her face. "You don't trust me?"

She bites the side of her lip. I know she trusts me. We have to trust each other when we're holding onto a secret bigger than either of us.

I keep the camera focused on her face while my other hand slides between her legs, rubbing her clit over her underwear. There's a change in her soft eyes; she blinks a few times before lifting her chin and letting out a breath. As I lowered the camera to where my hand was, I spit on my fingers, then slid her underwear out of the way. It's warm and slick behind the fabric, my spit unnecessary.

I look up at her, not that this is seen on camera, our eyes meeting while I rub the length of her soft folds. When I tease my thumb over her clit, she groans, pressing against my hand softly.

"Promise you won't show this to anyone." Her request is simple and something I easily agree with. It's a promise I keep even now. There are so many more videos that I've accumulated since then, but this one was the first. And it's my favorite because there's a hint of innocence to it. Not that either of us were innocent at this point.

I push a finger inside of her, just one at first, knowing she prefers two.

As I watch the video now, four years later, it makes me sad but it's also the quickest turn on other than Emma herself. I set my phone on my desk, leaned against the monitor, and pull my dick out. Rummaging in my top desk drawer, I find my small bottle of lube and squeeze some into my hand. In the video, I have two fingers knuckles deep inside her. The familiar, comforting sounds of her low groans can be heard. I'm hard, now and in the video.

Emma loves to fuck. She loves everything about it. Whore is a term of affection. My dirty little whore. Dirty little secret. Secret whore.

I wish my fingers were deep inside her now, pressing on her G-spot and making her convulse against me while she curses my name. Just like she's doing in the video.

The camera view changes as I prop up my phone on her desk chair beside the bed. Her face cannot be seen anymore, but her amazing body is right there front and center. I hover over her, tugging down her underwear as she lifts her hips. Then she pulls her bralette over her head, her perfect handful sized tits bouncing back into place. I lean over her, naked too now, and kiss her while she grabs my cock and rubs it over her weeping flesh. My mouth lowers to her breasts, sucking in the nipple of the one closest to the camera, as I push the head of my cock inside her.

I have to pause all other functions as my length moves into her on the first stroke. It happens every single time. That feeling of her muscles gripping around me, warm and wet, was like losing my virginity all over again every single time I fucked her. It was like winning the lottery. Being given a priceless gift.

Emma was a priceless gift. One I apparently couldn't afford.

It's maybe only two seconds, but I would give my life to be able to feel that euphoria. And it's only her that can do it. When I'm fucking someone else, there is no pause. Yeah, it feels good. I get off. But it's not sex with Emma.

And she thinks we can move on.

Things progress quickly on the video with her legs on my shoulders while I hammer into her. She is groaning and calling out to God, telling me not to stop. Telling me harder. Telling me she loves when I fuck her.

I know she loves more than just fucking me. She loves me.

I pull my dick out of her. "Roll over."

She follows my command, sticking her ass in the air, her cheek flat on the mattress when she looks directly into my phone. "Are you still recording?" I thrust inside her and her brows pulled together. "Fuck!" she calls out. "That's so good, baby."

Her hips are bucking back into mine and I know I'm about to blow—in the video and now. I grab her by her hair, jerking her head back and off the mattress. Her hand moves between her legs, her fingers going to work on her clit. A stream of nonsense laced with expletives runs out of her mouth as I fuck her as hard as I can. "Holy shit." She gasps when she brings herself to climax and I know I'm about to fill her up with my own release.

I'm about to blow my load sitting in my desk chair too but suddenly I have an idea.

Squirting a little more lube into my palm, I continue to stroke my member with rigor. I get up, go into Emma's bedroom, and open her top dresser drawer, grabbing the entire pile of clean underwear. I drop them onto her bed, spreading them out just as my balls tighten up. Closing my eyes, I visualize all the times I've fucked her over the side of this bed standing exactly where I am now.

My climax creeps in, like a generic, off-brand orgasm. I feel it but just barely.

It's always like that unless I'm with her.

No matter. While the climax is borderline unsatisfying, the amount of semen that comes out isn't disappointing.

For me at least.

And it's more than enough to coat the underwear laying on her bed.

Chapter Three

Emma

Our freshman year of college felt like freedom. We were in a new town where no one knew us, which meant we were free to be whoever we wanted to be.

River and I chose to be a couple.

In our minds, we were always a couple, but it had been a secret. Literally no one knew.

We both had relationships with other people during high school. Mine were fleeting, lasting a month, tops. I never let anyone do anything more than kiss me. Even that felt like cheating.

Cheating on someone who could never be mine.

River, however, didn't have the same restraint as me.

I'm not even sure it was restraint that I had. It was that I just wanted him and only him.

But he fucked Nora Chandler, this redhead who changed boyfriends more than anyone else, our junior year. He came to my house afterwards and cried himself to sleep in my bed beside me, refusing to tell me why he was so upset. I played with his hair and assured him everything would be okay, assuming his mom was drunk and lashing out like she often did.

Two days later, the rumor made it to me.

Apparently, he stopped before he finished, apologized, and said, "I can't do this."

After school, I went to his house, let myself in and went up to his bedroom to wait for him, checking his location constantly on my phone. I had a feeling he was checking mine too and that's why he went to McDonald's and the gas station before coming home. He knew I was pissed.

When I heard him ascending the stairs, I got off his bed and stood behind the door. As soon as he opened it, I jumped out and smacked him across his face. His hand grabbed my wrist before I could hit him again, so I lifted my other hand. He grabbed that wrist too and pushed me against the wall.

I was crying, a mix of anger and hurt. "Why?"

His face was redder than his normal ruddy color. "I'm sorry, Emma. I'm so fucking sorry."

It was there in his eyes that he was sorry. And I forgave him.

The Nora incident prompted a long discussion over several weeks about what the hell we were doing. We had to appear like normal high schoolers who weren't hiding something. Not everyone in high school dates and that was what I thought we should do. I pointed out that everyone already knew we were close so our friendship wouldn't set off any alarms.

River disagreed. We had both dated a handful of people at this point and he thought it would be more suspicious if we both stopped, especially right after he stuck his dick in someone else.

He promised he would never do it again. Promised he would only ever love me and that his love would last forever. Promised that someday we would figure it all out together and get married.

Turns out River is a liar.

I'm reminded of how vile River McIntyre is when I get home from work and find my underwear in a pile on my bed covered in his crusty ass seed.

My vision clouds. I'm fuming mad immediately, already trying to come up with a way to get him back. Yesterday, he tagged my car. Today, he jacks off on my underwear. I've really been trying not to engage with him and this bullshit he thinks is going to tell me how much he still wants me. If I ignore it, he'll stop eventually, right?

I go to the kitchen to get some paper towels so I can cover my hands when I pick up my underwear and toss them into the laundry basket. I'm distracted by my phone vibrating on the counter; Megan McIntyre's name displayed across the screen with a picture of her that's at least fifteen years old. Though I'm tempted not to, I answer it. "Hello?"

"Hey, Emma. Did I catch you at a bad time?"

If by a bad time she means did she catch me while I was trying to clean her son's cum off my bed? Then yes, this is a very bad time. "No, I just got home."

"Oh, okay, good." Her tongue clicks. "Do you know if River works the weekend of Mother's Day? We're trying to plan a brunch with Noni and want to be sure you guys can make it."

I walk over to River's desk in the living room and look at the calendar hanging on the wall beside it. It's still open to April, so I flip the page to May. "Hold on, let me check." In the time it takes me to check, I consider saying he's off even if he isn't. That way they will plan the brunch when he's working and— oops!— looks like I'll have to go alone.

Except Noni is inching ridiculously close to taking a permanent vacation and I would never forgive myself if it was the last chance River had to see her.

Turns out it's his weekend off. "Looks like he's off."

"Oh, good! We will plan on brunch on Mother's Day. And Saturday night we can go out for an early birthday dinner for you and Riv." I can hear the excitement in her voice. "Does that sound good?"

"Yeah, I'm writing it on the calendar right now." I'm not. "I'll tell River to see if he can get off that Friday so we can head up there when I get off work instead of waiting until Saturday morning."

While I'm talking to River's mother, I spot the travel size bottle of lube on the desk. River has lube in every room of our apartment. He used to keep it in his Jeep until it got really hot and leaked all over inside his center console.

After hanging up, I open the lube and empty it on the seat of his four-hundred-dollar gaming chair, watching as it drips to the carpet below. I roll my neck, close the cap, and set it back where I had found it. It doesn't seem like enough, so I find the lube from the bathroom, my bedroom, the kitchen— yes, the kitchen— and his bedroom.

I don't even know why he has lube in his bedroom. He never sleeps in there. We've had sex in there, but it's not one of our go-to spots. And it's not like he has anyone over.

Or maybe he does.

All the more reason to drizzle lube on his mouse, keyboard, and headset. I squirt it on his curved monitors, watching it run down the screen and then drip onto the desk.

Oops.

I'm positive replacing all that shit will still cost less than the damage he did to my car.

Before returning to the cum stained underwear in my bedroom, I text River. *Thanks so much for the present you left on my bed.* I add several heart emojis. *Call me on your lunch.*

When I'm on my way back up to the apartment from the laundry room, I spot Lillian, our downstairs neighbor, with her son Paxton. I can't stand her. She gives me 'pick-me' vibes so hard. Plus, I'm pretty sure River is fucking her.

"Hey, girl!" she calls out.

I force a smile and direct it at Paxton. "Hey, Paxton. How was school today?"

"Good," he says, uninterested.

"Have you guys checked out that new club that opened downtown?" Lillian asks. "Club W?"

I nodded. "Yeah, I went this weekend. It was okay."

"I'm thinking about going Friday while Pax is at his dad's. You wanna go?"

River is off this Friday. If I go out while River is off, I'm likely to have a repeat of the other night. "Maybe. Text me later this week and I'll let you know."

I'm eating the Mexican food River ordered for me the night before when he calls. "Hey," I say flatly when I answer.

"Hey, babe. What's up? You liked your present?"

I roll my eyes. "Stop calling me that."

"Calling you what?"

"Babe."

He hesitates. "What am I supposed to call you?"

"Em. Emma. Emma Lynn. Emma-lemma-ding-dong. I don't give a fuck. Just stop with the babe."

"Whatever." His tone is deeper. He's pissed and I'm fucking ecstatic.

Time to make it real. "Aunt Megan called earlier—"

"Don't call her that."

I laugh. "What?"

"You're just trying to piss me off now. Do you actually need something?"

"Yeah. Take off work next Friday so we can go home for Mother's Day and see Noni one last time."

"One last time? Is she sick?"

"No, just old. So, we need to assume every time is the last time."

"God, and I thought I was the fucked up one."

"No worries. You definitely are." I spear a slice of steak from my fajita platter with my fork. "Oh, and they're treating us to a birthday dinner that Saturday. And so, since I don't want to drive up there Saturday and drive back the next day, I need you to take Friday off so we can go up there when I get off work."

"Why don't you just take Monday off?"

"Why don't you just jack off? Maybe on your own fucking clothes."

He chuckles. "I fucking love you."

I hung up on him.

I hung up on him because I fucking love him so damn much that it's painful. Like, my heart literally aches for him twenty-four-seven.

Yes, his mom is *technically* my *step*-aunt. Megan McIntyre's sister, Christy, married my dad when River and I were ten. Christy met my dad when he brought me to River's birthday party in first grade. The following weekend, she brought River to my birthday party, anxious to connect with the single dad she met the week before, I guess. That's when my dad asked her out and they've been together ever since.

It was exciting. Me and River were friends but then we got to be cousins. No one else we knew had a cousin in the same grade. We were inseparable and no one tried to stop it. Everyone said how cute it was that we were so close. When we said we were boyfriend and girlfriend, everyone laughed, amused by our innocence.

Until it wasn't cute or funny anymore.

Over dinner one night in the fall of sixth grade, Christy looked over at me as I rambled on about something that happened at school, while feeding my little brother Eli bites of jarred baby food. "Emma, you know River can't actually be your boyfriend, right?"

"What do you mean?"

"He's your cousin. Your cousin can't be your boyfriend."

I was fucking mortified. River and I had pretended to get married a hundred times. We'd made lists of baby names and picked out what kind of dogs we wanted. He was going to be a lawyer like his dad, and I wanted to be a doctor.

When I told him what Christy said, his reply was simple. "They can't tell us what to do."

As we grew older and became more aware of the truth of our relationship, we learned that legally there is nothing stopping us from being together. We *can* get married. We *can* have kids, and it would be without complications because we aren't blood related.

The problem was that no one would accept our relationship. Not our friends and definitely not our family. It became a wedge between us as we became more conscious about what we said and did around others.

And then suddenly everything was a secret because we were afraid.

Now we're here. Facing the reality that we should have accepted when we were kids. There was no way to continue our relationship. It had to end.

It was time to figure out how to let go and learn how to love someone else.

I have no idea what time it was when River came to bed that night. All I know is that I sleep like I'm dead and nothing he does when he comes home wakes me.

Except when he rips my fucking underwear off and sucks my clit into his mouth.

"Oh, my... fuck." I reach under the blanket and run my hands through his hair, pulling his face against me tighter. One of his arms is wrapped around my thigh, reaching up into my T-shirt and tugging gently on my nipple. The fingers of his other hand are probing deep inside me, tickling my most sensitive spots.

Fuck the rules. Fuck this being wrong. I can't even think straight with the quickness he's bringing me to the verge of ecstasy.

No one will ever know my body like River does. I've tried. I've fucking tried. They lick at my center like it's a fragile piece of glass that's gonna break when they apply too much pressure. Like it's some rare food they've never tried and are afraid they won't like. They couldn't find a clit if it had a lighthouse beacon pierced through the center of it.

River knows what I like. He knows my pussy isn't breakable. He knows what a clit is and what I want him to do to it.

I told him no more but when he does shit like this, I question if I will ever really be able to walk away.

He throws the blanket off us; his mouth and fingers still working me like a skilled pianist on opening night. My climax ebbs forward and I start to groan, crying in sweet agony, pulling his hair so hard I think there might be a bald spot when we're done. My whole body is thrumming, vibrating from his touch.

Just as my orgasm falls into position, ready for take-off, he lets go of my clit and pulls his fingers out of me. He stops twisting my nipple and flicks it once—hard.

River rolls to his side. Lifting my head, I let go of his hair and look down at him. He's illuminated by the light of the TV that I leave on when I'm home alone. "What the actual fuck?"

He's grinning and shirtless, only wearing his uniform pants. They're unzipped and I can see the outline of his dick pressing against the fabric of his boxer briefs. "What's the matter, babe?"

"You're just gonna leave me hanging?"

Sitting up, he looks over at me. "Sorry about that. I keep forgetting we broke up." He uses air quotes when he says, *broke up.* "I mean..." He cocks his head and runs a finger down the inside of the thigh closest to him. "Unless you want me to..."

"I want you to fucking die." Not really. Because there is no fucking way I could live in a world where River is no more.

Fuck. Why is this so hard?

"But not until you finish this." I reach out for his hair, planning to direct his face back to where it belongs.

Jumping from the bed, he lets out a laugh. "Not so quick." He reaches out for my hand. I give it to him, and he pulls me from the bed before giving me a light shove into our stark living room. He yanks my hands behind my back, holding my wrists together. We walk over to his desk, and I remember what I did with the lube.

Fuck.

River doesn't say a word. But he also doesn't let go of my wrists. He runs his fingers across his keyboard, and I bite back a smile. He's pissed, and I realize he didn't bring me out here because he wants to eat me out somewhere besides my bed.

His slick fingers rub across my swollen, hungry center and I shudder at his touch.

Then he tugs at a wire that connects his headphones to something else, pulling it loose from both ends.

I roll my eyes, realizing what he's about to do. And sure enough, he starts wrapping the wire around my wrists, securing them together. I pull my hands away, turning my face toward him. "I don't have time for this shit. I have to work in the morning."

One of his hands comes up around my throat, holding me in place with my back pressed against his front. "And I'm wide awake, pissed off, and bored." He squeezes my neck gently. "I just wanna hang out with my favorite cousin and have a little fun." My skin prickles when he moves his hand up to my chin and pries open my mouth, hooking two fingers on my cheek. "Is that so much to ask?"

He's pressing against me, his erection hard on my lower back. I want him. I just don't want the games. Not tonight.

I jerk my head to the side and tug my hands away from him, realizing they're already bound by the wire which he's holding in place. "It is, River." My words come out garbled with his fingers in my mouth.

My attempts at pulling away fall flat as he jerks my arms back to him, quickly tying the wire, before spinning me to face him. His eyes are dark but, fuck, if I don't love when he looks at me like this.

"Why are you doing this to me?" he asks. "You can't fucking deny that you love me. You can't deny you don't want to be with me." I swallow down the lump in my throat and divert my gaze as his eyes glaze over. "You would rather just be miserable the rest of your life than figure out how to make this work?"

I look up at him. "Fine. Right now. Call your mom."

He shakes his head, frowning. "Why? So that you can walk away again when they all object and toss out ultimatums?"

I step closer, pressing my front against him. He doesn't touch me, just lowers his forehead so it's resting on the top of my head. I wish my hands weren't bound because I want to hold him. Hold him and tell him lies. Tell him it's all going to be fine when I know it never will be.

Chapter Four

River

I'm not sure why Emma thinks the two of us going to Club W with Lillian is a good idea. Particularly since she has accurately accused me of fucking our neighbor multiple times. It's whatever, I guess.

I offer to drive. Emma still has a rental, and Lillian has a booster for Paxton in the back seat of her car and fuzzy pink puffballs hanging from the rearview mirror. Plus, I get to control the music if I'm driving. It's a rule we've had since we turned sixteen. Whoever is driving gets to control the music.

Not that we can hear any music over Lillian's incessant talking.

"Fuck, you talk a lot," Emma says, mirroring my thoughts. "Doesn't your jaw ever get tired?"

"Only when I eat pussy," she replies.

Emma and I exchange glances, waiting for Lillian to laugh or say she's kidding.

She doesn't.

"Seriously?" Emma turns in her seat to look at Lillian.

"Hell, yeah! I love going down on bitches, but it's a hell of a lot more work than sucking cock."

Emma faces forward and picks up her phone.

"You wanna go down on Emma?" I snicker.

Emma jerks her face in my direction, daggers from her eyes shooting me. She looks so pissed off and I want to grab her face and kiss it. Without warning, she grabs one of the rubber ducks from the dashboard of my Jeep and whips it at me. It hits my shoulder and falls onto my lap.

"For sure," Lillian says. "You're gorgeous, Em. I would go down on you in a heartbeat. We can do it right now if you're up for it. River can watch."

Now I turn around, tossing the duck back onto the dash. "You're fucking with us."

She shrugs. "Kinda. I'd prefer not to bang in a car but sometimes you gotta do what you gotta do."

"I cannot," Emma starts, "think of a single scenario where fucking in a car is a 'gotta do what you gotta do' type situation."

Oh, I definitely can. When we were in high school, we fucked in the car. Hers. Mine. Our parents'. We fucked anyplace we thought we wouldn't get caught because the chances of getting busted at home were higher than anywhere else. It was without a doubt a 'gotta do what you gotta do' situation.

"I'm just saying, I would definitely be down for having a threesome with you both." Lillian pauses. "I get so jealous hearing you go at it like you do. The other night was, what? Two or three times? I'm not even gonna lie. I can easily get myself off just listening to you guys."

Even if I tried, I couldn't count the number of times I've woke Emma up by sucking on her clit. My whole plan Monday night had been to make her sit on my lubed-up desk chair to get her ass nice and slick. Then

I was going to push her face-down-ass-up on the floor and slide my cock right into her slick asshole. Remind her what the lube is actually for. Then once I unloaded in her ass, I was going to flip her over and go to town on her clit as a thank you for letting me defile her time and again.

But really, I just wanted to hear her scream my fucking praises while she came on my face.

Instead, I started crying like a baby as the truth sank in. There is nothing that I can do to save us.

We didn't fuck. And maybe we never would again. It's been two months since we had actual sex.

After I got a grip on my emotions, I untied her, and we went to bed. After a moment, she started rubbing my cock, whispering how she wanted to make me feel better. But no matter how hard I fucked her face, banging her head off the wall as I pushed into her as far as I could, and no matter how fucking loud she screamed in ecstasy while suffocating me with her slick flesh, it was nothing but a piece of duct tape on a sinking ship.

And we were both drowning.

Since she decided we needed to move on and declared there would be no more sex, I'd gone down on her at least once a week thinking it would serve as a reminder of what she was losing, but all she did was remind me of what she was hoping to gain. And they were things I couldn't give her.

An honest, open to the public relationship.

Marriage.

Maybe kids.

We really should've listened when they told us we couldn't be boyfriend and girlfriend.

"How do you see a threesome working?" Emma asks Lillian. "I've never had one."

"Mmm. There's a lot of ways. But the first thing that comes to mind is me eating you out while River fucks me from behind."

I give Emma the side eye. She's got her phone in her hand recording the conversation.

"That sounds hot as hell," she says. "Has River fucked you from behind before?"

My eyes meet Lillian's eyes in the rearview mirror. She's faltering. Definitely faltering.

"What?" She stutters over the simple word.

Emma faces her. "No, it's totally cool. We broke up, like two months ago."

"You did?"

She nods, looking at me now. "He's a great fuck, isn't he?"

Lillian lets out a breath.

Before she even speaks, I know how this is going to end.

"He really is. If you all are down, we should definitely hook up when we get back home. That would be so amazing."

"I never ate pussy before." Emma bites the inside of her lip and rocks in her seat a little. "Think you could teach me?"

My dick springs to life just like that, even though I know none of it will ever happen.

"Holy shit, I would love to."

Emma turns and smiles at Lillian. "Yeah?"

"You're gonna love it."

"I can't believe you get off listening to us fuck."

"It's so hot. You guys are hot." Lillian blows out a puff of air. "Hell, I'd be down to just watch you two go at it." Then she screws up her face. "Nah, I'd get jealous. I gotta get some dick too."

Emma doesn't say anything for a moment before turning around, looking down at her phone. "Oh, good. Makenna and Jack are already there."

I almost feel bad for Lillian.

"Who are Makenna and Jack?" she asks.

"Just some friends."

Jack is the only person who lives in the area who knows me and Emma are stepcousins. He didn't think it was that weird, especially after I told him how it all played out.

"You smoke?" Emma asks Lillian. "Weed?"

I fight against the eyeroll.

"I do."

"Makenna has some." She looks over at me. "Riv can't smoke because of his job."

It's true. But it's also Emma's way of keeping not-so-innocent Lillian outside while me and Jack go into Club W. That way me and him aren't accomplices to whatever she and Makenna are going to do to her.

When we got to the bar, I spot Jack's lifted black truck near the back of the parking lot. He and I both work at the prison. We went through training together. On a break one day, we were both texting and let out a sigh at the same time. We looked at each other.

"Women," he said. "Am I right?"

We've been friends ever since. And after hearing all about Makenna, it was no shock when her and Emma hit it off too.

Jack and I head into the bar, leaving the three girls to, well, to kick Lillian's ass. I just hope she has money for an Uber.

And maybe to move.

"Didn't you tell me you fucked your neighbor?" Jack asks as we wait for our drinks.

The music is loud as fuck, the bass shaking my bones. There's a lot of people here, but it's not crowded. It was almost ten o'clock, so it would probably fill up soon.

I shrug. "I don't remember."

"She's not even that hot." He lifts off the bar. "I mean, I'd fuck her, but that's not the point."

I scoff and shake my head. "Gotta get my dick wet somewhere."

"You still cut-off?"

The bartender sets our whiskey and Cokes in front of us. Handing over my debit card, I tell him to open a tab.

"I think it's really over," I tell Jack. "She was looking at apartments on her phone yesterday."

Jack's eyes are on me as I look for a table. When I spot one, I point to it with my drink in my hand and start in that direction. The club is dark. The walls are painted black. LED lights line the dance floor and walking paths. It appears all the lights are connected in some way with how a constant flow runs throughout the room, the lights changing color like they're being chased.

My phone vibrates in my pocket as we push through the crowd. When we get to the table, I pull it out to see a text from Emma.

Where are you guys? Did you start a tab?

Right side in the back. And yes.

I stare across the club at the bar we'd just left, spotting my gorgeous fucking girlfriend. Her dark blonde hair hangs loose around her shoulders with soft natural looking curls giving it body. And speaking of body, her scarlet-colored dress accents the curve of her hips, her waist, her tits, ass, and thighs.

Emma is very self-conscious about her body. She's always carried a little more weight than she likes, especially around her middle. It seems like a million years ago when she used to try to hide it from me, but I love every inch of her amazing body.

"Fuck, she looks hot," I tell Jack.

"I did not expect that."

"What? For her to look so hot?"

He chuckles. "If you could peel your eyes off your fucking cousin's ass maybe you would see that your neighbor is still with them."

She was.

I frown. "Yeah, I didn't expect that either." I shove his shoulder. "Don't fucking call her my cousin."

"Tell me, River. How old were you exactly when you learned how to play the banjo?"

I don't want to laugh but I do. "I'll bust that banjo upside your big ass head."

The three girls make their way toward us, drinks in hand. Emma comes up beside me, so close our legs touch, but she doesn't look at me.

"I'm high as fuck right now," she tells me between sucking her drink through the two stir sticks that are in it. "I'm gonna drink this and go fucking dance this shit out."

"Why is Lillian still here?" I say into her ear.

She looks at me. Her pupils are huge, surrounded by a ring of soft brown iris. "We brought her here."

"I thought you guys were gonna kick her ass."

Laughing, she throws her head back. "Why? Because you fucked her?"

Our eyes met and I can tell she's waiting for an answer. I shrug.

"Fuck whoever you want." She looks away.

"I only wanna fuck you."

Her eyes landed back on me accompanied by a disapproving look. "You've been saying that since we were sixteen, yet what's your body count?"

The thing about that, though, is the fact that since we were sixteen, we have flip-flopped back and forth about what our relationship is. Fear would settle inside one of us, telling us we were wrong, that we would get caught. Our families would be ashamed and disown us. It wasn't wrong to feel that way because it always was and always will be a possibility.

It was a risk we couldn't afford to take.

But, fuck, we were almost twenty-four. We're adults now. If we wanna be together then we should fucking be together.

But with the constant back and forth for all these years, pushing away and pulling back in, I'm not sure what she expected from me.

"You act like you don't have one of your own," I counter.

She tips her head to the side, her tongue playing with the stir sticks in her drink. "At least mine's in the single digits." Finishing off her drink, she set the plastic cup on the table. "Lillian is gonna teach me to eat pussy later," she says loudly. "Who wants to watch?"

Jack's eyebrows shoot up. He tosses a look at me. "I'm down."

"Are you serious?" Makenna asks Emma, ignoring Jack. "I didn't even know you were into that."

"Not sure I am." Emma shrugs. "But we're gonna find out later." She rounds the table, calling out, "Time to dance," as she leaves. Makenna follows, drink in hand.

Lillian's gaze shifts between me and Jack. "Who's your friend?" she asks me.

"Jack," I tell her. "He's with Makenna."

She nods, looking him up and down as she does. "Nice."

A few minutes later, Lillian joins Emma and Makenna on the dance floor. Me and Jack get into a conversation about a couple of inmates at work and stop paying attention to the girls. I go to the bar and order another round of drinks. When I get back to the table, Jack points out at the dance floor. The first thing I see is Lillian making out with Makenna. Like, Lillian has her hands inside the back of Makenna's skirt, hiking it up so anyone and everyone can see her ass. Their mouths are locked, and Makenna's hands are in Lillian's hair.

I sit down beside Jack. "She wasn't kidding about liking pussy, I guess."

"What?" he asks. Then he shakes his head. "Not them." He points again. "Emma."

I try to zero in on where Jack is pointing but don't see her. "Where?"

He juts his hand forward. "Literally right across from us at the bar."

My stomach drops when I see her. She's straddling some dude's lap; her head tossed back as his lips graze over her neck. I'm on my feet instantly, on my way to her. Adrenaline pumps through my veins, fire ignites in my core, but I can't fucking beat this guy's ass without risking my job.

And she knows it.

By the time I get to her, their mouths are locked, and his hand is kneading her tits—*my fucking tits*—through her satiny dress.

Grabbing her by the shoulders, I pull her off him. He stands, trying to adjust his tiny hard-on as he does.

She shoves me, yelling something as she does, but all I hear is Jack. "Bro, that's the guy she left with last week."

I smirk. "Good. That means I already know where you live, fucker." Lifting my hand, I press two fingers against his temple. I pull them back like I'm blowing his brains out just as he jerks away from me.

"I didn't know she had a boyfriend, man," dude says.

"I don't," Emma says, pushing herself between us. "This is not my boyfriend, Tom."

He looks at her and shakes his head.

"Tom?" I ask him.

"Not even close," he says. Then he turns and walks away.

Emma watches him for a second and then faces me, pushing both hands into my chest. "What the fuck, River?"

"Did you really think I would sit by and watch you make out with some dude?" We're screaming but it all just blends into the music. "You're literally directly across from where we're sitting."

"Fuck," she says, pressing her fingers to her own temples, like she can't comprehend what's happening. "When are you going to get it?"

I grab the back of her head and bring her face to mine. "I'm not going anywhere. Not now. Not next fucking week. Not ever."

She pulls out of my grasp. "Good. Where's your phone?"

"Why?"

"Let's send a group text right now to our parents."

I pull my phone out and hold it out for her. She doesn't even look at it. "Go ahead."

She stares hard at me for a moment longer before grabbing my phone. She enters the passcode and turns to walk away. I think about stopping her, but instead I exhale and watch her go.

Jack puts his hand on my shoulder, and I feel like I'm about to cry. I look over at our table, seeing Makenna and Lillian surrounded by four or five guys. I drop my head back and groan. "I'm ready to go."

We shove our way through the crowded club until we get to our table. Jack walks up behind Makenna, his hand encircling her waist as he kisses her neck. She turns her head, smiling at him, and their lips meet in a quick kiss. The guy she was talking to nods once at him and then turns his attention somewhere else.

Lillian is eating up the attention of three guys and I consider that maybe we won't have to give her a ride home. I scan the crowd for Emma, desperate to know if she really texted our parents.

If she did, our entire life would be about to change.

It's worth it. Whatever comes next is one hundred percent worth it. I will get down on one knee at a family reunion and never even think of another woman again if we could just get over this mountain standing in our way.

Jack leans over, shoving his phone in front of me. It's a text from my phone. *Please tell River to come outside.*

Nodding, I start toward the exit and then step out into the cool night air. The music can be heard as clear as day from outside. When I find her, she's leaning against the front of my Jeep Wrangler looking like a model. My phone's in her hand, her focus on it. "Did you do it?"

She looks up at me. "Hmm?"

"Text our parents."

A beat of silence passes before she pushes off the vehicle. "Come here." She holds her hand out and I take it, following her behind mine and Jack's vehicles. "Unlock the car."

My Jeep is backed into a corner spot in the last row of the parking lot, a building behind it. I pull out my key fob and click the button to unlock it. She opens the back hatch and lifts the glass. I expect her to sit inside, thinking she wants to talk about telling our parents.

Instead, she tucks my phone into her bra, grabs the waist of my jeans and starts unbuttoning them before getting on her knees in front of me.

I get chills at the unexpected action. She spits on my cock before stroking it a few times, then takes it into her mouth. I comb my fingers through her silky hair, pulling it back from her face. Our eyes lock and stay that way. I could look at her forever, mouth on my dick or not. Her perfect, plump coral colored mouth and dark eyes full of emotion combined with her perfectly proportioned features would always be the image of a goddess to me. There was no other woman in this world who could even hold a flicker of light compared to her.

Yet I keep letting her push me away just to pull me back in.

She pulls my cock out of her mouth and spits on it again, then starts jacking it with her hand. Her eyes are still on mine when she reaches back into her bra and pulls out my phone. Only then does she look away. A moment later, I can tell she's recording me.

My face, not my cock.

"Who do you belong to, River?" she asks me.

"You."

"Say my name."

"Emma."

"If I ever find out again that this dick has been in someone else's mouth, pussy, or ass, I will cut it off and choke a bitch with it. Do you understand me?"

I nod.

She stands, flashing a quick smile. "Good. Now fuck me like you hate me."

Turning around, she bends over, the upper half of her body leaning into the back of my jeep. With the flip of her hand, she lifts the back of her dress to bare her ass to the world. Her underwear, if she was even wearing any, is gone. The camera is still rolling on my phone, the camera flipped so we can both see ourselves. Her eyes are on me behind her as she waits for what she wants.

"No," I tell her. "I'm not yours. I was never yours and you were never mine."

"Shut the fuck up and do this, Riv." Her voice is commanding and normally I would be all about it, but my erection is already deflating.

"Sorry, Em, but this is what you wanted."

Emma turns around and faces me, sitting on the edge of the hatch. "What I want is your dick inside me."

My tongue wets my lips as I tuck my dick into my pants. I can't believe I'm turning down sex. "You want things I can't give you. So, like you said, there's no point in continuing."

Her eyes mist over. Emma doesn't cry often so I know without a doubt that I've struck a nerve. She looks away from me.

"You can get dick anywhere. So, unless one of us finds the courage to come clean to our parents, then it's over."

It's subtle, but she nods. We've both known for years this was never going to last. It's only hard because we let it go on for as long as we did.

That and the fact that we don't know how to live without each other.

I imagine someday when we both find someone else who is a fraction of what we have with each other, that we will still long for one another and crave the toxic chaos that has made us feel alive all this time.

Emma wipes her eyes and stands up. "Okay." She stops recording and switches to camera mode before holding my phone out in front of us. "Let's take a pic."

I lean in, my hand resting on her shoulder furthest from me.

Neither of us are smiling in the picture.

She closes out the camera app before opening my text messages. Her fingers move quickly across the screen as she types out the recipients.

Mom, Dad, Christy, Chris.

"What are you doing?" I ask, hearing panic in my voice.

She sends the selfie we just took.

I grab the phone from her hands before she can type anything more. "What are you doing?"

"Coming clean."

Frowning, I swallow hard.

Looking away from me, she bobs her head up and down. "Fine then. I guess this is what *you* wanted too."

CHAPTER FIVE

Emma

River had to work all weekend. I stayed in bed until he left Saturday afternoon and then made a mad dash to get dressed, make myself look presentable, and drive across town to look at an apartment that I had found for rent online.

The apartment we currently lived in was nice as far as apartments went. It was in a secure building, a part of a community with a fitness center and a pool. There was even a playground for kids, not that we would ever utilize it. The appliances were newer and everything was well maintained. We had two bedrooms and one bathroom, a large living room, and an eat-in kitchen. It was perfect for us.

You get what you pay for, I guess, because what I could afford on my own was a one-room apartment in a house that was renovated about fifty years ago into several apartments. The home was probably beautiful back in the day. The unit I looked at had worn out red carpeting and appliances older than me. The bathroom sink had no counterspace; not that I could get ready in there with the one overhead florescent light. The shower stall walls were yellowed and there were brown stains around the drain hole.

It was a big fat no.

As I drove back home, I considered my options.

My parents and River's mom replied to the picture of us with heart reacts and thanks for sending it. River didn't reply to any of them. While he was at work, he sent the picture to me. Then he sent a collage of four pictures. Us as kids, in high school, college, and now.

His text said: *Before. Beginning. Middle. End.*

I had to get away. It was the only possible chance to move past this crazy, toxic, unacceptable mess we'd gotten ourselves into. Since I clearly couldn't afford to live on my own, I had few options.

Try to find a roommate.

See if I could stay with Makenna and Jack for a while—though this would not put space between me and River like I needed.

Find a new job and move back home.

The more I thought about it, the right decision became obvious.

After our freshman year of college, we figured out that it would cost less to live in an apartment together off campus than it cost to live in the dorms. This was rather attractive to River's parents who were footing the entire bill for his education. I had scholarships and grants that covered my tuition and fees, but the dorm was out of pocket for my family. My dad and Christy have three kids at home still, while River is an only child. Needless to say, they too were thrilled to not have to pay as much. River and I both held part time jobs on campus to pay for food, gas, and other things. Our parents drove down here in a moving van and furnished our apartment with hand me down furniture and kitchen essentials.

It was like a dream come true. Like we were finally adults in a serious relationship, living together. The sky was the limit and nothing was impossible. We would talk about how someday we would finally tell our parents the truth and they would learn to accept it. We never considered there would be an expiration date on our fantasy.

By midterms, River was spending more time on campus than at the apartment, hanging out with friends, working out, playing pick-up games at the gym, joining gaming leagues. Meanwhile, I was at home, alone, keeping up with schoolwork and feeling sorry for myself. It seemed like everything else was more important to River than me.

It was the Friday before Thanksgiving of our sophomore year. We were due to go home for the holiday because it might be Noni's last Thanksgiving. We'd decided to wait until Saturday morning to leave because once we went home, our time alone was practically nil. I was waiting like a good little girlfriend at the apartment for River to come home so we could stay up all night having sex and then drive the four hours home on energy drinks and luck.

I had checked his location a few times. He had gone from the rec center on campus to the dorm he used to live in. When he left there, he was driving, and I thought he was finally on his way. I even texted him like a fucking idiot and said: *Can't wait for you to get here* with a kissy face emoji.

He never replied. He didn't open my Snapchats. An hour passed, and I checked his location again. I had no idea where he was. It was a location I wasn't familiar with. I almost called him but instead, I sent another text: *Hurry up, this bed is cold all alone.*

Shortly after that, he sends me a Snap.

Except he didn't mean to send it to me.

Obviously.

Because it's some girl sucking his mother fucking dick.

I never leave the house in pajama pants, but I didn't fucking change this time. I tracked his ass to some house I'd never been to, knocked on the door and was let into a party in full swing.

I found River in a bedroom with some mousy looking girl with a pointy nose and horse teeth and another girl with enough bleach in her hair to sanitize a locker room. Mousy was naked from the waist down, sitting next to him on the couch getting fingered, while Bleachy was kneeled in front of him with his dick in her mouth.

River is do-a-double-take gorgeous. He has sandy blond hair that's always been a little wavy. As we grew up, he let it grow out and embraced letting it be messy on the top. Just his hair alone gets him attention but when you add in his dark blue eyes, perfectly proportioned Greek nose, his symmetrical lips and flawless smile, plus the rosiness of his cheeks, he is literally the image of a male god. And that's not even paying homage to his chiseled chest and abs. Or what hangs between his legs.

Perfection.

And I know I'm not the only one who thinks so.

He's way out of my league but that doesn't mean he's not mine.

Before River even sees me, I've got both those bitches by their hair with my hands, pulling them to their feet. I'm so fucking pissed that I'm not even thinking. Not at all.

Except about killing.

Dismemberment crosses my mind. Definitely of these girls and possibly of River too.

Throwing River into a river.

I've got fifty pounds on either one of these girls easily. And while I'm really good at pulling hair and grabbing faces and clothes, there are two of them. If either of them knows how to actually fight, they could take me. I want to believe River wouldn't let them, but at this point, I don't think I know him like I thought I did.

I let them go and hit River upside his head so hard I can still hear it. His face jerks to the side from the force, but he recovers immediately and grabs my wrists.

"Chill out," he yells in my face. His pants are still unfastened but at least he pulled them up and tucked himself in. "What are you doing?"

I struggle to get free, but he's not letting me. "Me? What the fuck are you doing?" Looking behind me, I see Mousy buttoning her jeans. Bleachy is waiting by the door. There's three or four people standing in the hallway looking in. "Did you fuck him?"

They don't answer me.

I look at River. "Did you fuck them?"

"No, babe, no." There's liquor on his breath.

"You're drunk."

"Maybe a little."

The fire of my anger starts to die down, but I am far from done being mad. "Why?"

He sucks his lips between his teeth and shakes his head just a little.

Hurt is outweighing the anger. "Let's go."

"Can I let go of your hands without getting hit again?"

"For now," I whisper.

He chuckles and loosens his grip, kissing the back of each hand. "Let's go." Sliding his fingers in between mine, he holds one hand, letting the other fall to my side as he leads me from the room.

We ignore the yells and jests as we make our way out of the party. I hear someone say, "She's stupid as fuck taking him home after that," and it pushes me over the edge as we walk out the door.

"I am stupid," I blubber as we walk, pulling my hand from his. "Fuck you, River. Fuck you and fuck all of this."

"Where's your car?"

I'm tempted to tell him to walk or find his own ride, but I would have to revisit my dismemberment plans if he went back into that party. "I bet if it had two legs and a pussy you could find it."

He chuckles, pointing out my white Toyota on the other side of the street. "There it is."

When we got home, I made him shower before he could get into bed with me. I drew the line when he kissed my neck, his fingers grazing over one of my nipples when he put his arm around me.

"Don't touch me."

He pulled away. "I'm not trying to do anything. Fuck, Emma." The sigh he let out carried the weight of the universe. "I'm sorry."

I didn't say anything right away. It wasn't an apology that would make it better. There might not ever be anything that would make it better. "Nothing is happening between us until you get tested. And I wanna see the results."

When I tell River not to touch me, it doesn't mean don't hold me. No matter how angry I am at him, he is my comfort. Even when he is the one causing the pain, he is the one who can take it all away.

His hands run through his hair. "That's unnecessary."

"Don't tell me what's unnecessary." My throat starts getting thick again.

"I didn't fuck either of them."

My hand flew in his direction, smacking him in the nose with my knuckles. It really was an accident, but I was glad it happened. "I don't fucking care, River!"

"Ow!" He sat up quickly, rubbing his nose. "What the hell, Em?"

His glare crushes me, so I roll onto my side, facing away from him. I don't want to hurt him, but damn, he was hurting me.

And I allow it.

I accept it.

We move on.

The next day, we drove the four hours home for Thanksgiving break. The events of the night before had not been forgotten. Initially, I planned to give him the silent treatment for the whole drive. But when he reached over and grabbed my hand while I drove the first leg of the trip, I pulled away.

"C'mon," he pleaded. "We're gonna be apart for a week."

I guffawed. "Are you fucking kidding me right now? You didn't give a shit about being apart last night."

He sighed loudly and leaned his seat back, shielding his eyes with his forearm. His indifference crushed me, and I started crying. Sometimes he made me feel so small and insignificant. Like I was nothing more than someone to bide his time with until he found someone he really liked. Nothing more than a live-in fuck buddy he could experiment with.

"None of this is real anyway," River said in the passenger seat beside me. "Probably should just stop acting like it is."

My breath left my lungs as I stared at him, unmoving, unemotional while I was crashing and burning. Not real? If this wasn't real, then what was? If this wasn't real, then why did I feel like I was dying?

After I look at the apartment, I call Makenna and tell her what I'm considering. She tells me she's supportive of whatever decision I make, but adds, "If you're serious about being done, you really have no choice. Otherwise, you're just gonna keep getting sucked back in."

Then she tells me that she and Jack took Lillian home with them the night before. "And she really can eat pussy," she adds with a laugh.

I made out with Makenna once while she groped my boobs. It was so uncomfortable that I knew it wasn't for me, and therefore the idea of a threesome with River and another girl never enticed me.

"Did you let Jack fuck her?"

She sighed. "I did. He was all turned on from watching us and I felt bad for him just sitting there wanking it. But, like, I was on her face while he was fucking her. And he was messing with me, making out with me and shit. Like she was just a prop or something."

"Why do you sound like you didn't like it?"

"No, I did," she assures me. "I just kinda felt bad for her. Like we used her."

"I think that's what she wanted. Some people get off on that."

Makenna didn't say anything for a moment. "Do you?"

"Do I what?"

"Do you get off on being used?"

I let out a quick chuckle. "I'm not having a threesome with you and Jack."

She didn't laugh. "That's not what I mean, Em." I wait for her to continue. When she does, I swear a little piece of me dies. "I know River's your cousin."

River didn't come home from work until nearly five in the morning. The only reason I know this is because I woke up around four to go to the bathroom and was all alone. I checked my phone for a text but didn't have one. Usually, if he decides to go somewhere after work, he lets me know. The fact that he didn't text spoke volumes. But I refused to text him. Instead, I lay in bed imagining a million whores he's putting his dick in and every single one of them is skinnier and prettier than me. And every single one of them is not the daughter of the man his aunt decided to marry without realizing she was ruining my whole fucking life.

When I hear his key in the apartment door, I roll to my side so that my back faces the bedroom door and pretend to be asleep. He goes straight to the bathroom. When he comes out, his shadow looms in the doorway for a long moment before he comes in. I'm surprised that he rounds the bed to my side. My eyes close quickly. He stands there while my heart thuds in my chest, afraid he knows I'm faking my slumber. I don't want to talk. I don't want to hear his lies about where he was.

To be completely honest, I don't know what I fucking want.

Yeah, actually, I do.

And I can't have it.

River gently pushes my hair back from my face as he lets out a sigh. His words are as light as a feather falling in the night but weighty enough to crush my soul. "I love you."

CHAPTER SIX

River

There's a mission that needs accomplished when I get off work Saturday night. Jack declined joining me, insisting he needed to get home to make sure things were cool with him and Makenna after he stuck his dick in Lillian the night before right in front of her.

I swear, their relationship is more fucked up than mine and Emma's.

The previous Saturday night, I declined the invitation to Club W with Emma and our friends. There was a tournament in the gaming community I'm a part of that I'd been looking forward to for weeks. I was pissed that a new club decided to open the same weekend. When I was eliminated in the tournament early on, I was even more pissed. After sticking around online as an observer for a while, my frustration was not waning by any means. I had texted Emma and told her I was killed but she didn't reply.

I needed her to tell me I wasn't a fucking loser. I needed her soft eyes and the tickle of her fingers on my arm.

So, I went to Club W. It was packed and I had to park down the street a bit and walk. As I'm coming up the block, I see her exit the club with a guy. His arm is around her waist. Her face turned toward him. They walk to her car and stand beside it, talking for a minute before they start making out. She has her hands on the back of his head, and his are inside the back of her bubblegum-pink skirt, cupping her supple ass with his greedy claws.

Something washed over me. An emotion. I never know what to call it. It's like being punched in the gut, feeling like you're about to die, mixed with a rage strong enough that I could probably kill someone.

Emma doesn't make me feel rage. She does the opposite. I don't know how. Even when I do rage around her, it's never directed at her.

But I needed her that night.

Just like the night I slashed all four of her fucking tires.

I was not and am not doing well with her telling me we are over.

After she told me that bullshit, she stopped sharing her location with me, leaving me no choice but to put a tracking device on her car. The service requires an app on my phone which I have to delete and reinstall regularly because we have never hidden our phones from each other.

As I walk back to my car, I reinstall the tracking app and sign into it. Then I follow them to an apartment complex a few miles from downtown. He's driving a black Chevy Malibu, *Schmiz 1* on his license plates. I park my Jeep and turn the lights off so that I appear to be just another tenant getting home, when in reality I'm the psychotic fucking moron who fell in love with the one girl who was off limits.

After I see what building they go into, I watch for a light to go on in one of the apartments. Second floor on the right. Then I waited about thirty minutes, debating on going up there and pulverizing dude and carrying Emma away like a prize.

It's tempting. And would be so fucking satisfying.

Except she only likes that side of me when it comes to sex.

I drive home and get the black spray paint that's been sitting under the kitchen sink for over a year. We tried spray painting an old end table black. It ended up being the wrong type of paint and we ruined the table. We tossed the table but not the paint.

I needed her and she wasn't there because she was letting someone else fuck her. She couldn't even reply to my text. So, I left her a message she wouldn't miss in the form of black spray-painted letters on her car.

Now, this Saturday night, I have a new mission. This time, the results will be much more satisfying than tagging Emma's car.

I drive alone to the same apartment complex where *Schmiz 1* in the black Malibu lives. When I don't find his car, I take a wild guess and creep through the parking lot at Club W, easily spotting his vehicle. I park and consider my options for a while before driving back to his apartment to wait for him.

I parked about a half mile away before walking through the night to sit along the tree line between his building and the one next to it for about two hours. There's only one entrance into the parking lot and I have a perfect view of it.

It's nearly three thirty in the morning when he gets home. He gets out of his car, stumbling onto the sidewalk in front of the building as he tries to lock his car with the key fob.

I advanced on him so quickly that even if he would've seen me coming, he wouldn't have been able to react. He's lying on the sidewalk after I tackle him, his keys skidding across the unforgiving ground. I grabbed his shoulder and turned him over. There's already a scrape on his forehead from where he hit the pavement when he went down. My fists are flying, his head jerking from side to side with each blow.

Schmiz is saying something, groaning, his hands coming up in his defense, but I don't hear or see anything because my ears are ringing, and my vision is clouded with red images of Emma on his lap last night. I want to unsee them, but I can't. I want to believe she only did it to make me jealous, but I can't be sure. She said we need to move on, but I don't want to move on. And every possible thing she wants to move on to must be destroyed so she can come to terms with the cold, hard facts that I am the one she is supposed to be with whether we tell our family or not.

If she wants to get married, then I will marry her.

If she wants kids, there is no reason we can't have them.

If she wants me, I'm hers.

We don't need the approval of anyone. It's why we chose the same college four hours away from home. It's why we don't tell anyone we are related. It's the why for so many things.

She thinks she's not good enough for me. Thinks because her body is more filled out than she likes it that I couldn't possibly want her as much as I would want someone with less curves. She thinks pushing me away and messing with these fuck boys is going to deter me, but it just makes me want to fight harder for her.

I leave Schmiz moaning on the sidewalk and hightail it out of there.

I'm in love with Emma Novak. I don't remember a time when I wasn't. A million mistakes have been made over the years, more mine than hers. But this is the longest she has ever called it quits.

When I get home, she's asleep. I'm exhausted from everything and want more than anything to curl up beside her, but she doesn't want that anymore.

She doesn't want me.

When she gets out of bed to go to the bathroom the next morning, I wake from the spot where I'd fallen asleep on the couch. I turned my head to see her glaring at me from the hallway. "Hi."

She goes into the bathroom. The door locks behind her.

I face the TV sitting across the room from me. It must've shut off at some point after I fell asleep, my reflection staring back at me in the smooth black, reflective surface. I'm shirtless, my hair is a mess. Sitting up, I run my hand over the top of my head while waiting for her to come out of the bathroom and ask me why I slept on the couch. Ask me where I went after work. Ask me to lie beside her and watch movies until I have to work.

None of that happens.

She doesn't even look in my direction as she returns to her bedroom, slamming the door behind her.

I wait, knowing that when Emma is mad, it's best to just let her be mad.

Except waiting is not my forte and there's a tingle in my bones that won't let me wait. It feels like my skin is being peeled away from my body the way the outside of a potato or a carrot is removed. One swift slice after another.

In the kitchen, I pour a bowl of her favorite cereal. She likes to add the milk herself, insisting I use too much, so I pour some into a glass. Then I fill another glass with orange juice for her. We don't have any trays so I can't exactly be fancy, but I balance the two glasses on a dinner plate in one hand and carry her cereal in the other. When I get to her bedroom door, I cradle the bowl in the crook of my elbow and turn the nob as I nudge the door open with my foot.

Emma is lying on her side, the blankets pulled up to her shoulders. Her face is creased with sleep lines, hair in a messy top knot.

"Good morning." I try to sound like the world isn't crashing down around us.

She doesn't reply.

"Thought you might be hungry."

"What is it?" she asks.

"Cinamon Toast Crunch." I lower the bowl so she can see it. Then I nodded toward the plate with the glasses on it. "I didn't add the milk."

A war rages on her face as she contemplates whether to accept my pathetic breakfast. I toss her a smile in an extra effort to slice through the tension in the room.

She sits up.

The invisible fence around her dissolves.

I wait for her to get comfortable with her back against the headboard and the blankets smoothed across her lap before handing her the cereal bowl. She takes it and then reaches for the milk. I hand it to her and watch her pour about half of it into her bowl. She holds it out for me to take back and I do, setting it on the nightstand on my side of... err, the opposite side of the bed.

She takes a bite, her eyes anywhere but on me. I hold out the orange juice; she drops her spoon and takes it, setting it on her nightstand. "Thank you."

"You're welcome." I took her thanks as an invitation to sit on the bed, unsure why I felt like I needed an invitation.

"Did you use a condom?"

My eyebrows lowered. "What?"

She shoves a spoonful of cereal into her mouth. "Last night," she says while chewing. "With whatever hoe you were with until five in the morning."

I stare at her profile, trying to pick up on her intention. Was she asking if I used a condom because she wants to fuck or is she asking because she needs something else to hold against me? "I wasn't with anyone last night."

Emma snorted. "Probably someone you work with."

I immediately thought of the one coworker I had banged. Jaci Carls. It happened one time before I found out she was engaged. When I asked her about it, she shrugged and said, "So? Don't you have a girlfriend?" That had been six months ago, and I never even told Jack, so I knew Emma didn't know.

Not that I had been with Jaci the night before.

"I wasn't with anyone," I say quietly.

Emma stops chewing and looks at me. "Then where were you?"

I want to remove the hard edge from her eyes. I want to close the gaping canyon between us that just keeps growing deeper and deeper with every passing day. "I sat outside dude's apartment building and beat his ass when he came home."

Her lips quipped down. "What dude?"

I shrug, my eyes falling on my scuffed-up knuckles. "Schmiz 1."

"Schmiz 1?"

"Dude whose lap you were all over the other night. The one you were with last weekend."

Her jaw falls open. "His name is Schmiz 1?" Except she says it like it's one word, Schmizwon.

"I don't know what his fucking name is. That's what his license plate says." But then I realize something and look at her. "You don't know his name?"

She's focused on her cereal. "Tucker, I think. Something with a T." Her eyes find me again. "You know I'm not good with names."

We're quiet for a long moment while she finishes her cereal, and I think maybe the tension is gone and there's hope we can have a conversation about the future.

Holding her empty cereal bowl out toward me, she says, "I'm gonna start looking for a job back home."

She may as well have hit me upside the head with the bowl. I took it from her, staring into the caramel-colored milk left behind, dyed by the cereal. "Why?"

"Because the closest prison from home is over an hour away so the chances of you following me are slim." Reaching up, she pulls the hair tie from her hair. Sandy blonde locks fall around her face. "We need space between us. It's the only way."

"I don't want space, Em."

She closes her eyes and sucks in a deep breath through her nose. "There is no future for us, Riv. We gotta stop."

Setting her cereal bowl on the nightstand, I grasp at the straws in my mind. The same ones I've been grasping for years. The ones that have nothing except dead ends and disappointment written on them.

She talks about how she has never been good enough for me, but I don't see it that way. I'm not good enough for her. Emma is smart and assertive. Responsible. She makes decisions based on facts, not feelings. I don't think she has ever realized how small I feel around her sometimes.

"I can get a job with the police department. Maybe in one of the nearby towns or something."

Her head falls back. "River, stop. Please."

"You act like I can just fucking stop how I feel, Emma. It's not that easy for me. When I think about the future, I'm not thinking about marrying someone or having kids. I am thinking about you and only you. You think you can just move back home and leave me here? Like I have ever gone a day without you? How the hell do you think that's ever going to work? You think *you* can be away from *me*?"

She's shaking her head. "I didn't say it was going to be easy. But we have to do this. We need time apart to find... whatever it is we're supposed to find."

"I already fucking found what I need to find. Don't you get that?"

"Then why on earth do you keep fucking other girls? If I'm enough, if I'm the one you see in your future, then why are you constantly fucking around?" She pauses, but not long enough for me to respond. "Because you know when it all comes down to it, none of this," she points back and forth between us, "is real. You said it years ago and I should've listened to you then, but I didn't because I wanted to believe this *could* be real. But it can't and now we just need to face it and move on."

"It's real if we say it's real. That's all that matters, Em."

Her eyes twitch as she stares at me.

"I refuse to believe all this means nothing."

Over the last nine years since we moved our relationship from kissing cousins to something darker that neither of us could quite grasp, it's been routine for one of us to freak out every couple of months. The difference between our freak outs is that when I do it, it's in response to getting caught with someone else. When Emma does it, it's because she is battling her internal moral compass and our agreed perception of the fact that our parents would never accept our relationship.

"But it does," she tells me. "It means nothing. It never did."

CHAPTER SEVEN

Emma

"Hey, Ems," my dad says when he answers the phone. "How are you?"

I sigh. "Okay, I guess."

He hesitates. "That sounds like the opposite of okay. What's going on?"

"I don't know," I lie. "Been thinking about looking for a job back home."

"I thought you loved your job."

I do love my job. Kinda. As a health educator with the local health department, I work with community entities to provide information about family planning—a fancy way of saying safe sex—and prevention of sexually transmitted infections. A lot of my job involves travelling to the counties we serve, visiting clinics and doctors' offices. I provide them with condoms and at-home test kits for STIs and pregnancy that they can hand out to people in need. My goal in obtaining my degree in public health administration had been to work to educate teens on the risks associated with having sex at a young age. Most people don't realize that the risks span far beyond getting an STI or becoming pregnant.

Teens who engage in sex are also more likely to have future reproductive issues, depression and anxiety, substance abuse issues, suicidal ideation, and long-term relationship issues.

Even if someone had told me of the risks at fifteen, I still would have done it.

"I do love my job," I tell my dad. "But I think I just want to be closer to home." *And away from River.*

"Is River gonna stay down there alone?"

I'm not surprised that's his first question. "Not sure, really. We haven't talked about it much." It's no secret that River and I are close. Our family just doesn't realize the extent of our closeness. "There's not a prison anywhere near there so I'm not sure he would even consider it."

"True," Dad says slowly. "Honestly, we had always just assumed the two of you would come back up this way after college. Your mom and I were surprised when you said you were staying."

Christy is not my mom. I've never called her that. Yet my dad insists on referring to her in that way. I guess it makes it easier, especially given that she is the mother of his other three kids. But calling her my mom makes River seem even more... related.

My parents split up when I was about six months old. They met in the hospital emergency room where my mom worked as an admissions clerk while attending college part-time. She was eighteen when they met, nineteen when I was born. My dad was a twenty-four-year-old medical student.

After my parents split up, my mom dropped out of college mid-semester and moved back in with her mom an hour away from where my dad lived in Chicago. Sometime around my first birthday, she moved in with her boyfriend Joel, taking me with her. I have no memories of this period of time in my life. What I know is what's been shared with me by my grandmother, my dad, and from the photos.

A week before my second birthday, my mom and Joel got into a fight. I guess they were always fighting. Like, knockdown, drag out fights. As in, my mother was getting knocked down and dragged out. It's believed that Joel hit my mom on the side of her head several times with one of her dog statues that she collected. The dachshund to be exact.

My mom loved dogs but never owned one. She and my grandmother always lived in apartments where dogs weren't allowed. Instead of having a real one, she collected replicas. Little ceramic and porcelain figurines, stuffed animals, plastic toys.

After Joel battered my mother, he left for his twelve-hour shift at a factory. When he came home, he found me in a shitty diaper asleep on the kitchen floor with a pack of hamburger buns. I had eaten through the plastic bag to get to the bread because my mom hadn't fed me all day. He immediately started yelling to wake up my mom. When she didn't wake up, he grabbed her by her arm and realized she was dead.

Instead of doing the right thing and calling the police, he changed my diaper, put me in my crib with a bottle, gathered some clothes and left.

The next afternoon, a neighbor called the police to report that I'd been left home alone two days in a row based on the fact that I'd been crying for two days. My mom and I were found, and the next day Joel turned himself in.

He's still in prison.

After that, I lived with my grandmother for a few months before I came to live with my dad. He dropped out of medical school and took a job in pharmaceutical sales. We moved to Thomas City, my dad's tiny hometown in the middle of nowhere.

When my dad refers to my mom, I know he's talking about Christy because we rarely talk about my real mom. Every once in a blue moon, he will get a look on his face and say something about how an expression I made, or whatnot, reminded him of my mom.

"Yeah," I tell him. "I thought I could do it, but I don't know. Me and River work opposite shifts. Most of my friends moved away. I just feel like if I moved home, I would feel less... lonely."

"Well, Ems, I hate to hear that you're feeling that way. It's unlikely there's a job open at the health department here, but you could try Peoria maybe. Or the hospitals might have something."

I nod. "Yeah, that's what I was thinking."

"Do you have a timeline of when you're wanting to do this or are you just gonna wait and see what happens?"

Tears nip my eyes. "No timeline. Just thinking about it. I might hop online later and see if there's anything that looks worth applying to."

What I'm saying hits me. Moving away from River. Not seeing him daily. Not having him beside me while I sleep.

Letting him go.

I think of the scene in *Titanic* then. The one where Rose lets Jack go and he fades away into the bottom of the ocean.

River won't be fading away into the bottom of any ocean, but he will fade into the background of my life. He has to.

"What's with this ex-boyfriend who keeps vandalizing your car?" Dad asks.

I groaned, not surprised Christy told him about the spray paint last weekend and the slashed tires two weeks before that. "Just some guy who couldn't accept that I was dating someone else." I pause. "They arrested him," I add quickly. Then I remember how River supposedly beat up... whatever his name was last night. "And I ended things with the new guy."

"Does this have anything to do with why you want to come home?"

"Kinda, yeah."

"Does River know this guy? The asshole one."

I make a face. "Yeah, River knows him alright." I knew where my dad was going with this. "He confronted him once. It's not a big deal. Since he was arrested, I should be able to get restitution for the damage."

After Dad and I talk a while longer, and he fills me in on what my siblings are up to and how he had re-stained the deck, we get off the phone. I wish I could say I felt better. That some epiphany happened while I was talking to my dad, but there was no change.

I have to leave. There is no point in staying here another night knowing nothing is going to change.

I cried as I packed my clothes and toiletries. I debated leaving a note but decided against it. Once everything was in my rental car, I stared up at the living room window of our second-floor apartment thinking about how the last time River held me, I hadn't known it would be the last time.

Choking back a sob, I go back up the stairs and into our apartment. We have a dry erase board in the kitchen that I thought would be helpful for making a list of things we need to grab from the store. It worked for about a week. Then River started drawing penises, boobs, and stick people fucking in a variety of positions on it. Currently, there was a drawing of a female pole dancing on it while other stick figures watched, holding out what was supposed be debit cards. I erase the artwork and write, *I love you. I'm sorry.*

For a long moment, I stare at it. My final words. I know they're not really final, but they are ending an era that has lasted most of my life.

I erase the apology. I'm not sorry. I don't regret that it happened, just that we couldn't... that I wasn't... Yeah, I don't know.

That night, after checking into a hotel and ordering DoorDash, I shut off my phone. Then I turn it back on because I'm so used to being able to check social media a hundred times a day. But then shut it off again about thirty minutes before River gets off work.

The night drags on and I get little sleep in the unfamiliar bed all alone. When I woke up in the morning, I immediately picked up my phone, forgetting it was off. I leave it off until I get to work.

My co-worker Carla comes into my office while I'm waiting for it to power on. She makes small talk with me about the weekend while I sign a birthday card for someone in the food inspections department. I can hear my phone vibrating beside me and fight to look over at it until she leaves.

It's not a surprise that River tried contacting me. I'm not even sure I'm surprised by the fact that there are thirty-three text messages and seven voicemails. When my office phone rings, I'm just opening my messages app.

"This is Emma," I say into the phone when I pick it up.

"Emma, you have a guest up front," the receptionist tells me.

"Okay." I swallow, knowing damn well River is my guest, and that I was stupid not to realize he would come here when he wasn't able to reach me. I could say I'm busy or about to go into a meeting, but he would probably just sit in the lobby and wait for me all day.

He is making this way harder than it needs to be.

When I open the door to the reception area, he's leaning against the wall in a pair of joggers and a hoodie. His hair is a mess. His cheeks are red, and his eyes look a little puffy.

He pushes off the wall when he sees me and follows me without a word back to my office. When we get to the small space, he steps inside while I shut the door. Instantly, he picks up the framed photo of us that sits on my shelf. "Surprised this is still here."

I grab the picture frame and set it back on the shelf. "What do you want, River?"

He sits in the chair across from my desk. "Don't insult me with dumbass questions."

I roll my eyes as I take a seat behind my desk.

"Where did you stay last night?"

"Don't insult me with dumbass questions."

"It's not a dumbass question, Emma. Fucking had me worried sick that something happened to you."

I shrug, noticing his right hand is swollen and bruised. "I left a note."

"No, you didn't. You wrote a lie on a dry-erase board. Because if you loved me, you wouldn't have done that."

"I did what needed to be done. We aren't going to be able to move on if we live together and share a bed." I lower my voice. "If we keep messing around."

He scoffs, a smirk dancing across his mouth. "Yeah, fuck how we feel. Fuck how being apart makes me physically sick." His jaw clenches. His anger is coming straight down the pipeline. I stand, preparing to tell him he needs to leave before he explodes and embarrasses me. "Not once have you asked me what I want. And when I try to tell you how I feel and what I want, you just discount it as something meaningless." He stands too. "Can I get someone else? Of course. I can get fifty fucking girls by this time tomorrow if I want. But I only want to be with you. I don't give a fuck about our parents or anything else. You're stuck on shit that doesn't matter, Emma, and it's going to be the death of both of us." Turning away from me, he grabs the doorknob. "I'll see you tonight." He looks back at me. "At home."

And then he's gone. I stare at the open door to my office for a long moment after he leaves. Why does he have to be so damn callous? Mr. 'I can get fifty fucking girls by this time tomorrow' can fuck off. Like, why would he think reminding me of how he could get anyone he wants is going to make this any better?

I hope everyone he fucks for the rest of his life feels like a bowl of wet noodles.

I pray that every orgasm he has for the rest of his life feels like a wet dream.

After work, I'm still pissed and don't even consider going home. My car was finally ready, and I picked it up at lunch. I'm glad to have it back. The insurance company paid for the rental, but the amount it covers is only enough for a tiny hatchback car. At five-foot-seven, I like having my space. I may not be what most would consider tall, I'm average when it comes to height, I suppose, but I like to have my space.

At the hotel, I changed into pajama pants and a tank top. I leave my bra on because I ordered DoorDash again and don't want to show off my perma-hard nipples to the delivery person. I start an episode of *House Hunters* on TV while I wait for my food and find myself thinking about house hunting with River. The people on the show are always talking about needing space for entertaining, but River would be more interested in a dedicated gaming space and maybe a sex dungeon. I scoff at the thought, almost disgusted with myself for even thinking about house shopping with him.

I glance down at my phone to see how much longer until my food arrives, realizing River has not called or texted once since he left my office earlier. Frowning, I pick up my phone and open Snapchat to see if I missed anything. He rarely posts on Instagram or Facebook, but I check them anyway. Nothing.

In a way I'm relieved, but at the same time, I'm concerned. It's not like him to be... silent. Maybe he's finally getting it. Maybe he's finally seeing it my way.

I'm still not sure that's what I want.

But I also don't want him to keep pushing me to keep living this double life with him.

I toss my phone aside. I'll shut it off before I go to sleep just in case he decides he's done being silent when he gets off work.

Right before the house hunters on the show are about to reveal which house they chose, there's a knock on my door. It's perfect timing as a commercial comes on. I jump up and go to the door, opening it without looking through the peephole.

It's my food alright.

And River.

He stands there with his perfect fucking smile, holding my food in his hands. "Why am I not surprised you ordered Mexican?"

"Why aren't you at work?"

He shrugs. "Wanted to see you."

"How did you know where I was?"

His smile fades, which is a nonanswer all on its own. He pushes forward over the threshold into my room. I don't budge. He still manages to get around me, throwing off my balance as he does. I keep the door open, my eyes following him as he sets my food on the little desk beside my purse.

"Why aren't you at work?" I ask again.

He comes toward me, his narrowed eyes shadowed as he licks his lower lip. "Like I said, I wanted to see you."

When he reaches me, I step aside for him to exit the room. "And now you have. Thanks for stopping by."

He rips the door from my hand, slamming it shut as he shoves me against it with his weight. His hand grips my throat, and he pushes his forehead against mine.

My breath catches and my knees wobble slightly. I close my eyes, his warm breath on my face, traces of wintergreen tickling my senses.

"I'm not going anywhere." He pushes tighter against me. "Ever."

It's a really shitty spot to be in. I desperately want to lift my face and kiss him but just as equally, I want to tell him to get the fuck off me and leave me alone.

The grip he has on my throat tightens just slightly as I hear the sound of him unbuckling his belt. Opening my eyes, I lower them to see him quickly pulling the black leather strap loose. Once he has it undone, he quickly tugs it through the beltloops and away from his body.

"River," I say, barely a breath behind his name.

He pulls away from me as he lifts the belt and wraps it around my neck, flashing a smile as he pulls the strap loosely through the buckle. I tug at the loop around my neck to keep it from being too tight, knowing at this point, I would not be successful in removing it.

The throbbing between my legs doesn't want me to remove it anyway. But I need to use my head and not my fucking clit to make decisions. River pulls the belt tight, my hand still in it. My head jerks forward.

"Fucking stop," I tell him.

"Move your hand."

"No, just take it off."

He cocks his head. "What's the matter, Em?"

I look up at him with watery eyes.

When I don't answer him, he backs up from the door, leading me toward the bed. I manage to pull my hand from the belt as we walk; he doesn't pull it tighter. He sits on the bed when he reaches it, pulling me to stand between his legs. Letting go of the leather strap, he puts his hands on my ass and squeezes, pulling me back with him as he lies back on the bed.

I struggle against him for a moment, as I land in an uncomfortable position on top of him. But when I try to move, he grabs the belt again. I'm straddling him when he lies back, his feet still on the floor. I can feel his hard length pressing against my thigh. As much as I hate to admit it, I'm turned on as hell. I'm like one of Pavlov's dogs when it comes to River. All he has to do is give me a certain look and I'm ready to spread my legs wide open for him. Add in being rough like this, and an inferno of fucking desire rages inside me.

That look, the one that melts me, is written on his face like my own destiny. "Come here and kiss me," he whispers.

I deliberate but a second before I lean down, bringing my face to his.

Chapter Eight

Emma

Within minutes of my nonverbal consent, River has peeled off my shirt and is undoing the clasp of my bra. My cleavage spills out into his hands, and I straighten my posture. River sits up, his hungry mouth immediately descending onto one of my peaks while he rubs the other one with his thumb. My head falls back as I let out a groan of pleasure.

River's belt still hangs loose from my neck, and I reach up to take it off just as I feel the nerve tingling sensation of his teeth on my nipple. I rock my hips against his knowing I am not going to stop him no matter what my brain tells me.

Just as I start to pull the leather strap of the belt through the buckle, he grabs the end of it, pulling it tight. It was unexpected; my head jerks as I make a gagging sound. He moves his mouth to my other erect bud; his eyes flipped upward to my face.

"Be a good girl, Emma."

He's rolling his hips, his hard cock pressing against my center. The throbbing heat between my legs is desperate for him. I tug at his crewneck sweatshirt, pulling it up and over his head to reveal the defined muscles of his chest and abs. He returns his attention to my breasts, licking circles of pleasure around my nipples while holding one mound in each hand, pushing them together so he can swiftly move back and forth between them. My hands run across his chest, the peach fuzz on his pecs as soft as velvet.

"Fuck," I mutter, overcome with desire.

River drops my breasts, taking hold of the belt in one hand and giving it a firm tug. Our eyes meet. "Get on your knees," he tells me.

I slide off him and onto the floor as he wraps the end of the belt around his fist a few times to shorten the length of the hold he has on me. Like I would even go anywhere if he took it off. Not that I want him to take it off. I like River being in control. He knows me and my body. He respects my boundaries.

Sexually, at least.

When he rises to his feet in front of me, I can see the bulge of his arousal through the dark denim he's wearing. He gives the belt a slight tug and I look up at him. Our eyes meet and he nods, giving me permission to unfasten his pants. In a frenzy, I unbutton, unzip, and lower his jeans and boxers, noting some of his precum was wasted on the fabric. His cock springs to full attention, practically hitting me in the face.

I run my tongue across his tip, tasting his precum, my eyes turned upward to his face as I do. My hand runs the length if his smooth rod. I've never seen a dick more perfect than River's. It was the first one I ever saw and for years it was the only one I saw in person, and maybe that's why it's the image of perfection.

Once I've gotten all his precum, I spit on the shaft and move my hand more vigorously up and down. He pushes his fingers through my hair, gripping the back of my head, urging me to take his organ into my mouth. Licking my lips, I wrap them around his head, teasing his tip with my tongue briefly before sliding more of him between my lips. River exhales above me, and I look up at him to see his eyes are closed. His lips are slightly parted, his tongue resting on top of his lower teeth as he relishes in the pleasure I'm giving him.

He is the most beautiful man I have ever seen. Hands down.

His hips begin to thrust against my mouth, gently, and his eyes open. For a moment, he watches as his cock slides in and out of my wet lips.

I'm taken aback when he pulls it out of my mouth.

He tugs on the belt, urging me to stand, and I do so. Then he removes the belt from around my neck. "Take off your pants."

I push them down, letting them fall to my ankles and then kick them to the side. My eyes fall to his dick fisted in his right hand. I'm tempted to shove him backward onto the bed and climb on top of him. The throb in my heated center is starving for attention. I want to be filled. I want to feel him pounding into me so hard that I see stars. I want to fucking come over and over while he fucks me into oblivion.

He knows this. He knows how much I love to fuck.

He also loves to torture me.

"Turn around."

I do as I'm told, hoping he's going to bend me over and impale me from behind. Instead, he grabs my arms and begins wrapping the belt around my wrists, securing them with a double cuff. I press my thighs together to try to get some relief as he's securing the belt.

River chuckles, sliding a hand between my legs from behind and into my wet center. I flinch at his touch, not expecting it. "Soon enough, babe. Be patient." He rubs the length of my lips with his knuckles a few times, drawing a groan from me as I try to move against his hand.

He removes his hand and spins me around, pulling my face to his. His tongue dives into my mouth like a pleading cry for this to never end and if I could control it, it never would.

"Get back on your knees," he whispers when he pulls away, tugging at my lower lip with his thumb. I get down on one knee and then the other, careful to keep my balance without the use of my arms, and look up at him, my mouth open and ready to take him. He smiles and my heart melts. He puts two fingers into my mouth and tugs my cheek. "You're an eager little slut tonight."

Fuck, yeah, I am. His words damn near push me to insanity. All I can do is press my thighs together to get any type of relief. Without my hands, I can't do anything to pleasure myself and he knows it. He likes it.

River's hand rips across my face. As soon as I feel the sting, he is already rubbing the cheek he hit. "Separate your legs."

"Please," I beg.

He scoffs. "You really think..."

I suck my lips between my teeth and push my legs apart, feeling cool air touch my warn, wet skin.

His fingers are in my mouth now, four of them, as he pushes them to the back of my throat causing me to gag. He pulls at my cheeks with both hands so hard I think my lips will split. "Ready, babe?"

He doesn't wait for a reply. The force of his cock against the back of my throat makes my eyes water immediately. He's gripping my hair for leverage, holding my head still while he fucks my face.

"Oh, my fuck, yes, Em," he says. "Keep your eyes on me."

They are on him. I couldn't look away if I tried. When he's fucking me like this, his whole face changes. River is mesmerizing. He looks angry, like he's hate fucking me, and I know my pussy is weeping, desperate to get the same treatment my mouth is receiving.

His thrusts slow as he pushes himself all the way in, his balls resting on my chin as he pinches my nose closed. Holding me in place while he quickly taps his dick against the back of my throat, I feel his throbbing length on my tongue. His body twitches against my face as I start seeing stars on the edge of my vision. My lids feel heavy, but I want to watch his beautiful face while he uses me to reach euphoria.

Just when I think I'm going to pass out, he removes his cock from my mouth. It's still rock hard, streams of saliva and precum hang between his engorged head and my lips. I stick my tongue out to pull them into my mouth, ready to taste him again already.

River pulls me up roughly with my hair and I cry out. He shoves me onto the bed. Using my legs, I scoot toward the center, fully expecting that I'm about to get the life fucked out of me, but he grabs me by the ankles and pulls me back, spreading my legs wide as he does. "You wanna come on my face, don't you?"

"I just wanna come," I tell him. I'm lying on my side because it's too uncomfortable to be on my back with my arms secured behind me.

Using two fingers, he spreads my folds to expose my clit. "So fucking wet." His thumb grazes lazily over my bud of nerves causing me to arch my back.

"Please, River," I beg. "Please."

He keeps rubbing, applying just a subtle amount of pressure, while stroking his cock with his other hand. "Please what?"

"Make me come. Please." I don't even care how desperate I sound. This man drives me insane.

"What do I get?"

"Anything. Whatever you want. I promise."

His thumb stops moving. "Anything?"

I'm not sure what has him hung up. We've done just about everything there is to be done. He knows practically nothing is off limits. Especially with the right amount of lube.

He kneels on the bed. I twist my body to take his cock into my mouth again in hopes that he will reciprocate on my lower half. With a hard tug to my hair, he stops me from getting any closer. Our eyes meet. "Anything, Emma?"

"Anything, River. I'm yours."

He straddles my face at an angle, respecting that I can't lay flat on my back. My mouth hangs open in wait. "Damn fucking right you're mine." He punches his cock all the way into my mouth hitting the back of my throat. I gag but recover quickly when I feel his mouth on my pussy, sucking and licking like it was a fucking pie eating contest. His fingers are digging into my inner thighs, holding them apart. I want to grip my legs around his head and fuck his face like he's fucking mine, but he's in full control of everything.

Sometimes I'm in control but, honestly, I love it more when River is calling the shots. There's something so exhilarating about letting go and giving in and watching to see how much pleasure you can give another person. I could never let anyone else do the things I let him do to me.

Like control my fucking orgasm.

He's exclusively sucking on my clit like he's trying to suck a too thick milkshake through a straw, and I can feel my release building in my core. It's like a trail of gasoline has been set fire throughout my body and its headed straight for my center where it's all about to combust.

River pulls away, leaving my jewel aching.

"What the fuck?"

He falls beside me on the bed. "Get on my face. I wanna watch you come."

My eyes bug. "I can't get up."

He lets out a low chuckle, sits up, and helps me onto my knees. Before he lies back down, he brushes my cheek with his knuckles and gives me a kiss, sucking my lower lip between his.

I try to center myself over his mouth, but I quickly lose balance, my knee landing on his chest. His hands grip firmly to my hips, urging me to try again. I lift my arms slightly from where they rest on my back. "It'd be easier if..."

His lips quipped upward, amused by my plight. "You got this, babe."

When I try again, I get my leg the rest of the way over him and look down. He lets go of my hips and reaches up, cupping one breast in each hand.

"So fucking perfect," he tells me with his eyes on my chest. Then he looks at my face before lowering his hands onto my ass and squeezing. "C'mon."

I inch forward on my knees until I'm centered over River's mouth. His death grip on my ass is urging me to lower myself onto his eager lips, and I give him exactly what we both want. It's been minutes since my orgasm was about to crest but it takes no time for the burn to build back up inside me. River's lips and tongue go to work, absorbing my vigorous motions over his face. The urge to lean forward is excruciating as my body wants to fold against itself to find that fleeting high of an orgasm, but if I do, I will fall forward face first with nothing to catch me. The friction is intense. So intense that I'm barely even aware that River is a part of all this anymore. He becomes an object for me to use to bring my release.

I'm vaguely aware of the sound of my groans as I grind myself against him as my climax starts to bubble up. "Oh, my God," I call out, followed by a long, drawn-out nonsensical sound as the orgasm bubble bursts inside me. Pressing harder against his face, I try to drag it out as long as I can, without realizing that I've leaned forward too much.

When my face plants onto the mattress, I twist to my side immediately, panting like I'd just run a marathon. I can still feel the aftershocks of my climax in my bones.

River rolls to his side and buries his face in my pussy. My little bundle of nerves is on fire, and he fucking knows it. He goes straight for it, sucking it in between his lips. "Fuck," I say, meeting his eyes as I wrap my thick thighs around the back of his head. I thrust my hips trying to bring on another explosion as soon as possible.

But I'm already thinking ahead to the next step. River has not gotten off yet. I drew a line saying no sex and we've held to it, only doing things like we're doing right now. But usually, those sessions have him getting off first and then me because after I come, I'm fucking done. I am not working to make him get off. Which means he's anticipating being able to fuck the shit out of my exhausted body.

Before I can decide what to do, I'm coming again. I gasp as my body goes rigid. A prolonged groan slips between my lips uncontrolled. "Holy shit," I say as my second orgasm tapers off. I drop my legs, letting River free.

He doesn't move immediately but pulls his face back as his fingers slide through my wetness. "You're so fucking wet, babe."

"No shit," I breathe out.

His eyes find mine. "I'm going to fuck you."

It would be a lie if I said I didn't want to feel his cock inside me.

He gets up on his knees, lifting one of my legs and resting it on his shoulder. The shine of my juices covers his beautiful face. "Is that okay?" The head of his dick slides across the slick folds.

My nod of consent is barely complete when he shoves his dick into me. "Holy fuck, Em, I missed this pussy." His eyes close as his body stills. I can feel him twitching inside me.

I'm still on my side, one of my legs on the bed, his legs on either side of it. The resistance of him holding my other leg is just enough for me to push against in an attempt to feel him deeper inside of me. Ever since the first time we had sex nearly nine years ago, when he first enters me, he pauses. I used to think it was some sort of battle in his conscience over fucking his cousin, but he later told me that the initial thrust inside me was a feeling unrivaled to anything else and that he wanted to savor it.

I just wanted to be fucked.

He opens his eyes and begins to stroke his cock inside me. "I love you, Emma." His brows are pulled together. "I love you so fucking much." He shakes his head and looks away. "I wish you fucking understood."

"I love you too," I assure him, but he's pumping into me now and I'm not sure he's listening.

"I can't let you go. I won't." His words come out through gritted teeth. "I won't."

I barely hear him. His length is deep inside me, filling and stretching me. This position allows him to move deeply within me. The tip of his cock is tapping my cervix gently, providing an amazing blend of pleasure and pain. Exactly what he knows I like. He's grunting with every thrust, his eyes closed now, and I fear he's going to blow already. It's been so long since I was decently fucked, and I am nowhere near ready to have this end.

His mouth falls and his eyes spring open as he pulls himself from inside me, dropping my leg in the process. Without a word, he grabs the belt around my wrists and uses it to turn my body over so that I'm on my stomach. "Ass up, babe."

I work to get on my knees, sliding forward on the bed until my head hits the upholstered headboard. He pulls me toward him some, being considerate of my head hitting the headboard with what he's about to do to me. My face is smashed between the pillows, and I want to grab them and move them but can't. I'm about to ask River to do it, but then I feel his face between my legs again. This time though he's licking upward from my throbbing, swollen pussy to in between my ass cheeks. I groan, enjoying the sensation of his stiff, wet tongue circling my puckered hole.

He chuckles lightly as he straightens behind me. "You ready?"

I nod.

"Tell me what you're ready for."

"I'm ready for you to fuck me."

The head of his cock is pressing against my opening. "Tell me you want me."

I try to look back at him but can barely see him behind me. He's just a blur of skin and hair. "I want you, River. I want you to fuck me. Fuck me hard."

"Fuck, yes," he says, surging inside me.

I love this position. He's reaching parts of me he couldn't hit before, and I'm lost in a sea of oblivion in no time. Everything seems to slow and when he pulls back in between his thrusts, I am desperate for him to push back into me, gifting me with the hurt that feels so good.

I don't ever want it to end.

River said he can't let me go and I don't want him to. I don't think I can let him go either. And yeah, maybe at the moment I'm a little distracted by how perfectly he's fucking me, but I really do love him.

The mind-blowing sex is definitely an added bonus.

I'm brought back to the present, where I'm in touch with what's happening outside of my body and not just the phenomenon he's creating inside of me, when he starts rubbing his thumb over my unoccupied tiny hole. I arch my back, his cock hitting on a new angle as he spits in between my ass cheeks.

My constant low groan has stopped, unsure if he thinks he's going to try to fuck my ass with spit alone. It's not that we haven't, but it's just not as enjoyable without lube. Even he agrees.

His thumb presses against the hole until it enters. He spits some more, sliding his thumb in and out of my ass slowly, and in no time, I'm lost again in the sensations. He keeps spitting, replacing his thumb with one finger, and then two. They circle and probe delicately inside me. between him fingering my ass and impaling my vagina, I feel full, and a tickle starts to grow inside of me.

"Holy fuck," I mutter. "Don't stop. Don't ever fucking stop."

The speed at which River is ramming into both of my holes is quickening. I feel full but light at the same time. Almost like I'm suspended midair. It's like a fucking drug. The tickling in my abdomen is growing, spreading throughout my middle before an explosion I've only felt a few times before ripples through my entire body and soul with hurricane force. I'm crying out from the sheer force of it, my body shaking with convulsions.

Vaginal orgasms are not a myth.

"I'm gonna come," River declares. He pulls his fingers from inside me and grips my hips, pulling my extra skin so tightly I know I'll have bruises, as he throttles his rock-hard member into my convulsing flesh. "Oh, my God, Em. Holy fuck!" With the word *fuck*, he gives one final hard, painful thrust into me, making me cry out from the force of it, before he lets out a low, long groan. His motions slow as he empties himself inside me, his entire body twitching.

The moment comes too soon. He pulls out of me, and I fall flat onto the bed, exhausted. Carefully, he unfastens the belt from around my wrists and rubs the flesh that was tucked under the leather. His fingers tickle along the length of my spine. "I'm gonna get some washcloths."

My eyes are glued to the curve of his perfect ass retreating to the bathroom when I realize I allowed the rules to be broken. I said no more sex but threw it all to the wind when he showed up, took off his fucking belt, and reminded me who was really in charge.

And maybe I'm just high on residual orgasms right now, but I have no regrets.

CHAPTER NINE

River

After I gently clean Emma up and put her water on the nightstand beside her, I ask if she needs anything else. She looks up at me with fear in her eyes before shaking her head. "I'm not leaving," I say, unsure if that's a reassurance or if she was hoping for the opposite. She doesn't say anything, so I sit beside her on the bed. "Sit up. Let me rub your shoulders. I know they have to hurt."

She sits up with her back to me, and I begin to rub her shoulders, upper arms, and shoulder blades, paying close attention to the way her body reacts to my touch. "Why aren't you at work?" she asks quietly.

I exhale, not at all surprised that she still wants an answer to one of the first questions she asked when I arrived. "Because Em..." Every possible way to say what I need to say is going to make me sound like an obsessed, possessive asshole. Which, let's face it, I am. It will also give her the opportunity to retort with the fact of my infidelities. I choose a different approach. One that I'm not ready to admit is accurate. "When I have cheated on you, it's been because I'm afraid. Afraid that we would get to a point of no return and not be brave enough to... to take the leap.

That we would forever be stuck in a rut together of this fantasy where we're together but we're not. And I get in my head and convince myself that all of this means nothing.

"But Emma..." I stop rubbing her shoulders and crane my neck to look at her face. There are tears on her cheeks. "This is what I want. You're all I want. And I'm not just saying that because of the sex. You're a part of me and I can't fucking live without you being this person in my life." She turns her face away from me. "Not my cousin. Not someone I see on holidays and shit. You're the one I want forever, and I know you feel the same way. And we are just going to have to own up to it and come clean."

She sniffles, lifting her hand to her face. "You really think they're just going to be, like, okay, cool, so happy for you guys?" Her hair shifts when she faces me, tickling my bare chest. "They're not, Riv, and then we're gonna have to deal with that and with the disgusted looks we get from everyone for the rest of our lives."

I shake my head. "I do not care. We never have to go back home again. We can make our own family."

She looks away from me. It's not the first time I've said these things. "River..."

"We need to stop letting our fear make decisions for us."

"What if they disown us or whatever? Shame us. Banish us. I don't know."

I kiss her shoulder softly, trailing my lips toward her neck. "Let them. As long as I have you. That's literally the only thing that matters."

Her sigh is as heavy as bricks. She leans back against me, and I fold her into my arms. "If only that were true."

We sit silently for a moment, a home improvement show playing on the television. I know what I have to do and there is an ache in my gut because of it. When Emma's stomach growls, I'm reminded of the Mexican food I hijacked from the DoorDash driver. She clutches her stomach and giggles. "Sorry I interrupted your dinner," I tell her.

She pulls away from me to get out of bed, but I don't let her go. "I'll get it for you."

While she situates herself against the headboard, I find her tank top and toss it onto the bed within her reach. Locating my boxers, I pull them on before opening up her food containers revealing her usual steak fajitas and guacamole dip with chips. After handing her the food, I pick up my jeans from the floor and pull out my cell phone.

My eyes are on Emma when I sit back down beside her. She's watching the demo team on the TV tearing out a kitchen sink with great interest as she eats. My phone is open to my mom's contact. I let out a sigh and call her.

Emma looks at me. "Who are you calling?"

"My mom," I say just as my mom answers. "Hey, Mom."

Emma stops mid-chew, her eyes rounded at me.

"Hey, hon," my mom coos. "I thought you worked on Monday nights."

"I took tonight off," I tell her.

"Oh, okay." The slur in her voice is slight.

I glance at the alarm clock on the nightstand beside me. It's seven-thirty. Hopefully she's not too sloshed yet. Then again, I haven't lived at home in years and really have no idea what she does all day now that she doesn't have me to pretend to take care of. "I just wanted to let you know that I took that Friday off so me and Em can come up that evening. And Emma is taking Monday off so we can have two full days at home."

"That's awesome." I can hear genuine excitement in her voice.

Emma's staring at me. She didn't take Monday off. But she will now.

"I, uh…" I falter with my words and meet Emma's gaze. "When I'm there, we have something really important to tell you guys." Emma's eyes fall before she turns away, setting her plastic fork atop her fajita meat.

"Oh?" My mom's voice rises as she drags out the syllable. "You're gonna make me wait until then?"

I rub my thumb on the outside of Emma's elbow. "Yeah, it's kinda something we need to share in person. Probably at the brunch on Mother's Day so everyone is there." The ache in my gut is growing despite thinking taking the first step would make me, *us*, feel better.

Emma faces me with fire in her eyes. It's a fight not to smile at her. I want to grab her face with both hands and kiss her until her eyes are soft again.

I finish up the conversation with my mom and end the call. Emma's staring at the television again, but I can tell she's not really watching it. "Hey," I say quietly.

"Are we really gonna do this?" Her voice is strangled over her words.

Just saying 'yes' doesn't seem like it does our situation justice. So, I choose my words carefully. "I'm gonna marry you, Emma Novak, and I don't care what anyone says about it."

We were almost fifteen when I first realized the complexity of our relationship. Ever since I could remember, Emma had been my best friend. No one at school gave it much thought because we were cousins. At home, both of our parents were sure to remind us plenty of times that we were cousins. But it was only because we were friends that my aunt Christy met Chris Novak in the first place. And it was shortly after they met that I decided Emma was my girlfriend.

After Christy married Chris, and thus everyone throwing a wet blanket over mine and Emma's young love, we dropped the boyfriend-girlfriend label. It didn't seem like any big deal at the time because we were still friends and—even better—now we were cousins, which was far superior to being friends.

Except as we got older, those cutesy little feelings we had for each other didn't fade. Our hormones and bodies started changing, hers more than mine at first, and I found myself wondering what she looked like without her clothes on. And then I would scold myself for thinking of my cousin that way. I felt ashamed of the things I thought and tried to avoid her.

Despite my efforts, we couldn't stay apart. Because underneath all of it, we were friends. And that was exactly how she saw me. I was scrawny and wore braces. She was tall and curvy and will always be the prettiest girl in any room. My friends talked about her changing body, and I knew she would end up falling for someone who was more her caliber. One of the guys whose puberty had arrived when hers had.

Emma and I spent a lot of time together. Doing schoolwork, going to games, hanging out, watching movies. It was a friend zone I couldn't escape.

During ninth grade, my puberty arrived with a crash and a bang. I grew six inches and gained fifty pounds between the start of school and our birthday in May. My body ached and I was in pain from how quickly I grew. My mom repeatedly took me to the doctor to figure out if there was something wrong with me. I was uncomfortable with myself all the time. My posture was slumped, and I kept my head down. School was a nightmare. I had gone from being a skinny little dweeb that could sometimes make people laugh because I was funny, to being one of the tallest guys in our grade in the blink of an eye. Everyone stared at me, and I felt one hundred percent like a freak. When people laughed, I was sure it was at me or about me. I fucking hated myself.

But when I was with Emma, I felt normal. I was myself again. I latched onto her during my freshman year in high school and fell so hard for her that I still haven't picked myself up off the floor.

The first time I kissed her was a complete fluke that was not planned. It was Christmas and we were celebrating at Noni's house. Uncle Gary always dressed up like Santa and handed out gifts to all the kids. Me and Emma, being the two oldest, got to be Santa's helpers. Noni sent us out to her garage to get the sacks full of gifts. Once we retrieved them, we were supposed to plant them on the porch and then pretend they suddenly appeared, drawing the other kids to the door and window to see. Then Uncle Gary would come around the corner of the house in his Santa suit acting like his sleigh had just landed and tell everyone how his elves had put the gifts on the porch.

It was the third year me and Em were the secret helpers.

"Holy shit, it's freezing," Emma said when we entered the garage. "Why can't Christmas be in the summer?"

"Probably should take that up with Jesus. Maybe the Virgin Mary," I suggested.

She gave me the side eye. "Did you just say virgin?"

I chuckled. "Did you?"

"I suppose I did." She looked around the garage. "There's three bags."

I eyed the overflowing sacks of gifts. "We can each grab one and then I'll come back for the last one."

"Okay."

We each picked up a big sack of gifts and hoofed it in the frigid temps back to Noni's porch, snow crunching under our feet. We set our bags down in sync, looked at each other and ran back to the garage. "I said I would get it," I pointed out. I reached the garage first thanks to my new and improved extra-long legs. I stopped just inside the door and turned around as she slammed into me. My arms went around her as I struggled to keep my balance.

She didn't pull away. Breathless, she lifted her face to look up at me. Her cheeks were red from the cold and strands of her caramel-colored hair hung across her forehead. Her tongue slid between her lips, wetting them.

I didn't even think about it. It just seemed like exactly what I was supposed to do. What I was always meant to do. There was no fear or second thoughts. My mouth lowered onto her soft, damp limps. There was a lingering hint of peppermint and hot cocoa between us. Her hands pushed gently against my abdomen, but she didn't pull away. Our lips mashed together softly, like we were skating on thin ice and everything would break if there was any sudden movement.

When we pulled apart, it was together. Her eyes were full of questions I wouldn't have the right answers to for years, and my stomach was full of butterflies that would never fly away.

"We need to get Santa's last sack." She was breathless when she spoke.

But I didn't give two fucks about the sack, Christmas, or any of it. "I'm gonna marry you someday, Emma Novak, and I don't care what anyone says about it."

The day after I called my mom with promises of big news, it was my regular day off. Because I work every other weekend, I get alternating Tuesdays and Fridays off. Convincing Emma to skip work wasn't as hard as I expected. We needed the time to talk and get our ducks in a row now that the groundwork has been laid. She never finished her fajitas last night, but the hotel had a full hot breakfast available. I figured that after we ate, we would check out and go home.

Emma woke up with other plans. Plans she wanted to share with me. It was barely six in the morning when I woke up to getting my dick sucked. Months had passed since the last time that happened.

While I'm usually the more dominant one in our relationship sexually, she takes her moments, and I revel in them. Just like I revel in all the moments with our clothes on that she calls the shots. As she wordlessly mounts me, bringing me inside of her, I stare up, completely enthralled by her mere existence and know I can't let our fear hold us back any longer. I can't let her talk me out of telling the truth. I want her and only her and I will give my last breath fighting for us.

Chapter Ten

River

In the mix of everything that happened since I followed Emma to her hotel, I had completely forgotten what I had done at home. "Fuck," I mutter as Emma stands in the entrance of our apartment slack jawed.

"What did you do, River?" she hisses.

I walk around her and survey the damage with fresh eyes. There are multiple holes in the walls. My desk and everything that was on it are on the floor. The coffee table, which I threw at the TV, is halfway on the entertainment stand, halfway on the floor. The TV is pushed into the wall and I'm fairly certain the screen is broken from the coffee table hitting it. The only thing still in its place is the couch because I sat there and cried like a baby after letting my anger out.

"We won't get our deposit back," she points out. Like that's the only problem.

"I was upset." I run my fingers along the cracked drywall closest to me. "I can probably patch these up. Watch a YouTube video or something."

She gives me the side eye before going to her bedroom with her purse and tote bag. I follow with her suitcase. "Babe," she says with a sigh. She doesn't need to continue. I didn't make the bed. It's one of her biggest pet peeves.

"I know, I know. Sorry." Leaving her suitcase in the doorway, I go to the bed and begin smoothing out the covers before setting the throw pillows in their place.

When I finish, I look for her approval. She's smiling. "Thank you. But I also realized that if the TV out there is broken, we're gonna be spending all our time in here."

There is no TV in my bedroom. We never sleep in there so there is no point in having one. It's basically a place for me to keep my clothes and shoes and offers a great front for when our parents visit. Emma even messes up my bed when they visit to make it look realistic.

"That TV is definitely broken." I stand behind her, pulling her into my arms as I kiss the top of her head. "And my favorite place to be is in your bed."

She spins in my arms, resting her hands on my chest. "Mine too."

"Second favorite place to be is anywhere you are."

We don't often say *I love you*. I'm not really sure why. Maybe it's the whole cousin thing. Maybe it's because both of her parents toss the phrase out constantly at every juncture. You're going to the kitchen for a snack? *Love you!* Going to the bathroom? *Love you!* Taking a phone call in another room? *Love you!* Pulling a blanket over your lap while watching a movie? *Love you!*

The words are meaningless. What matters is knowing you are loved. The actions that are shown assure us we are loved. My dad, being gone more than home, did not tell me that he loved me or my mom. My mom being drunk more than sober did not tell me that she loves me. Uncle Chris and Aunt Christy allowing me to stay at their house when my parents were fighting because my mom was drunk and my dad was always gone, showed me they loved me. Emma, living a secret life with me for nine years, shows me I am loved.

Which maybe explains on some level why I'm scared of coming clean. My dad is an asshole. When I was little, I would get spanked for bad grades or getting into trouble at school. Dad would use his hand on my bare ass. Then it was a hairbrush until the hairbrush broke. Once I was taller and bigger than him, he would get in my face and scream, his breath reeking of bourbon while he pushed me into a corner, antagonizing me to get me to hit him first. I never did. I always stood there and took his abuse *like a man*, as he would say, while my mom watched without intervening.

The only thing I learned from that was how much it sucks to get yelled at and hit. It didn't make me get better grades or behave at school, but it did teach me who I didn't want to be. Which is why I rarely raise my voice and try my hardest not to lash out at Emma. When I drink now, I know my limits, though that wasn't always the case.

My dad is a very public person. Weston McIntyre, or Wes Mac as he's more commonly known, is a United States senator. And because of that, when I got arrested for public intoxication shortly after turning twenty-one, it made the news. As if everyone didn't already think of me as the black sheep of the family, that cemented it.

Emma bailed me out and we never planned to tell anyone what happened. Word spread and my dad showed up at our apartment screaming with rage. I tried to tuck my tail between my legs, actually feeling badly that I brought public shame to his name, but when he punched me, the smidgen of respect I had left for my dad went out the door with him.

That didn't mean I wasn't afraid of his reaction to finding out about me and Emma. It could easily go public and embarrass him. There is so much more to *us* than being cousins though we know that would be the only part anyone focused on.

Emma pulls away from me. "Let's get it cleaned up."

"I'll do it. It's my mess."

"It's my fault."

I raise my eyebrows. "It's not your fault I have anger issues."

"Maybe not, but I'm still gonna help."

We don't say much at first. I start with my desk, throwing out the items she poured lube on the other day. I'm assuming the monitors weren't affected by the lube, but I may have wrecked them by throwing them to the floor. Something to worry about another day.

"I, uh, told my dad I was thinking about moving home," Emma tells me as she brushes chunks of busted dry wall into a dustpan. "So, if your mom tells Christy we have big news, they're all going to assume it's that we're moving back home."

I looked across the room at her. She's crouched down to the floor as she picks up bigger chunks of drywall from the carpet. "I mean, we could still do that if you want to."

Her eyes go wide as she sits on her bottom. "You say that like they're going to be okay with this. That the people we grew up with are going to be cool with this." She scoffs. "Could you imagine our kids going to Thomas City Elementary and having Ms. Bristol as their teacher? Have the kids of the people we grew up with in their class? Our kids would be ostracized worse than us." She shakes her head. "Not happening. If we're doing this, then we're staying right here. Or going somewhere else entirely."

My smile spreads from ear to ear.

She lets out a nervous laugh. "Why are you smiling like that?"

I shrug. "Thinking about having kids with you, I guess."

"We're a long way from that, buddy." She stands, picking up the dustpan as she does. "Buying a house, getting married." Her eyes settle on me. "Step one, telling the truth."

"Step one is easy," I tease, straightening my desk chair.

Emma snorts as she leaves the room. "Yeah, that's why we've not done it in nine years."

"Nine years ago, we didn't know it was going to become *this*."

She wears a grin when she returns to the living room. "Oh, so you just thought you could fuck your cousin and move on with your life."

My smile fades. "You know I hate when you say it like that."

"I do."

"Then why do you do it? Makes me feel like some inbred freak."

Obviously, we know there's nothing inbred about this. But that doesn't remove the label of cousin from describing our relationship.

"You know," Emma says. "There are people out there who legit fuck their blood cousins and siblings and even their own kids. We are not them. And we have to remember that and stick to the facts of our situation. We are not related by blood. We were friends before we became family, and we have continued to be friends." She pauses and looks at me. "But what we share isn't going away. We tried that. Now we have to try something new. And it might be uncomfortable for us and for them, but if they actually love us, they will grow to accept it and be okay with it."

Fuck, yes. Emma is on board. "I wanna kiss you right now."

She cocks her head. "What's stopping you?"

I screw up my face like I'm trying to come up with a reason. "Probably the fact that you're my cousin and our parents would disapprove."

Her head falls back as she laughs. "Probably shouldn't tell them how many times you've made me come in the last twenty-four hours, should I?"

Crossing the room to her, my gut grows tight. "I'm about to add another one to it."

She backs up. "Only one?"

I grab the back of her head and pull her face to mine. Her hands rest on my hips. "I'm gonna make you come so many times and so fucking hard you're gonna need to take the rest of the week off work from exhaustion." I lower my mouth to hers and nip her lower lip with my teeth. "You're gonna be screaming my name so loud the people down the block will be looking for a fucking River." My hand slides between her thighs and rubs her through the fabric of her jeans. "I'm gonna pump so much cum inside you that your birth control is going to be calling the police for back-up."

She laughs, but I try not to smile. I press my already growing cock against her hip. "All I'm hearing is a lot of talk with no action."

My mouth devours hers, our tongues dancing together as she slips her hands inside my shirt. Her fingers rake across my chest leaving tingles of electricity in their path. I lift her by the thighs and wrap her legs around me before carrying her to the couch. Laying her down across the length of it, I hover over her and break our kiss. She places her hands on my cheeks and our eyes meet. "Are you ready?"

Her eyes twitch. "For what?"

My original intention was to ask if she was ready for me to fuck her. But there is something bigger at stake. "To spend the rest of your life with me."

She blinks a few times, clearly not expecting that. Then she runs her hands behind my head and pulls me closer to her. "I can't imagine it any other way."

Resting my weight on my knees between her legs, I unfasten her jeans, tugging them down before I stand and pull them the rest of the way off.

She peels off her socks and tosses them to the floor before bending her legs at the knee and spreading her thighs to show me her whole world. For a moment I pause and appreciate her beauty and perfection. I will never, ever grow tired of Emma. I love her more than I can ever love myself. Her happiness, her needs come before mine in every aspect of life.

She's so good to me. Way better than I deserve. Especially with all I've done to hurt her.

I kneel on the floor beside the couch and run my fingers through her slickness a few times, my eyes on hers, before one finger slithers inside her. Slowly at first, probing as deep as it can. She bites her lower lip when my thumb presses against her clit. A flood of nostalgia rushes into me, recalling long ago when we first started to explore each other's bodies. How we had no idea what we were doing and just did things we'd heard about or had seen in movies.

The first orgasm Emma ever had was from me doing exactly what I was doing now. I didn't even know what or where a clit was when I fingered her back then. But as I rammed my fingers inside her while we sat on the couch in my game room, her pants barely pulled down, her body suddenly went stiff before she made a sound and then shook like she got the chills.

"Holy shit," she breathed out. "I don't know what you just did but it felt good." I had stopped moving. She looked at me. "Like, really, really good."

I know what I'm doing now. There is no doubt I can make any girl come but I never try with anyone else. Making Emma feel good is part of my purpose in life, I suppose, and over the course of time, I have figured out how to make her come with my hand, mouth, cock, and toys. I know her body better than I know anything, even myself.

My two middle fingers are inside her, curving to hit the G-spot just as she likes. Her back is arched as she thrusts her hips against my hands. The sloppy sound of my fingers in her wetness has my cock desperate for attention, not to mention the feel of her pussy walls gripping my hand. I'm avoiding her clit on purpose because I know she likes what I'm doing and as soon as I touch her there, she will explode.

Using my left hand, I free myself from my pants and start stroking. Emma looks at me as she turns her head, opening her mouth for me. I shake my head. "Don't worry about me."

I spit into my left hand and rub it over my head and then down my length while Emma lays beside me moaning and thrashing about. Her hand hovers over her center and I know she wants to come. She's desperate to touch herself and get the rush that she craves. But I beat her to it, rubbing my thumb over her bundle of nerves in quick circles, she quickly arches her body off the couch and yells out. "Oh, my fuck. Fuck!" She thrusts into the air as I hold onto her sweet spot as long as I can to draw it out for her. The sweet aroma of her has my mouth watering and I'm desperate to bury my face between her legs and lap up every drop of her.

She falls back to the couch and opens her eyes into mine. "Holy fuck, Riv."

I pull my fingers from inside her, gathering up as much wetness as I can before rubbing her juices all over my cock. Still stroking, I rise up beside her face, resting my knees on the couch cushion. My dick is several inches from her mouth and that's okay. She licks her parted lips, eyes on the quickness with which I'm jacking myself off.

Out of the corner of my eye, I see her own hand slip between her still spread legs, rubbing over her engorged clit. My balls grow tight, and I can feel my fuse about to blow. I'm panting and I can hear the thud of my heart in my ears over the roar I let out as my seed comes out in several spurts all over Emma's lips and face. She props herself on her elbows, tongue extended, and I push forward onto her tongue, letting her run circles around my head before she opens her mouth all the way, sucking my length clean while she stares up at me.

My dick falls from her mouth with a pop, and I hit it against her cheek a few times, smiling at her. "You're such a good little whore," I tell her affectionately.

She smiles back, wiping her fingers along her face to gather errant ejaculate. Then she licks her fingers clean. "Only for you."

CHAPTER ELEVEN

Emma

River is a fucking asshole.

Like, seriously.

It wasn't always this way. But when he grew up, so did his ego.

That's not to say he doesn't have a sweet, caring, considerate side, because he most definitely does. But sometimes his cockiness makes me want to throat punch him. And it's always at its worst when were about to have a big blow up, which is usually brought about by him fucking around with someone.

It seems like we're through the worst of his hoe days, but there is still the unaddressed issue of him and our neighbor Lillian. I'm sure there are others I don't know about, but the air needs cleared, nonetheless.

We're watching some stupid action movie where a cop comes out of retirement because he's apparently the only person on planet Earth who can track some serial killer, and I'm bored. River eats these movies up. He doesn't always want to work at the prison. He wants to be a 'real cop,' as he calls it, and someday become a detective.

"Hey," I say as the retired cop combs through some top-secret documents he shouldn't have access to. "We need to talk about the bitch downstairs."

He glances at me quickly from his side of my bed. "Do we?"

"Yeah, we do. And we also need to talk about how Makenna knows we're related."

Swallowing, he picks up the remote and pauses the movie. "I'm gonna assume Jack told her."

I raise my eyebrows. "Why does Jack know?"

"We were fighting, and I was pissed and drunk."

"Ah, yes. The age-old excuse."

He looks down. "I didn't know he told Makenna. But to be fair, it was before you met them."

I let out a laugh. "So, she's probably known since before I even met her."

After Makenna dropped that bomb on me the other night, I hung up on her. My two lives didn't intermingle. Like oil and vinegar. They refused to coexist in the same space.

Unless that space is this apartment, my bed, or the fold of River's arms. He is my whole fucking life and those are the parts that truly matter.

"She implied that you're using me."

River chortled. "Using you?"

"For sex, I guess."

"You know that's not true."

"Do I? Because if you're comfortable telling Jack *that*, then what else have you told him? And what are they saying behind our backs?"

"It's not like that, Em."

"They're saying I'm stupid to think my smoking hot cousin really wants me when he could have 'fifty other girls by this time tomorrow.'"

River twists himself, and he is suddenly on top of me, glaring down with anger in his eyes and I fucking welcome it.

"The whole world knows you're out of my league," I remind him. "I don't need to hear it from my so-called friends."

"Shut up," he growls.

I push at his chest. "Get the fuck off me."

He moves his hands from where he's pinned my shoulders down to around my neck. I lift my chin to give his hands more room because he doesn't scare me.

"Tell me how you ended up sleeping with the skank downstairs."

The tightening of his hands is subtle. "You cut me off."

I narrow my eyes. "I will cut *it* off."

He smirks. "Nah, you like it too much."

"I can find fifty other dicks by this time tomorrow, Riv. Guys love these thick thighs."

His smirk fades as anger darkens his eyes.

I wink. "No worries, babe. I'll FaceTime you so you can watch."

He rolls his neck, popping it. "You really don't think I'll kill a man?"

I shrug.

His face lowers to mine. "I'll get away with it too."

"I hope so." I bring my hand up to his cheek and pat it twice. "Not sure what I would do if I didn't have you to use me."

A smile plays on his lips as his hands tighten even more around my throat. "This is what you wanted, isn't it?" His tongue darts out quickly, wetting his lips. "Is your pussy dripping yet, whore?"

There *is* a tingle between my legs, but I'll never admit it out loud. Not that I can. When I open my mouth to speak, I realize his grip is tighter than I thought and the pressure on my windpipe is making it hard to draw in a breath. I touch the back of his hand.

He lets go and I take in a breath.

"All that is done, Em," he says, sitting back down on the bed. "I'm not fucking around with anyone ever again. You mean too much to me, and I feel like we've reached a fork in the road. If we're putting it out there for our families, then we have to be solid. I only need one girl, not fifty, and you're the girl I pick." He looks at me lying beside him. "The end."

I rub my throat for a moment before reaching under the blanket to press my fingers against my center and soothe the ache. "The end?"

He cups himself between the legs. "This will never touch anyone else." Reaching over, he grabs my crotch. He laughs when he discovers my hand is already there. "Are you masturbating?"

"I had an itch."

He gives me a skeptical look. "My little whore likes getting choked a bit too much." His hand presses against mine, pushing firmly against my center. "Emphasis on the '*my*' part."

Letting go, he picks up the remote and starts the movie again. I sigh, well aware he never gave me an answer about Lillian at all.

It reminds me of all the times before when he would admit to being with someone else but nothing more. Which was almost worse than knowing the details. For some reason, my sick mind craved the specifics.

A couple years ago, we had a huge blow up. The weight of our lies was on me that day and I was caught up in how the us we pretended to be would only ever be make-believe. I told him all of this was fake and never meant anything to me. And then he left after shoving me into a wall with tears in his eyes. I told him I would see him in hell or the next family reunion. I cried myself to sleep, completely sure it was really over. I'd said too much and made him cry.

When I woke up at three in the morning and he wasn't home, I checked his location. I didn't know where he was other than an apartment building right off the interstate. I started calling on FaceTime.

After five times of him not answering, I got dressed and went looking for him. Usually when I did this, I would find him drunk, sometimes even passed out. But every time I went on a mission to find his dumb ass, I entirely expected to find him with someone else.

I stared at the apartment building I'd tracked him to with no way of knowing which unit he was in. His car was parked on the street in front of the building, and I had parked behind it. I got out of my car and looked into his windows for a clue, not that there would be one. As I walked back to my vehicle, River returned my call on FaceTime.

"It's just my cousin," he was saying when I answered. "Chill the fuck out." His face came into view, but he wasn't looking at his phone. His eyes were focused on something in front of him, his cheeks bright red, eyes drooping from the effects of alcohol. He flashed a lazy smile when he looked at the phone. "Hey. You called."

"Where are you?"

"At this girl's house." He looked in front of him. "What's your name again?"

I recognized the look of concentration on his face. His set lips and pulled together brows. My heartrate quickened. "What are you doing?"

"Anna," he said quickly. "Her name is Anna."

"What are you doing, River?"

He looked right at me. Like he could see my soul, raw and open. "I'm doing Anna."

I stopped walking. "You're fucking some bitch with me on the phone?"

He screwed up his face. "Who cares? You're no one to me." He squint-ed at the phone and then the camera flipped.

Anna's ass took up the majority of the screen. She's bottoms up on a bed, and I can see River's dick sliding in and out of her.

I was sure I would be sick. "Are you fucking kidding me right now?"

"Nah, definitely not." He flipped the screen back to him and dropped the phone on the bed beside him. "You told me to go. Told me what we had wasn't real."

I turned and walked into the lobby of the building. "Show me the condom."

"What?" he asked, glancing at the phone. "Look at me, Em. I wanna see your face."

A line of chrome mailboxes occupied the wall to the left of the door in the lobby. I scanned them for the name Anna. Apartment 3B is Anna Cartman. "I wanna see the condom, River."

"Who the fuck is that?" Anna asked.

"Shut the hell up," he told her.

I started up the stairs. "Condom now or I'm cutting it off when I find you."

He laughed and pulled his dick out of her, dangling it above the phone. "Happy, bitch?" he asked without looking at me.

Happy is not a word I would use to describe any emotion I had at that moment.

"This is what you wanted so don't even act like you're mad," he told me. "Put your ass back up here," he instructed Anna.

"Get off the fucking phone," she retorted.

"This is not what I wanted, and you know it," I said.

"Is she your girlfriend?" Anna asked.

"Nah," River told her. "Just my cousin." He's looking straight at me when he says it. Then he's looking at her again. "Let me fuck your ass."

"Stick your dick in her again and I'll cut it off," I said.

Laughing, he picked up the phone, flipping the camera again just in time for me to watch his covered dick push against her nasty hole while she calls out a stream of profanities before falling forward onto the bed.

"I am on the third floor of this apartment building, Anna," I said loudly. "Unless you want me to start yelling and beating on doors to let all your neighbors know that you're letting some dude with a girlfriend fuck you in the ass after you just met him, you're gonna get out from under my man and come open your fucking door."

"Fucking chill, Emma," River said. "I'm almost done."

Like I gave a fuck that he was almost done. What, did he think I'd just chill while he blew his fucking load in that bitch's ass? "I am counting to five. One..."

There was rustling on his end of the phone. River groaned. "Fucking come on!"

"I gotta live here," Anna told him.

"Two..."

The FaceTime call ended.

The door to apartment 3B swung open with Anna standing in the doorway, a blanket wrapped around her. "I didn't know he had a girl-friend," she told me. "I'm sorry. I don't want any trouble."

I took in the sight of her. Her hair had obviously been dyed blonde and not dyed well. She was heavier than me, her black eye makeup smeared under her eyes. What struck me the most was that she was at least ten years older than me and River. *At least.*

River appeared from the hallway, buttoning his pants as he spoke, advancing on me quickly, getting in my face. "I'm gonna fucking kill you, Emma. You can't fucking tell me you don't want me and that I'm worthless and mean nothing and then show up while I'm trying to move the fuck on—"

I slapped him across his face so hard my hand stung. He grabbed me by the throat and pushed me against the door frame. My breath slipped out of me at the force he used.

"I'm calling the cops," Anna announced.

River let go of my throat and grabbed my hair, dragging me into the hallway. I flailed my arms at him, trying to get his hands out of my hair. "Let go of me!"

"Shut the fuck up," he hissed. "Thanks to you she's calling the fucking cops."

"And pulling my hair helps that how?"

He let go, shoving me into the wall as he went around me. I followed him down the stairs quickly. When we reached the last flight, he stumbled and rolled headfirst the rest of the way down. My heart leapt into my throat. I stopped on the second step from the top and stared at him lying on the ground with his arms and legs spread wide. He's staring at the ceiling and for a second, I wondered how badly he was hurt.

Then he let out a laugh. "Fucking trash pussy wasn't even worth all this." He started to get up. "I'm sorry, Em. Can we just go home?"

I didn't answer him as I descended the stairs. Did he really think that little apology was going to make what happened okay? When I reached him, he tried to put his arm around me, but I shoved him away. He took the hint and followed me outside to my car. Pointing at his car, I reminded him, "You drove here."

He looked at his car parked in front of mine. "I can't fucking drive. I'm so sloshed right now I might as well be my mom." The laughter that came out of him sounded manic and completely unhinged.

"You wanna leave it here and let the cops run your plates so they can come looking for you?" I unlocked my car. "She saw you put your hands on me."

His head dropped back as he looked at the inky night sky. "Fuck!" Staggering, he walked to his driver's side door. "Follow me, okay?"

I stared at him as I got into my car and shut the door. He stared back at me, and I had half a mind to run him over. But then he got into his car and the thought died. A full minute passed before he pulled out onto the road. By the time we got to the end of the block, I could tell he was drunker than I thought he was. He was swerving, nearly hitting parked cars. Speeding up and slowing down. When he reached the stop sign, he put his car in park and got out before walking back to my car.

"I'm gonna kill myself, Emma."

That was pretty extreme, even for drunk River. "What?"

"I can't drive. I'll end up killing myself or someone else."

"What were you gonna do? Sleep at that whore's house all night."

He smiled at me, letting out a chuckle under his breath. Then he reached into the window and ran his fingers along my jaw. "You're my whore and when we get home—"

I pushed his hand from my face. "Go one more block and turn right. There's a shopping center. We can leave your car there."

He nodded and headed back to his car. Miraculously, we made it to the shopping center. He got into my car and immediately leaned over for a kiss.

I shoved him away. "I'm never fucking touching you again."

River leaned on my shoulder. "Doesn't mean I'm not gonna touch you."

"Not with that nasty dick you're not." I pulled out onto the road. He sat up. "You saw the condom."

"I don't give a fuck. You wanna call me on FaceTime while you're fucking some dusty old bitch and think you're ever gonna fuck me again? What the hell is wrong with you, River?"

He was quiet for a minute. "A lot." There was a pause before he continued. "Probably started when I popped my cousin's cherry." The crazed laugh busts out of him again, sounding like a cross between a laugh and a cry.

I swung my arm, hitting him in his howling mouth with the back of my hand. "Call me your fucking cousin again, you piece of shit."

He started screaming then, just a loud, constant scream, while he beat his fists on the dashboard of my car and doubled over.

I took my foot off the accelerator, honestly scared of him for the first time in a long time. I wasn't sure if I actually hurt him with my backhand or if he was just having some sort of astronomical meltdown.

Then he looked at me, storms raging in his blue eyes. He leaned all the way over, getting in my face and obstructing my view of the road. "Who the hell do you think you are?" he screamed, his spittle hitting my cheeks and lips. "My fucking father? Are you my dad now, Emma? Are you him? 'Cause you're making me feel like he does!" I've stopped driving, the car at a standstill in the middle of the road, my body trembling. River pulled back some and looked in front of us. "Drive!"

I took my foot off the brake and started driving, eyeing him the entire time.

"You know there's a way out of all this, right, Emma?"

I didn't answer.

"We can't be together. We can't be apart. So, you know what we have to do?"

At that point, we still had another ten minutes to go. I felt like I was gonna throw up. My whole body was tense with fear and adrenaline.

River grabbed the steering wheel and turned the car into the oncoming lane. "What do they say in *Romeo and Juliet*? Something something with a kiss I must die?"

I struggle to push the car back into our lane. Thankfully, there were no other cars in sight. "You're scaring me, River. Stop."

He let go of the wheel. "I haven't even given you a reason to be scared yet. Just wait until we get home."

I looked over at him, unsure what he meant. He's pulled my hair, put his hands on my neck, shoved me and pushed me, but never really hurt me. Were any of those things okay? No. But neither was me slapping him. River has anger issues. He always has. The number of times I've seen him flip out and break things, even when we were kids, and then flip a switch and bawl like a baby were unfathomable. But there was something different that time. Maybe it was the alcohol. Maybe he used something else, drugs or something. I don't know.

What I did know was that he was quoting a play famous for lovers who die, trying to cause me to wreck the car, and talking about things being worse when we got home. When I reached the next stoplight, I turned right instead of going straight.

"Where you going?" he asked.

I sucked in my breath. "I'm scared, Riv. I can't take you home like this."

"What?"

I glanced at him. "We're going to the hospital. You're drunk and I don't like the things you're saying."

"No, the fuck we're not. Go home."

I shook my head and pulled into the parking lot of the hospital emergency department. "I'm not going to tell anyone you put your hands on me as long as you don't tell anyone I did either."

"I don't give a fuck about that. Take me home, Emma, I'm fine."

I pulled into a parking spot and turned off the car. "I'm scared of you right now." As I opened the door to get out, he grabbed a handful of my hair and pulled me back.

"Start the fucking car and take me home!"

It was a fight not to scream out, but I didn't. Instead, I threw the keys into the parking lot.

"What the fuck did you do that for?" he yelled, letting go of my hair.

I jumped out of the car before he even had his door open. Grabbing the keys off the asphalt, I started walking toward the entrance to the emergency department as a security guard came outside, his eyes on me.

"Everything okay?" the man asked.

I looked behind me to see River standing beside the trunk of my car. "He's drunk and saying things about dying."

"Emma, no," River pleads. "C'mon. Let's go home. I'm fine."

"You're not fine," I told him.

"You're gonna ruin my future."

I didn't understand what he meant because, quite frankly, our future was already pretty fucked up just from the toxic relationship we'd been entertaining for years. I was pretty sure neither of us would ever be okay.

River took off running in the opposite direction.

Tossing a glance at the security guard, I jogged back to my car, got in, and went after River. After scouring the streets for fifteen minutes and repeatedly calling his phone, I spotted a few police cruisers with their lights rolling.

The police found him before I did.

I parked my car on the dark side street and walked over to them, seeing River in handcuffs with a tear-soaked face. "I'm his cousin," I said loudly so River wouldn't call me his girlfriend. "I was trying to take him home, but he started talking about dying and I got scared."

An officer shined a flashlight at me. "What made you scared?"

I wasn't entirely sure if Anna had called the police, not that it would matter. We would never tell anyone how we'd hurt each other. "I was afraid he might hurt himself when we get home."

"You weren't afraid he'd hurt you?"

I screwed up my face. "No."

The officer turned away from me. "We're taking him back to the hospital. After he's cleared, he can call someone to pick him up."

"I'll just go up there and wait."

The officer looked at me again. "It will be several hours before he's even sobered enough to be evaluated. Go home and get some sleep."

River was sobbing loudly, and my heart broke in half. "His dad's a senator. Wes McIntyre."

"He mentioned that."

Of course he had. Tears burn the back of my eyes. "Can I give him a hug?"

I'm surprised that they let me. When I wrapped my arms around River's waist and leaned on him, he said, "I'm so sorry. So, so sorry. I didn't mean to scare you."

"It's okay, babe," I replied without thinking. "I'll see you in the morning."

He kissed the top of my head. "I love you. Please don't ever leave me."

I shook my head, glancing at the cops. "We'll talk in the morning."

"Thought I heard you say you were cousins?" one of the officers asked as I started back to my car.

"Fuck that cousin shit," River said. "She's my everything."

To this day, I'm still not sure what happened at the hospital, but the call I got in the morning was not from there. It was from the jail. He'd been arrested for public intoxication.

And then we discovered he'd left his phone at Anna's house. Luckily, she was nice enough to give it to me, thoughtfully adding in that I was worth more than a man who cheated on me and treated me like shit.

River's dad got him a lawyer. Once he went through anger management classes and attended a few therapy sessions, the charges were dropped.

I had no idea that being arrested or hospitalized for mental health could prevent him from working in law enforcement. That night was a turning point for River, though. He stopped drinking so much and lashed out at me less. Things were good between us for nearly a year after that.

Now, two years later, I'm lying in bed beside him, planning to give up our big secret in less than a week, and all I can think about is my need to know when and what he did with the nasty neighbor downstairs. I'm thinking about Makenna telling me how Jack and her both fucked Lillian and find myself feeling a little envious. Kinda turned on if I'm being honest. Not that I want Lillian to go down on me or want to watch River fuck her. I'm not sure what I want other than to know. Maybe it would help me understand what I'm lacking that he needs.

"Babe," I say, still paying no attention to the movie. "I want you to tell me about Lillian."

He lets out a sigh and pauses the movie again. "Why?"

CHAPTER TWELVE

River

I lie in bed for an hour after Emma leaves for work on Wednesday. An overwhelming feeling of anxiety has been building inside me since I called my mom Monday night. Emma is right. They are not going to be okay with this.

It's not like we ever thought they would be. It's why we've kept it under wraps all these years. We've had ample opportunities to stop. To walk away from this dysfunction. But now we are at the precipice of changing everything, specifically our future.

Since I'm the one who decided to get the ball rolling, I need to be the one who says what needs to be said. Which means I need to organize my thoughts into relevant points. Anticipating that we will be met with resistance, everything needs to be thought out ahead of time. I need a comeback for every jab that comes our way. And not just some witty, sarcastic comeback, but a valid, logical one.

My dad was a lawyer before he became a politician. He'd urged me to go into law, but I was never interested in thinking that deeply about things. This is the first time I've ever regretted my decision. If I've ever needed to win an argument, it's this one. I don't want to lose my family, our family, but I will sacrifice all of them for Emma. I meant it when I told her we could make our own family.

They're not going to stand in our way.

After I get out of bed, shower, dress, and stuff my face, I find one of Emma's cute little notebooks that she loves to buy insisting she's going to start journaling or some shit. This one has a deep purple cover that says 'You're Bold. You're Beautiful. You're Badass.' There's nothing written inside of it.

I get comfortable on the couch with the notebook and a pen and start writing my speech. We would arrive home on Friday night. On Saturday, they were planning something for our birthday which was still a week away. Sunday was Mother's Day brunch at my parents' house with Noni. That was when I thought it would be the best time to make our announcement. Everyone would be there. It would save us from rumors and misconstrued facts getting spread around.

Emma and I are the oldest of our generation. Uncle Gary and Aunt Kelly have two kids. Kyler just turned nineteen. Jordyn is the next oldest after us at twenty-one and she has a baby. Emma has three half-siblings. Elijah is about ten years younger than her, followed by Cora and Wyatt. Then there's Uncle Jake. He has four kids with three different women and has never been married. Jake is the youngest of my mom's siblings by several years, so his kids are all pretty little.

Luckily, I'm an only child since my parents are terrible. I've wondered a few times if they intentionally never had more kids, but didn't care enough to ask.

Contact with my dad's side of the family is minimal simply because of politics. They don't agree with my dad's views, and quite frankly neither do I. It was the reason we moved to little Podunk Thomas City from Chicago.

I add another fact to the list of reasons me and Emma are meant for each other. We were both born on the same day in the same Chicago hospital and then later ended up in a town that's three hours outside the city with a population of less than five thousand. Things like that don't just happen. Our fate was written in the stars the moment we were born, and no one can tell me otherwise.

I've made a lot of mistakes with Emma over the years. Sometimes hurting her was intentional. No matter what the circumstances were, the reasons were based on the fear of losing her. Our relationship has always operated on a cycle of highs and lows. At our lows, we pushed each other away because we were convinced that we could never be anything more to one another. The highs came after the lows and were full of emotion and feeling and amazing fucking sex. Before we moved downstate for college, our relationship had been our little secret. We told no one. After we broke the ice between us with that kiss in Noni's garage, all bets were off. We were inseparable. The best of friends.

Friends who were *step*cousins.

Friends who made out when no one was around.

Friends who crossed off every first with one another.

Every. Single. One.

We lost our virginity on the floor in my family room while *Grey's Anatomy* played on Netflix. Emma had wanted to be a doctor and was obsessed with that show, determined to be a real life Meredith Grey.

Our senior year in high school, my mom walked into my bedroom while Emma was on top of me. My mom apologized for not making dinner and said she was going to bed.

My mom never made dinner if my dad wasn't home by that point. Her coming into my room without knocking had been completely unnecessary.

Emma sat frozen on top of me for a moment after the door shut. Then she jumped up, ran to the bathroom and vomited.

We thought it was all over. I was positive my dad and Uncle Chris would kill me. Emma was hysterical and could barely calm down enough to leave the bathroom.

"Okay," I told her. "Let's think about this. My mom didn't even say anything about what we were doing. She was passed out when we came up here. Chances of her remembering any of this tomorrow are slim, if she even realized what we were doing."

And I was right. It never came up.

At that point, we'd already both chosen to attend Illini South University four hours away from home. We were more cautious after that, but also more adventurous, doing things in places other than our houses, which sometimes meant having to improvise *how* we did it.

Before we even left for college, I knew how much Emma liked sex to be rough. I'm not sure where it came from, but shortly after we moved on campus, she got drunk and asked me to fuck her like I hate her.

"Like I'm a whore or something," she slurred quietly while tugging at my waistband.

"What does that even mean?" I asked with a laugh.

She got all red faced trying to explain what she wanted.

Safe to say I figured it out. And a whole lot more. There are limits and things that are definitely off limits. And that is okay. It's perfect. Emma keeps me more than satisfied.

When I've been with other women, it's never been because I needed sex. Until recently, at least. In the past, when Emma and I fought, it never lasted more than a week. Since moving downstate, the longest we ever went without having sex was two weeks after I called her on FaceTime while fucking someone else. I always use condoms and get tested regularly.

Emma didn't sleep with anyone but me until we were twenty. When I found out, it was the one and only time I honestly contemplated suicide.

But you can't feel jealous over something that's not actually yours and never was yours.

Two months ago, when Emma decided our relationship needed to end, I hadn't taken her too seriously, figuring it was another of our cycles. Not much changed. I still slept in her bed. We never talked about what came next. No one mentioned living separately. I still ate her out with no objection, but she rarely reciprocated and refused to allow me to take things any further. I tried waiting her out, pushing her to just let things go back to normal.

Now she wants to act like she doesn't understand how I ended up with Lillian.

I skim over what I've written, satisfied so far. Over the next few days, I can add anything else I think of. I snap a picture of the speech and send it to Emma. *Preparing for my state of the union address lol*

She reads it immediately. *OMG. This is what you're gonna say?* Before I reply she sends another text. *You can't read from a notebook*

I assure her it's just for reference and that I'm not going to read it from the notebook.

I feel a sudden illness coming on. May have to stay home this weekend, she texts.

My cheeks balloon as I blow out a puff of air. *It's time. We have to do this.*

The three little dots indicating she's replying pop up and disappear several times before she says, *I know.*

CHAPTER THIRTEEN

Emma

My workday ends before I'm ready on Friday. It's weird, though. A big part of me is ready to get this over with while there's a fraction of me that is so afraid everything is going to fall apart.

This morning, I took River's Jeep Wrangler to work while he kept my Toyota Camry so he could have it packed up and ready to go when I got home. Even though his Jeep is newer, my car gets much better gas mileage.

River opens our apartment door for me as I reach the top of the stairs. "I just gotta change," I tell him.

He follows me into my bedroom. "No quickie?" I'm tempted when I sneak a glance at his cute little smirk. Especially when he grabs my hip and pulls me to him. "It's gonna be days..." He drags out the s in the last word.

I leaned into him, breathing in his fresh, clean scent. "Let's just go."

He accepts my decision and sits on the bed, watching as I change into leggings and a crew neck sweatshirt. By the time we hit the interstate headed north, it's about six o'clock. Even without stopping, it would be ten before we get there. But considering we will need to eat and use the restroom, it'll be more like eleven.

"Where's that notebook with your speech?" I ask him a few miles up the road.

He looks over at me from the driver's seat. "In my bag. Why?"

"Was gonna read it again."

"I can just give it to you from memory if you want."

Nodding, I agree. "That might be a good idea. Practice, you know."

I watch as the cityscape fades into the corn and soybean fields that will make up the majority of our view on the drive home as River rambles about our fate being written in the stars and that if Christy had never taken him to my birthday party, there would have been no cause to question our love. That just because my dad married her didn't mean we couldn't love each other too.

I let out a quick laugh in the middle of his speech. "How far do you realistically think you're going to get before someone interrupts you?" My eyes land on his face as he frowns.

"Should I just cut to the chase? Like, 'So, me and Emma have been together for nine years and are tired of keeping it a secret' or something?"

"Yeah, that would probably be a better way to start. Then they can be mad or whatever and *then* you can regurgitate all that lovey-dovey-written-in-the-stars bullshit."

He huffs a little laugh. "Are you making fun of my speech?"

"Nah. I love that side of you."

"I hope you love all sides of me. Especially given what we're about to do."

We're quiet for a moment. "Nine years," I say quietly. "How do you figure nine years?" I turn my head to look at him.

He glances quickly in my direction. "First real kiss."

"At Noni's on Christmas?"

Nodding, he says, "We were fourteen. Now we're about to be twenty-four, but it's only May, so nine and a half years."

"I can't believe we're gonna be twenty-four by this time next week. Like, are we officially adults now or not?"

Our conversation continues for a while until I put on Taylor Swift despite his protests because he's the one driving. After we stop to get dinner at Subway, we get back in the car and I know I'm going to doze off now that my belly is full, so I let him put on his early 2000s grunge music. The first song that plays is one I hate, and I voice my distaste.

"What?" he asks with a laugh. "Mile 258 is legend. They didn't make any bad music."

"Isn't that the band where the guitarist tried to kill the lead singer?"

River chuckles. "Yeah, but he ended up dead anyway." He looks at me. "You watched the documentaries with me. It was all very suspicious."

I roll my eyes. "Maybe you can crack that case back open someday, Detective McIntyre."

The next thing I know, we're pulling off the interstate. I look around seeing nothing but darkness. "What are we doing?"

"Fucking."

I jerk my head in his direction. "What?" Then I see his dick in his hand and roll my eyes. "Seriously?"

"It'll be super quick." He looks at me as he pulls onto the frontage road. "I don't want to wait four days."

"We've figured it out before."

"This time is different." He parks the car and shuts the lights off. "We don't know how any of this is gonna go." He gets out of the car and comes over to my side, opening the door. "Pull your pants down. Let me get you wet."

"This is stupid."

"This is so fucking hot. I'm about to explode just thinking about it."

I get out of the car and look toward the interstate we just exited. We're far enough away that no one can see us. Before I can even start to pull my leggings down, he's doing it for me, opening the back door at the same time.

He rubs two fingers softly over my warm center. "Lay down back there so I can go down really quick." Leaning forward, he kisses my lips hastily. "C'mon, Em. I need this. I need you. I don't want to blow this on your clothes."

"Then stop jacking it, idiot," I say as I sit on the edge of the back seat, my legs still outside the car.

River kneels in front of me and lifts my legs, causing me to tip backward so that I'm on my back. He shoves his head between my thighs. My leggings are like a rubber band holding my thighs tight around his head, but it doesn't slow him down. His tongue is lapping along my labia, wetting it thoroughly. Two fingers slide inside me and curl directly into my G-spot and I completely forget that we are on a frontage road in the middle of nowhere. My back arches as I grab a handful of his blond hair. My pleasure groan is constant, and I can't seem to understand why we ever stop having sex. Between what he's doing with his fingers and the way he's eating my pussy like he's at a watermelon eating contest, I am completely turned on and it's probably not even been two minutes since he started.

The man is magical. And he's mine.

Far too soon, he pulls his head from in between my legs, reaching his hand out for me. "Get out."

I take it and he pulls me to my feet before practically shoving me toward the front of the car. He pushes his weight against me, his hand guiding his excited cock to my center. I place my hands on the hood of the car and push my ass toward him a little and he moves his body into mine before wrapping his arms around my waist and letting out a pant.

"Holy fuck, Emma."

He holds onto my middle as he impales me with so much speed and force that I'm almost like a ragdoll in his arms. My hands are no longer on the hood of the car. They are extended out in front of me, at my sides, everywhere, as my subconscious searches for reality. Because where River takes me when he fucks me is otherworldly. I don't see. I don't hear. I can only feel. And it fucking feels amazing. I love it when he is rough with me. I live for it. Used to be that I thought something was wrong with me because I always wanted him to go harder and faster, but no, it's just good that way.

That doesn't mean I don't enjoy slow, sensual sex, because I do. But this frenzied fucking madness where I am living in nirvana is far superior.

River's hand comes around my throat tightly, pulling me back and flush with his body. We're both grunting with each thrust, his breath hot in my ear. I try to get my bearings and reach between my legs and press against my throbbing pleasure center, knowing River isn't going to do it for me. And I don't want him to. I want to be in the exact position I'm in with his hand tightly around my throat and his arm holding me against him while we're connected by his best weapon.

When I touch my clit, it's almost too much. I pat it several times before I start rubbing, and I feel my knees go weak. "Oh, fuck. Fuck, fuck, fuck." I want to stop but I can't. Whenever I come, it makes him come, and I'm not ready for this to end but I want to, I *need* to come.

"Come on my dick," River commands. "C'mon. Fuck, you feel so fucking good."

"Don't stop," I beg. "Please. Don't stop."

"I don't want to, babe. I don't." He's panting, barely able to get the words out. "So fucking good."

My orgasm crests and I open my mouth, letting out a sound as the explosion rips through me, shooting fireworks through my limbs. I keep rubbing, trying to get another one, but I can feel the sudden change inside me as River's own climax builds. "No, no, please, please don't stop."

"I'm... fuck, Emma, fuck." He's delivering his final thrusts inside of me, filling me with his creamy ejaculate. "Holy shit," he mutters finally as he stills. "That was so fucking..." His hand lowers from my throat and loosens around my waist.

There are tears in my eyes when I lean forward onto the hood of the car, using my hands to support my weight. That's how good it was. I'm crying because it's over. I press my hips against his groin, and he flinches, moaning. "Please," I whisper.

He pulls himself from inside me and grabs my arm, spinning me to face him. "You're such a needy little slut."

"I really am," I agree.

His hand lifts to my lips. "Open up." I do, and he slides his fingers into my mouth, giving me the wetness off his cock. I didn't see him touch himself, but I know the taste. It's him mixed with me. Our eyes stay locked as he dips his hand between my legs. A smile quips on his face. "You're gonna like this."

When his fingers slip past my lips this time, there's an entire dollop of his cum. I lap it off his fingers and then take his hand, sucking each finger clean hoping to get him aroused again. Shadows flash in his eyes and I reach between us for him, finding it more flaccid than hard, but that doesn't deter me. "Please," I beg again.

He pulls back, his cock falling from my hand. "We gotta keep moving."

"I hate you," I say as I pull up my leggings. "Like, legit fucking hate."

Grinning, he fastens his pants. "But you love this dick."

I let out a breathy sigh. "I do love that dick."

Turns out we were only a few miles away from our exit when River pulled over. It's a quarter after eleven when we stop at the truck stop at the Thomas City exit to use the restroom. I do my best to clean myself in the bathroom, so I don't walk into my parents' house smelling like sex.

When we get back into the car, I drive since we'll be dropping River off and I'll keep my car with me. "Why do I feel like we're going to our own funeral?" I ask him on the twenty-minute drive from the interstate to Thomas City.

"Because we both know there's a good chance my dad's going to kill me."

I look at his model-worthy jawline and features illuminated by my dash lights. "I don't think it's going to get out of hand like that."

He huffs. "Nah, he'll keep his cool in front of everyone and then blow a gasket later."

I shrug. "Well, I'll reserve a hotel room tonight for Sunday. That way, once everyone knows, we don't have to pretend anymore. We can just be together."

He looks at me for a long moment. "I can't decide if you're serious or still thinking about sex."

My head falls back as I laugh. "I was one hundred percent being serious. We're adults. Our parents can't tell us what to do. They will either deal with it or they won't. All that matters is what we want."

Taking my hand in his, he gives it a squeeze. "You seem a lot more confident than you did earlier."

I nodded, realizing I'm feeling pretty fearless right now. "Probably still high from that roadside fornication."

That earns me a belly laugh from River. "Roadside fornication? Yeah, you're definitely high on something."

My heart swells. I love him so much. I might be feeling invincible at the moment, but I know it won't last. This weekend is going to take a toll on both of us.

River leans over and kisses me a block away from his parents' house. We don't speak as he gets out of the car. He gets his rolling suitcase from the trunk and looks back at me as he unlocks the door to go inside.

Five minutes later, I pull up at my parents' house and text River, *Miss you already.*

Miss you too. Love you.

Love you too.

Chapter Fourteen

Emma

I barely slept last night. The living room couch is pretty comfortable at my parents' house, so that wasn't the issue. The issue was that I was alone. On a couch. Without River. And I couldn't keep the TV on because it would wake up my brother Wyatt whose bedroom was closest to the living room.

When River is at work, I keep the TV on for background noise. I fall asleep with it on nightly, and he shuts it off when he comes to bed.

The hotel room idea sounds really good about now because I'm not sure I can do this for three nights in a row.

River texted me about an hour after I dropped him off to tell me his dad wasn't even home, and his mom was slurring her words and trying to make him a hamburger. When we were little, I was envious of his bigger house and the fact that he had a mom. As we got older, I realized how shitty his home life was, and my envy was replaced with empathy.

When I got home, my siblings and Christy were all asleep. My dad was awake, reading a thick hardcover book under the light of a lamp. We exchanged pleasantries about my drive and the late hour, and he went to bed.

I was awoken around seven-thirty in the morning by Cora and Wyatt, who were super excited to see me. It wasn't that I wasn't excited to see them too, I was just tired.

Christy made pancakes and bacon for breakfast, which I eagerly devoured. Me and River rarely ate food at home. And if we did, it was microwaved.

"You wanna come shopping with us?" Cora asks me. "I need a dress for a dance."

My eyebrows shoot up. "A dance?"

She nods. "It's my first one."

Cora is twelve and in seventh grade. But in my mind, she's still a little kid, maybe six or seven years old. "Yeah, sure."

I've always loved the dining room at my parents' house. There's a big bay window with plants on the sill and plenty of sunlight bathing the room with brightness. But I think it's the memories this room holds that makes me love it so much. Countless meals, board games, crafts, science fair projects, and homework. It's the gathering room in our home. We spent more time here than in the living room.

"What's on your neck?" Eli asks from across the table.

My hand comes up to my neck defensively. "I... I don't know."

"Looks like someone strangled you," Wyatt points out. He wraps his hands around his own neck and makes choking sounds. Then his body goes limp in his chair as he fakes his own death.

My dad lifts his head and looks over at me, then back at his food.

I know exactly what's on my neck. And my ten-year-old brother is spot on. I get up from the table and go to the bathroom, pretending to have no idea what they're talking about, while I try to come up with an excuse.

I inspect my reflection, easily making out the vague outline of River's hand. Letting out a heavy sigh, I pull my phone from my back pocket and take a picture and send it to him with the word *Thanks.*

I go back into the kitchen with a smile. "So, my friend Makenna is having a masquerade party for her birthday, and we were trying on different costumes. One of them had this neck thing..." I wrap my hand around my throat. "It was super tight, and I hated it, but I didn't realize it left a mark."

"Do you have a picture?" Cora asks. "Mom, can I have a masquerade party for my birthday?"

"I don't, but I can Google something similar." I pull my phone out again and open my browser. Cora leans in to watch as I'm typing. When the search loads, I click on images. As I'm scrolling down the screen desperately looking for something that goes around your neck, River's reply pops up at the top of the screen. *Lmaoooo you fucking loved it.*

I slide the notification away but not quickly enough.

"What did River say?" Cora asks. "Are we gonna see River today, Mom?"

Before I can reply, River texts again. *Can't stop thinking about it tbh.*

"I don't see anything like the one I tried on," I tell Cora, locking my phone. "And yeah, I think we're all having dinner together tonight for our birthday."

"I'm not going," Eli says. "Unless I get to drink."

I narrow my eyes at him. "You're fourteen."

He shrugs. "Like you didn't drink at my age."

"I didn't." It's the truth too. I did other forbidden things instead. "Yeah, okay."

"You're going and you're not drinking, Eli," Dad says. "Now stop."

Eli rolls his eyes.

I feel like I've entered another dimension. I feel old. Really, really old. Cora going to a dance. Eli drinking. What's next? Wyatt going to college? Being nearly ten years older than Eli, I've always felt a little removed from them. And when I left for college, I thought my dad and Christy were relieved because now they got to be a real family without me lingering around like a black cloud. Not that they ever made me feel that way, but it was so obvious there was me and then there were the kids. Not to mention that Christy is barely fifteen years older than me and my dad almost ten years older than her. People often mistook me and Christy for sisters and assumed my grey-haired dad was both of our fathers.

Life was so much better downstate where I got to live my lies with River.

Our birthday celebration was at a newly reopened pub and eatery in the town square called The Last Day. I know from Facebook that it's owned by the brother of someone we graduated high school with. Lacy Taylor was one of the girls River dated after he insisted that he needed to keep up the farce.

Not that our parents know any of that or would remember the three-week fling River had with her or realize that her brother owns the place where they planned our birthday dinner, or that Lacy Taylor is still as smoking hot as she was in high school, but I wasn't happy.

When I texted River to tell him where we were going, he said *I heard that place is cool.*

To which I pointed out *Bryce Taylor owns it.*

Yeah, I know.

And then I remembered that I couldn't be jealous when he wasn't even mine.

But now he is. And we are one day from telling the world.

Okay, just our family. But it's a start.

There are two heavy, solid wood tables pulled together to accommo-date our large family. Aside from the six in my family and the three in River's, our cousin Jordyn shows up with her boyfriend, and our cousin Kyler. And somehow River ends up sitting at the other end of the table with Jordyn and Kyler, while I'm stuck beside Cora listening to her tell me a never-ending story about how some girl in eighth grade was caught vaping in the school bathroom.

I'm on my second beer and cashing in on some stuffed mushroom appetizers when I spot Lacy Taylor behind the bar. My eyes dart to River but he's oblivious. I'm bouncing my leg as I chug the rest of my beer. Christy is deep in conversation with Aunt Megan. Dad is listening earnestly to Uncle Wes. Eli and Wyatt both have their noses in their phones while Cora gives me the latest updates on who is and isn't getting invited to someone's house to swim over the summer. My anxiety has me on edge and I need to move.

"I have to pee," I tell Cora as I stand, my eyes on River. He looks up at me and smiles. I force a smile back before going to the bathroom. I just need a minute. No, what I need is something more. But since River can't calm my nerves right now, I'm gonna have to get some shots.

Yes, that's what I'm gonna do.

When I open the door, River is standing there. He's looking down the hallway. "You okay?"

I nod.

"You don't seem okay."

"Lacy Taylor is here."

"Did you talk to her?"

I shake my head.

He looks at me. "I don't miss this place at all."

I smile, feeling some of the tension in my shoulders loosen. "Me either."

"We're definitely not coming back here to live."

My smile grows. He *can* calm my nerves without touching me. Fucking magical.

"I'm gonna get a couple shots I think," I tell him. "Want one?"

He shakes his head. "I'm good. Take my seat when you get back to the table. I'll pull up a chair. You don't need to sit all the way down there alone."

I feel bad about abandoning Cora, but I need to be close to River.

He goes into the bathroom, and I go to the bar. Lacy Taylor squeals when she sees me.

"Oh, my God! Emma, how have you been?" She rounds the bar and gives me a hug. "I haven't seen you in forever!"

I nod, faking a smile. "Yeah, we never came back after college. Living down by St. Louis still."

"That's so cool." She goes back behind the bar. "I don't think I'll ever leave this town."

I laugh. "I don't think I'll ever come back."

"I'm jealous, not gonna lie." She shakes her head. "What can I get you?"

I ordered my two shots of cinnamon whiskey and downed them after handing her my debit card to start a tab. As I turn to walk away, River reappears.

"Riv Mac!" I hear someone yell from behind me. I turn to see a couple of guys from high school smiling and waving at River. When I look back at River, he is wearing his overwhelmed face but trying to look brave.

I go back to the table and sit beside Kyler. Within no time, I'm in an adult conversation with Jordyn and feeling like myself again. It barely even registers when River pulls up a chair and sits on the other side of Kyler. But I do notice when Eli sticks himself between me and Kyler.

My little brother's puberty hit the same way mine did. He is already over six feet tall with weight to match. He played football and was on varsity as a defensive lineman his freshman year. Kyler, at nineteen, was smaller and looked younger than him.

"What are you doing?" I ask Eli.

"Not getting choked," he says.

My eyes went wide. "Do you wanna get choked, you little shit?"

Eli looks around. "Why? Is your boyfriend here?"

River is covering his mouth to hide his laugh.

"Eli, go sit down," Jordyn says. "And mind your business."

"You're just jealous 'cause that douchebag isn't choking you out like Emma's getting it."

Thank the stars none of our parents are paying attention.

Until now.

Jordyn's baby daddy shoots up, his chair tipping over. "What did you say, fucker?"

Now River is on his feet. "Okay, chill, Brody. He's fourteen."

"I don't care if he's eight! He doesn't need to talk to her that way."

River nods. "I agree. Eli is a punk. But you're not gonna fight him."

Kyler sighs as he stands, looking at Eli. "Let's go outside for a few."

As they're walking away, River's dad asks, "What just happened?"

"Eli was being mouthy," River says, taking his seat without looking at his dad. "It's fine."

The food arrives and I order two more shots. River moves to sit beside me. Kyler and Eli come back in, the distinct odor of marijuana following them. I look up to see my dad eyeing them, but no one says anything. It's nearly ten o'clock when Christy says they're gonna head home, which prompts River's dad to call it a night as well while his mom literally chugs a full beer.

"I'll be home in a bit," I tell my dad.

Somehow, Kyler ends up with a beer and it's just the five of us left. Me, River, Kyler, Jordyn, and her baby daddy who is apparently named Brody. We're all just talking and having fun. It's surprising, really, because for most of my life, I have wanted to scratch Jordyn's eyes out. But maybe now that we're older we can get along.

"Anyone wanna come smoke with me?" Kyler asks.

Brody is on his feet immediately, followed by Jordyn. With the three of them gone, River and I look at each other and laugh.

"One night down, one more to go," he says.

True, but two more nights alone on the couch. "We're taking a detour on the way to your house."

"Are we?"

I wrap a hand around my throat. "I need you to choke me out some more so Jordyn can be jealous."

His head falls back with laughter. "Somehow, I don't think Jordyn would be jealous."

My body tilts in his direction. "Still need you to do it."

"I'm gonna do that and a whole lot more." He leans close to my ear and rubs his hand along my inner thigh.

"Um, hello?" The sound of Jordyn's voice hits like a slap on the face.

Our bodies straighten as we look up at her, Kyler, and Brody. "Thought you were going to smoke?" I ask.

She points between us shaking her head. "What did I just see?"

River feigns confusion. "What did you just see?"

"Were you about to kiss her?"

I can't help it. Laughter rolls out of me. River laughs too. "What?"

"You were rubbing her leg."

"I *grabbed* her leg."

"You were definitely rubbing her leg, bro," Kyler says.

Brody chuckles. "Think we just figured out who choked her out."

"No, no, no," I say, still laughing.

But at the same time, River stands. "Okay, look—"

"I knew it," Jordyn screams. "I fucking knew it!" The back of her hand slaps Kyler on his upper arm. "I told you something was going on, didn't I?"

My laughing stops and I look around us. No one seems to really be paying attention to us.

River goes around the table to be closer to Jordyn. I stand so I can hear what he's saying.

Kyler rubs his arm where Jordyn slapped him. "I definitely need to smoke now." He picks up a lighter from the table and turns to head back outside.

"It's not what you think," River starts.

Jordyn narrows her eyes. "You don't know what I think."

"You're thinking this is some sick fucking bullshit and it's not."

"She's your cousin." She looks at me. "He's your cousin."

"Step," River points out. "We are not related by blood."

Brody laughs and I feel very disconnected from what's happening. It's our worst nightmare, our biggest fear, but I feel nothing.

"We are already planning to tell everyone tomorrow," River says, ignoring Brody. "Can you please just keep your mouth shut until then?"

Jordyn's face falls, like maybe what she just learned is sinking in. She glances at Brody and sits down. "Cousin fuckers," she mutters. "My cousins are cousin fuckers."

I wince. "Okay, that's harsh."

"What am I supposed to call it, Emma?" she asks. "This is sick."

River sits beside her. "It's not sick." He glances at me, shaking his head. "It's not even about sex. We love each other and have for a long time."

"Yeah, River," she says. "I love you guys too and I'm sure you love me." She jabs her finger in Brody's direction. "But it's not the same as the love I feel for him."

"Right, yes," River agrees. "But what if Brody's mom married Uncle Jake?"

She stares at River for a long time. "We're in our twenties. She's been in our family for as long as I can remember."

River shakes his head. "Just because our aunt married her dad doesn't make her blood."

I want to touch him, rub his shoulder, something to let him know I'm still here. Listening to him defend us to Jordyn has me swelling with pride and excitement. Maybe it's because I'm a little drunk, but I know he's not, and I'm not scared.

This is it. We're really doing this.

"How long?" Jordyn asks, looking up at me.

"Since high school," I tell her.

She keeps looking at me. "And this is what you want?"

I nod. "This is what I want."

Her hand rubs her throat. "I know he has a temper."

I touch my throat too. "No, that's from—"

"Nope, stop." Jordyn shakes her head. "I get it." She shudders. "I don't need details."

We all look at Kyler as he walks up. "What's up? So, are we all part of your big secret incest shit now too or what?"

Jordyn rolls her eyes. "It's not incest, dummy. They're not fucking blood related."

"People eat that shit up on the porn sites," Kyler says. "You guys could make bank."

"You're disgusting," I say.

"Says the one getting choked out by her cousin." Kyler guffaws.

River stands, moving uncomfortably close to Kyler. "Shut the fuck up." Kyler takes a step back. "We're telling everyone tomorrow. Please, can we just keep this between us until then? And after everyone gets the joy of watching my dad knock me out, you can make all the fucked-up jokes you want because we will be gone and out of your lives."

CHAPTER FIFTEEN

River

I barely slept last night after the shitshow that concluded our so-called family birthday celebration. Besides Jordyn calling us out and Kyler being a fucking child about it, I snapped at Emma and made her cry when we left the pub.

This whole disaster is my fault. She wanted to put distance between us, and I wouldn't let her because I'm such a fucking mess I don't know how to live without her. But I also don't *want* to live without her. I don't give a fuck what anyone says. Not her and definitely not our family.

Emma is mine.

"Maybe we can just tell Jordyn we were joking?" she said as I drove her car across town to her parents' house. "You know, like, take it back."

"What the fuck are you talking about?" My voice came out way louder than I meant for it to, causing her to flinch.

"Just, that, I don't know. Maybe it's not the right time."

I slammed on the brakes, stopping the car in the middle of the road. "Not the right time? Are you fucking kidding me right now? It's over.

Done. There are no more secrets. Even if I was going to remotely consider what you're suggesting, they are not going to keep their mouths shut."

"Yeah, but—"

"But nothing, Emma! There's no going back. By this time tomorrow, our entire family is going to be calling us cousin fuckers."

Her shoulders slumped as she looked out the passenger side window. "I'm sorry." The hiccup in her voice gave away her fight not to cry. "It's going to be okay, right?"

My fingers ran through a lock of her hair. "As long as we're together, it's going to be okay. Even if we are all we have left, it will still be okay."

There were tears in her eyes when she faced me. "You're sure?"

My knuckles ran across her cheek. "One hundred and ten percent sure."

Now, staring at the set dining room table and listening to Noni and Grammy fuss over Jordyn's baby in the next room, I am zero percent sure.

But I have to do this. For us. For me. For Emma. So we can stop feeling like we are living a lie. So we can move forward. So we can have a future together.

I put the salt and pepper shakers on the table and go back into the kitchen. My mom is pouring orange juice into her champagne.

"How many is that, Megan?" Dad asks her.

She finishes her pour before shrugging.

"We haven't even eaten yet."

When she sees me, she smiles. "Can you find out if anyone needs anything, hon?"

I gladly leave the kitchen. You'd think after twenty-five years my dad would stop harping on my mom about drinking. She's been to rehab at least ten times in my life. All while I was still living at home, so I imagine without me being here to give her some semblance of responsibility, it's gotten worse.

Between her alcoholism and my dad's abuse, it's no wonder I turned out the way I did.

In the living room, my eyes immediately landed on Emma. She's the image of perfection in her navy-blue flower print dress. The long sleeves are sheer. The V-neck and length that reaches nowhere near her knees would normally have me trying to sneak away to taste the sweet nectar between her legs, but it's the furthest thing from my mind.

She offers me a small smile and looks away. I look around the room, seeing all my cousins on my mom's side, minus Uncle Jake's spawn. With it being Mother's Day, they're probably with their own moms. Noni looks especially frail and small in Dad's recliner. Grammy stands beside the chair bouncing Jordyn and Brody's little girl on her hip. Jordyn and Brody are on the couch nearby, but they're both looking at me, as is Kyler, who is clearly stoned as fuck. Eli is sitting beside him and doesn't look much different.

Noni had one child. That child is Grammy. Grammy had four kids. Megan, Gary, Christy, and Jake, making Noni our great-grandmother and Grammy our grandmother. Noni has always been the matriarch in the family. She's the one that coordinated holidays, get-togethers, and family vacations. She came from a time when it was completely normal for women not to work. Noni always had candy hidden in glass bowls all over her house and treats for us when she came over. She came to all our events and games when we were growing up. It wasn't that Grammy wasn't there; she just wasn't there as much. Grammy always worked and since I can remember Jake still being in high school when I was little, I'm sure she was busy with him.

Seeing Noni look the way she looks today makes me want to turn back time and be a kid again. Because then Noni would be who she used to be, and I could get a do-over.

And in the do-over, I would still pick Emma.

After we have brunch, which is eggs benedict, fruit, and pastries that my mom had catered because no one wants to eat anything she cooks, I catch Emma looking at me. When I glance at Jordyn, she's got her eyes glued to me as well.

It's time. Because if I don't do it now, people will start leaving the table and then facts will get distorted, and everyone will be yelling 'cousin fuckers' at us.

I keep my eyes on Emma as I clear my throat, sitting tall in my chair. "If everyone could, uh…" Emma drops her eyes to her plate. I feel like I could pass out. Taking a sip of my water, I speak again. Louder this time. "Hey, guys." My voice wavers. "I have some news I wanted to share if everyone can listen."

Uncle Jake is beside me. "Hey!" he yells out when less than half our family looks at me. "River's trying to talk."

I feel a rush of blood to my head. They tell you to imagine your audience in their underwear when you're nervous, but this is my family and the only one I ever want to see in their underwear is the one I'm in love with. Plus, I feel like I'm standing in my underwear under a spotlight right now.

My non-existent confidence is waning.

"Oh, I think I know what this is about," my mom says excitedly, her words tumbling over one another.

Christy nods and points at Mom. "I think you're right."

They think we're moving home, just as Emma predicted. I clear my throat again as Jordyn says flatly, "Yeah, me too."

Emma has her head down, her hand shielding her eyes.

I'm gonna be sick.

Closing my eyes, I pull a deep breath in through my nose and blow it out of my mouth. "Emma and I are together."

The silence that follows seems to stretch on longer than the Mississippi River, but it was maybe five seconds, tops.

"As in you drove here together?" my dad asks.

I look at him. "As in we are in love and have been together for nine years and decided we need to tell the truth because we are tired of keeping it a secret."

"Come again?" Uncle Chris asks. Emma's shoulders shake as she cries across the table from me. I want to comfort her but I'm afraid to move. Uncle Chris looks at her. "Emma?"

She jumps up from the table and darts toward the door. I'm on my feet immediately, blocking her way. "No," I whisper. "It's over. They know now."

Sobs rack her body as she snivels in front of me, her mascara smearing under her eyes. I reach for her just as one of her knees buckles. She leans into me, gripping my shirt.

All eyes are on us and most everyone wears a dumbfounded look on their face. Jordyn is breaking off a piece of croissant for her baby. Kyler is smirking and trading knowing looks with Brody.

"So, like, Emma's your girlfriend?" Cora asks with a horrified look on her face. I nod. "But you guys are cousins! That's disgusting."

I open my mouth to speak but Jordyn beats me to it. "It's actually not, Cora. River's mom and your mom are sisters. But Emma has a different mom, which means she is only our cousin because your mom married her dad. That makes her our *step*cousin."

Jordyn is my new favorite cousin.

Other than Emma. Obviously.

"No." My dad stands. "No. Absolutely not. You guys *are* cousins. This isn't happening." He points at us. "What kind of fucking degenerate are you, River? God, Emma! I at least thought *you* had a head on your shoulders." He looks at Uncle Chris. "What the hell is wrong with these kids?"

Chris is taken aback. "Emma *does* have a head on her shoulders, Wes. And I don't appreciate you insinuating that she doesn't."

My mom stands and starts picking up plates from around her. "Well, this certainly is not the news I was expecting." She pauses and looks at us. "But I can't say I'm surprised." With a huff, she shakes her head and leaves the room. Christy follows her.

Before I can consider why my mom *isn't* surprised, my attention is drawn back to my dad.

"You're going to end this right here, right now, River. That girl is your cousin, not your damn girlfriend." He starts walking toward us and I instinctively back away. "What the hell is wrong with you, son? You can't marry your damn cousin!"

Emma lets go of me and stands on her own. "What are you gonna do, Wes? Hit him? Gonna show him how to be a real man? Hit your kid, berate them, tell them they're worthless their whole fucking life. Why don't you hit me? I'm just as much a part of this as he is."

My dad is stunned. Hell, I'm stunned.

"Okay, okay, stop all this nonsense right now!" Noni's wobbly voice yells out. "What is wrong with you people?"

Grammy reaches over and squeezes her hand. "Let's stay out of it, Mom."

Noni pulls her hand away. "Like hell I'll stay out of it." She shoots a glare at her daughter. "I am thrilled to hear this news."

"Are your hearing aids on, Noni?" Uncle Gary asks. "Did you hear what they actually said?"

Noni points at him. "You watch your mouth, Gary." Her hazy eyes find my dad and then us. "I remember long before Emma became a part of our family when her and River would just play together for hours. All the time. If you saw one, you saw the other. And there was one day, they were probably about eight if I recall. They were sitting at the table eating peanut butter sandwiches and I was struck with a feeling that they were gonna be married one day. From that day on, I watched them grow, and watched Emma become my granddaughter, always with that hunch in the back of my mind. Every step of the way, side by side." She laughs. "When Christy told me they got an apartment together, I knew then it was only a matter of time before they became more than friends."

"That wasn't nine years ago," my dad said. "Nine years ago..." He looked at us. "You were still in high school and living at home."

I lift my chin. "It'll be ten years in December."

"Now, like Jordyn pointed out," Noni says, either not hearing me or purposely brushing over what I said. "They're not blood." She shrugged and reached for her coffee cup. "I see nothing wrong with it."

"Yeah, well, Jordyn's an idiot." My dad scoffs. "She's barely twenty-one and has a two-year-old."

Jordyn balks. "Excuse me, but how is that your business, Senator?"

Smiling, I take Emma's hand in mine. She squeezes so tight I'm sure I'll have imprints from her fingernails.

My mom and Christy reenter into the room. "I've known about this for years," my mom announces. "I've seen them doing..." Her eyes dance over us with disgust. "*Un-cousinly* things."

Emma covers her mouth with her other hand. I bite the inside of my lip, feeling heat on my cheeks.

"And you never did anything to stop it?" my dad screams.

"No, and let me tell you why, Wes." She crosses her arms over her chest. "For one, I knew Emma was on the pill. And face it. We've ignored and neglected him his whole life. Gave him zero affection. All you ever did was scream and tell him about how you should have paid for me to have an abortion—"

"I never said that!"

He definitely said that, but I keep my mouth shut.

When my mom speaks again, she's quieter. "I never said anything because I was glad that someone made him happy and that he was getting affection from somewhere. So what if it's Emma? She's not his blood. She's the daughter of the man that my sister married. That's all."

Oh, but Emma is so much more than that.

My dad's face is so red that when he looks at us, I think he might have a coronary, and it wouldn't bother me if he did. "You're a fucking disgrace, River, and no longer my son."

Not completely unexpected, but my throat tightens up anyway. The burn behind my eyes lets me know I'm about to cry.

"Now that's going a little too far," Emma's dad says, standing. "While I agree this is very unconventional, I don't think it's cause for words that harsh. And quite honestly, I think you've said enough and probably should take a walk, Wes." He glances at us and then at Christy, before looking back at my dad. "I'll go with you. Give us some time to mull this over."

"Sounds like a fine plan," Noni agrees.

With a huff, our dads leave the room. No one speaks until we hear the front door of the house shut.

My mom is looking at me. "He's worried what people will say."

Emma nods. "That's why we never said anything before."

"We thought it would eventually go away," I add. "We tried to not let it come to this but then, it's like, we realized we're gonna be twenty-four and every time we try to move onto something else..."

Emma looks up at me. "We can't. And we won't."

"Okay, so," Cora starts. "If River is your boyfriend, is he still *my* cousin?"

Chapter Sixteen

River

My dad never says a word to me when he and Uncle Chris return from their walk. He doesn't even look at me and I conclude that he meant what he said. I am no longer his son.

I'm okay with that. He was a shit father anyway.

For the next hour, Emma and I stick close to one another and field the questions that come our way. Wyatt doesn't give a shit about any of it. Cora has a million questions, most importantly: will she get to be part of the wedding? Kyler and Eli pretend to choke themselves every time they look at us and I make a mental note to smack both of them later.

As far as the adults, Uncle Gary and Aunt Kelly say little. Uncle Jake says he knows it must've been hard to keep it hush-hush all these years but is glad we were able to let the truth out. He tells us there's nothing to be ashamed of.

"Your dad's a fucking prick, River," he says. "But I don't need to tell you that."

Jordyn leaves shortly after all the drama dies down. She hugs both of us. "Sorry if what I said was rude or whatever last night. It'll take some time to get used to."

Brody stood behind her, their kid screaming in his arms. "Good luck, guys." He flashes a grin before leading Jordyn away.

Christy approaches, an apprehensive look on her face. "We're gonna head home." She forces a smile. "Your dad would like to talk about this more." She shoots a quick glance behind her and whispers, "Without an audience."

When we got into Emma's car to go to her parents' house, it hit me. It's done. We did it. Everything is brand new from this moment on.

"Holy fuck," I say with a laugh as I start her car. "Holy fucking shit." She looks at me. "I can't believe we did it."

I pull out of the curved driveway and onto the street. "But we did."

"You did. You did it, River." When I reach the stop sign at the end of the block, Emma takes off her seatbelt, turns to me as she gets on her knees, and grabs my face. "I love you so fucking much right now." Her mouth crashes onto mine with a hunger only I can satisfy. I grab the back of her head, feeling our tongues intertwine and I know, I just abso-fucking-lutely know, I will never grow tired of the taste of her.

But I have to pull away. "I can't walk into your house with a raging hard on."

She laughs, falling back into her seat and grabbing her seatbelt. "We're getting a room tonight. No question about it."

Probably for the best considering that I'm not exactly welcome at my parents' house right now.

When we get to Chris and Christy's house, Emma walks right in. There is no one in the front room, but we can hear voices coming from the kitchen, so we go in that direction.

"I don't know," Christy says before we can see her. "Fifteen or sixteen maybe."

We pause just outside the entrance to the room.

"And you didn't think you should check with me before putting my daughter on birth control?" Emma's dad asks. There's an edge in his voice that I haven't heard often.

"She's my daughter too."

"No, no," Chris says quickly. "Clearly not. Because that would make what they're doing wrong."

Emma looks at me and I know her heart is sinking. It's okay, I tell myself. We still have each other. We knew this could be the outcome.

"Ten years in December," Chris says. "I feel like an idiot. They had sleepovers until they went to college... and we just let them. Thinking they knew better. And then *paid* for them to live together."

There's a lull in their conversation, and Emma leads the way into the kitchen. "Hi," she says easily. "We're here."

Chris stares at her for a long moment. "Yes, yes. Let's go in the front room."

"Where are the kids?" Emma asks.

"Eli went somewhere with Kyler," he explains. "We asked Cora and Wyatt to stay in their rooms for a while."

Emma looks at me. "Uh, so, I'm not sure if you know this, but Eli is smoking weed. And I'm pretty sure he's getting it from Kyler."

Chris lifts his chin and looks at Christy. "Mmm. Seems all my kids like to get things they shouldn't from their cousins." As soon as the words leave his mouth, he throws his hands up. "Uncalled for. I apologize."

Uncle Chris is a softspoken man of few words. But when he speaks, he means what he says. He never says things off cuff, so I'm honestly not sure how this is going to end.

In the living room, Emma sits on the couch and pulls her legs up beside her, covering them with a blanket. I sit beside her, careful not to touch any part of her. Chris and Christy sit in their chairs near the window.

"Emma," Chris says. "I honestly don't know what to say. This is not the future I had envisioned for you. And I don't mean that to sound harsh because I am beyond proud of you and all you've accomplished. But I'm confused because you just called last weekend and told me you were thinking of moving home and didn't think River would be joining you."

Emma opens her mouth to speak but Chris puts his hand up, stopping her.

"Plus, with your car being vandalized repeatedly, and those marks on your neck, quite frankly, your mom and I are concerned that there's more to the story than we're getting."

Emma looks at me. "There is." And I know she's got this. I don't know what she's going to say, but I'm gonna let her say it.

"I was seeing someone else for a few months. Trying to... not have feelings for River, or whatever. But the feelings never went away. And since we live together, well, no one really knows we're cousins down there. So, this guy, Tucker, he thought there was something going on with me and River." She looks at me. "And there was. He was right." She looks at her parents again. "So, he wanted me to move in with him and I wasn't about to do that because I've only known him for a few months. But I started staying with my friend Makenna some nights and he didn't like that because Makenna's boyfriend and River are friends. He assumed River was there and that's why he vandalized my car."

"Why did you say you wanted to move home just a week ago?"

Emma sucked her lips between her teeth and furrowed her brow. "Because I knew I would never find anyone else if River was always there. But then I realized, I don't want anyone else. And we have tried to walk away or whatever, a hundred times at least. And we just decided to stop fighting this and... and, and let the dominoes fall."

Christy exhales loudly. "They're falling alright."

"What about this?" Chris waves his hand in front of his neck and my blood runs cold.

"I told you. It was from a costume I tried on."

Chris studies his daughter as he considers her lie. "River, I sure hope you have enough sense in your head not to lay your hands on my daughter. I know what you've seen growing up, and you better realize that behavior is not acceptable."

Probably not the best time to point out that Emma loves when I put my hands on her that way. "That goes without saying."

"Mmm, yes, well I thought not fucking my daughter went without saying too, but here we are."

My face flushes and Emma laughs. "I know this will take some time to get used to," she says, "but I love him, and he loves me. And we don't care who doesn't like it or thinks that it's creepy or whatever. All that matters is that we know it's right for us."

"It'll definitely take some time," Chris agrees. "Just don't go rushing into having any babies please. I don't think any of us could handle that at this point."

We both laugh. "No worries there, Dad," Emma says, her eyes on me.

I feel like I can breathe for the first time in nearly ten years.

There are no objections when we say we're getting a hotel room for the night. Emma packs her things and tells her parents goodbye. They both work in the morning, so she won't get to see them again. I text my mom to let her know what's going on and that I will come by tomorrow to get my things after my dad has gone to work.

At the hotel, we stand there and stare at each other silently for a moment, smiles on both our faces. "This feels so good," Emma says.

It does. It really fucking does.

I go to her, pulling her face to mine with fervor. She begins unbuttoning my cobalt blue dress shirt, pulling it out of my slacks, and tugging it down my arms. Her fingers dance across my skin under my ribbed tank top. I pull my mouth away from hers and press our foreheads together. "You're so fucking amazing," I tell her. "The way you stood up to my dad like that."

Her soft sable eyes met mine. "You're the amazing one. All I did was stand up to a bully. You took on everyone else." Our lips come together quickly.

"*We* took them on." I run my fingers along the soft skin beneath the fabric of her V-neck dress. "And I have zero regrets."

Her arms come around my neck. "Me either."

I kiss down the length of her neck, pressing my face into her cleavage while I massage her mounds over her dress. She rubs her thigh against my groin, urging a groan from me. Reaching behind her, I unbutton the back of her dress and tug it down to expose her navy-blue lacy bra and immediately lift her perfect fucking tits out of it, letting them rest on top of the bra like they're on a display shelf. I lick her nipples alternately, switching back and forth between them, flicking them with my tongue and biting softly how she likes.

Emma's leg hooks around my hips as she presses into me, her hands on the little desk area behind her for support as her head falls back. "Fuck, babe. I need you," she whispers.

I pull my mouth from her pert nipple. "You have me."

"All of you."

I shrug off my dress shirt and pull my undershirt over my head before lifting my face to hers, planting a kiss on her chin. "I'm yours." My hands slip around her fleshy thighs, lifting them around my hips and begin rubbing her through her underwear. She's already damp to no surprise. I push my weight against her, my covered cock meeting her thigh. Pulling one of her nipples with my teeth, she lets out a yelp and I tuck my fingers around the edge of the fabric and inside her warm, slippery body.

She's stuck. Completely at my mercy. I'm holding her ass up off the desk just enough that if she tries to use her hands for anything, her head will hit the wall. I tickle her sensitive spot inside, her body stiffening in my hold as she lets out the low, constant moan that is music to my ears.

"Don't move a muscle," I instruct, letting go of her so I can unfasten my belt and pants. My fingers slow inside her and she adjusts her arms, just as I free myself from the confines of my slacks and boxers. I remove my fingers from her and slide her underwear to the side, allowing a quick glance at her shiny pink lips. My mouth is instantly watering at the sight, but my dick is hungry, and I know Emma is ready to be fucked.

Besides, I have the rest of my life to eat her pussy.

My excited cock breaches her entrance and chills run down my spine as she exhales. She lifts her head and looks at me. The expression on her face is erotic. Her eyes are hooded as she looks up at me through her lashes, lips slightly parted. Sandy tendrils of hair fall in her face as her chest heaves.

It's the most beautiful I've ever seen her.

I move slowly, stroking in and out of her, pushing deeper each thrust. She's gripping me, trying to keep me deep inside her, and I want to stay there where it's warm and safe.

"Why are you looking at me like that?" she whispers.

"You're just so fucking beautiful it makes my heart ache."

Her legs pull tighter on my hips. "Touch my clit and I'm gonna come."

I chuckle. "Definitely not touching it yet."

"Mother fucker." She begins to gyrate her hips, but I know at this angle and the fact that she still has her underwear on, it's not gonna happen. "Put me on the bed."

Letting go of her hips, I lower them to the edge of the desk and lift her dress so I can see her pink skin peeking out around my cock. "You're gonna come, babe. Don't worry."

She picks up her arms and one of her hands goes straight for her center.

I intercept it and grab the other one before she can even move it. "Not yet." She fights to get her hands free, and I shove my dick into her fast and hard. "Fucking stop, Emma."

"Fuck!"

I do it again. She yells out louder this time but stops fighting. I pull her up with her hands, backing away from her. Her legs fall to the floor as I grab the V-neck of her dress, ripping the sheer fabric down her front. I let it fall to her feet.

She stares down at it, wide eyed. "I just bought that yesterday."

Before she can say another word, I grab her hair and drag her to the full-length mirror hanging on the wall, shoving her face against the glass. "You ever seen a cock hungry whore before?" I push her head into the mirror again. "Have you? 'Cause there you are. Desperate and needy for cock." My hand grips tighter in her hair, pulling her scalp. She lets out a whimper, her eyes on my reflection in the mirror. "Don't look at me. Look at the whore." Her eyes shift to her own reflection. "There you go. Keep your eyes right there."

I push up against her forcefully, pressing her tits against the glass as I reach around in front of her with both hands, grab the seam of her underwear on one side and swiftly rip them so they hang open, exposing her light tuft of trimmed pubic hair.

"You wanna touch your clit, whore?" I whisper in her ear. She nods enthusiastically and moves one of her hands to do so. I press against her, feeling my cock rest against the top of her ass cheeks. "All I did was ask," I hiss. "I didn't say you could."

She reaches behind her and fists my cock with her clammy palm.

I have to fight back the urge to smile. "So fucking desperate." I push my hand between her body and the mirror. "Think I can make you come in less than a minute?"

She nods quickly. "Just touch it. That's all."

Using two fingers, I spread her lips, rubbing all along the inside of them, tickling over her clit. Her body slumps as she shudders.

Her head falls back on my shoulder as she faces me. "Please."

"Begging like a good little whore." I kiss her quickly. "Watch the whore. She's about to come on my hand."

Emma's head shoots up, her eyes falling to the reflection of my hand in her pussy. My saturated fingers press hard on her clit. She gasps, her mouth falling open.

"Watch your face, babe. It's fucking beautiful."

Her eyes travel up, alternating between our faces as I rub her clit until her body is limp, her forehead pressed against the mirror, inaudible groans slipping through her lips as she comes. Her body shudders against mine in the confined hold I have her in. She whimpers my name. "Do it again."

Ignoring her request, I wrap my arms around her, pulling her hips toward me and spreading her ass cheeks. Lining my cock up, I push the head inside her dripping center and then pull her body back against mine before pushing us against the mirror.

"Fuck, fuck, fuck," she yells out when I start hammering into her, the sound of her sweaty, slick skin on the mirror driving me wild. I'm ready to come almost immediately. The reflection of her face and tits smashed against the mirror is fucking hot. She has not stopped moaning and grunting, and I can feel the ball of fire igniting in my gut.

I pull my dick out of her, a stunned look registering on her flushed face. My hands take hold of her hair again and swing her over to the bed. She immediately rolls to her stomach and sticks her ass in the air. My mouth waters, craving the taste of her, but I'm ready to blow.

"Roll over," I command.

She looks back at me. "What?"

"On your back."

Emma does as she's told, pulling her knees up and letting them fall apart. Her underwear still hangs onto one of her thighs and her bra is below her tits. I kick off my shoes and pants before I get on top of her and join our mouths together, pressing my body against hers. She guides my throbbing dick inside her, and I wrap my arms around her head, pushing into hers slowly, feeling every inch of her insides and feeling her skin all along mine. I stare into her eyes, reveling in the newness of what we overcame today, my soul filling with the knowledge that Emma is really truly mine now.

"I love you, River," she whispers as we move together rhythmically. "I love you so much."

I kiss her, deep and slow, the same way I'm fucking her. "I love you." My voice cracks with emotion as I feel my climax rise up inside me.

I lose sight of reality for a moment as ripples of euphoria spread through me. As I pulse into her, I can feel her gripping me tighter, trying to milk every last drop I have.

Her thighs grip around my hips when I stop moving. "*This* is what you wanted."

I dropped my head onto her shoulder, breathing in the scent of her heated body. Her hands run through my hair, sending chills to every nerve ending I have.

Yes. *This* is what I wanted.

CHAPTER SEVENTEEN

Emma

River and I ride the high of our successful relationship reveal all the way home. Even going back to his parents' house at nine in the morning to find his mom already reeking of gin didn't dampen our mood. But like all good things, it has to end.

We get home with barely enough time for River to change into his uniform before heading to work. When we pull into the parking lot of our building and spot Jack's lifted pick-up truck, we exchange glances.

Jack's truck is all black. The paint, the rims, even the windows are blacked out. Even without his personalized license plates his vehicle is unmistakable.

"Is he picking you up or something?" I ask River.

He shakes his head. "Haven't talked to him since before we left."

We grab our suitcases and head inside. As soon as we step into our building, we spot Jack walking out of Lillian's first floor apartment. "Oh, hey," he says when he sees us. He's not wearing his work uniform. "I'm gonna..." He points at the door behind us. "Gotta change still."

Neither of us move out of his way. "What are you doing, bro?" River asks him.

Jack looks out into the parking lot. "I gotta go. I'll see you at work."

It's obvious what he's doing, and it pisses me the fuck off. "Wow."

River moves and lets Jack leave. I'm tempted to follow him and take a picture to send to Makenna, but I don't. Alternatively, I would also like to knock on Lillian's door and punch her. Instead, I follow River upstairs and into our apartment where he immediately goes into his bedroom to change. I toss my suitcase on the couch and unzip it. With being gone all weekend, I didn't get any laundry done and have to work tomorrow so my night alone will be spent making trips back and forth to the laundry room.

"Don't say anything to Makenna," River says when he comes into the living room. His eyes are downcast as he runs his belt through the loops in his pants. "Not yet at least." He looks up at me. "Let me talk to him."

I shrug. "It's obvious what he was doing so don't try to defend him."

"Maybe they broke up," he suggests. "Maybe he was there proposing another threesome or something. Maybe Makenna is cool with him hooking up with her."

I shoot him a doubtful look. "Maybe he's a cheating piece of shit."

River sits beside my suitcase and starts pulling his shoes on. "That's not like him."

It's really not. Him and Makenna are super into each other even if they do like to swing a little from time to time. "What ever happened between you and Lillian?"

He stands, his eyebrows raised. "You know I don't have time for this right now."

"You're never going to tell me, are you?"

"Why do you want to know so bad?" He goes toward the kitchen.

"Morbid curiosity."

The kiss he gives me when he leaves takes my breath and common sense away, along with my curiosity. After I start my laundry, I scour Netflix for a romcom I haven't seen before, settling on one that I have, and sit back on my bed with my economy sized bag of Skittles until the timer goes off on my phone to remind me to put the clothes in the dryer. Except when I get to the laundry room, all four dryers are full but not running. The clothes in them aren't even warm anymore. Since I only need one dryer, I pull the clothes out of one and place them in the basket sitting on top of it.

Our apartment building has four units. Me and River in one apartment, Lillian and her son below us. Across the hall from her is a woman in her sixties with a yappy dog. And across the hall from us is two Asian men who are usually wearing scrubs. So, when I see that the laundry I'm pulling out of the dryer is full of lacy thong underwear and little boy clothes, I realize it's Lillian's.

I hold up a pair of black panties and find myself getting angry over how tiny they are. I'm imagining River's hands gripping her narrow hips, her slender thighs wrapped around him. The image of her bouncing on his dick with no loose skin moving around, her perky little tits just barely jiggling. And when I go back to my apartment, it's a fight not to call Makenna and tell her what I saw earlier. Then I start imagining Jack fucking her, followed by the visualization of her eating Makenna out while Jack fucks her. I wonder if he finished inside her. I wonder if River finished inside her.

River claims to always use a condom. And I know he gets tested every so often too. I've even given him the home tests that I hand out at work for him to use. And the handful of times I've been with someone else,

I've practiced safe sex. Plus, I got on the pill at fifteen. Right after our first time. River is the only one I don't use a condom with and vice versa.

But we can never be too safe, hence the testing. Thankfully, neither of us has ever had any STIs.

It's not even that I think Jack is dumb enough to fuck Lillian without a condom, it's simply the fact that he fucked her at all. The fact that River fucked her.

Of all the fucking people in the world to get as a neighbor, why did it have to be her?

My anger is still simmering when I go back to the laundry room for my clothes. When I see Lillian's clothes still there, I debate whether or not to get scissors from the apartment and cut up all her little itty bitty slutwear.

I decide to do it.

I pull every pair of her underwear I can find out of the basket and cut them in some way making them no longer wearable. And then, because I took my stuff out of the dryer, I put hers back in. Hopefully, with her clothes being where she left them, she won't even suspect someone cut up her underwear.

The rush I feel is like winning the damn lottery.

River calls me on his lunch break. I'm giddy to tell him what I did, but there's something in his voice that gives me pause.

"What's wrong?" I ask cautiously.

"Nothing really. Just tired I think."

I bit my lower lip. River doesn't sleep much in general, so I'm a little surprised by him saying that. Especially since we slept a solid eight hours the night before. Well, at least I did. I guess I really don't know if he was sleeping. "Did you talk to Jack when you got to work?"

He lets out a weighted sigh. "Yeah and, according to him, it's not what we assumed."

A belly laugh escapes me. "Of course that's what he said."

"I don't know, Em. I kinda believe him." He pauses and lowers his voice. "He said Makenna's been spending a lot of time with Lillian. I guess she got a sitter for her kid Saturday, and they all went out. They ended up back at her apartment. Except this time, it was just Makenna and Lillian hooking up. Like, he wasn't included. Said it was like watching her cheat right in front of him."

I consider that. "Hmm. Even if that's true, I'm sure he didn't mind watching."

River scoffs. "Yeah. Not at first."

Unsure why that bothers Jack or River, I say, "That does sound odd."

Silence hangs on the line between us for a moment. "I'm super glad all that bullshit is behind us now."

"What do you mean?" I ask.

"You and me... I don't know. Just that we don't have to fight this anymore. Don't have to pretend we think we can find someone better. That we don't have a future, because we do and it's like a breath of fresh air knowing we don't have to deal with drama from other guys or girls ever again."

I'm grinning ear to ear, not that he can see it. It *is* like a breath of fresh air. "It's a new beginning."

"Whatever we did before is in the past and means nothing now."

We got off the phone a few minutes later but it was hours before I realized River never told me why Jack had been at Lillian's.

The following night when River got home from work at almost one in the morning, he woke me up to say happy birthday. Then he snuggled up beside me, chose something to watch on TV, and I fell back asleep.

In the morning, it wasn't my alarm that woke me up, but River, eager to have birthday sex before I went to work.

I spent a large part of my birthday at a rural health cooperative meeting where representatives came from other health departments, and we all discussed what was working in our areas and the possibility of combining some of our efforts. Because my program was going well in the counties our office covered, my direct supervisor, Carol, volunteered that we could possibly take over some of the other areas since the grants were set to be open for bids later this year.

I don't want that. I don't want to cover more area. Our health department already covers seven large, rural counties. Plus, the need for what I am doing is frowned upon in the most rural areas as many of the residents held highly conservative views on sex and reproduction. There was no way I would ever be allowed into any of the high schools to offer condoms or test kits, which was my goal, and it put into perspective for me that I am not doing what my original goal had been. I wanted to reach young people. Teens. Not pedal government handouts to clinics that probably threw them away when I left.

I was so caught up in the possible changes that I barely looked at my phone all day. By lunch, I missed calls from both my parents and had barely even noticed the Facebook notification saying River had tagged me in a post. Which was probably a good thing.

When I got home, I discovered River had left me with a giant gourmet cupcake on the kitchen counter. It's my favorite: chocolate cake with pale pink buttercream icing, topped with a beautifully crafted dark pink rose complete with green leaves and a bit of stem. Two candles are stuck into the frosting so that their wicks touch. A handwritten note sits beside the cupcake. *Happy birthday to my twin flame. Don't make plans for Friday.*

The cupcake is too pretty to eat, especially alone, so I decide to save it to share with River. If I go to bed early, when he gets home, I can get up and spend a little time with him.

After I shower, I sit down in the living room only to remember we still haven't replaced the TV that River broke in his rage fest last week when I left. Hard to believe it was just over a week ago I was entirely sure I had no choice but to walk away from the dysfunctional relationship he and I shared, and now, the whole future lay ahead of us with endless possibilities.

Besides the TV, we still needed to patch the holes in the walls, and he needed a new keyboard and stuff. Maybe if we pool our birthday money, we'll have enough to replace the TV without dipping into any savings.

I sigh and pick up my phone from beside me on the couch, intending to check out TV prices. Instead, I open Facebook with the knowledge that there will be a ton of birthday wishes I need to acknowledge. Before I can even get to them, I find myself staring at the top post in my newsfeed. The post River tagged me in seven hours ago that I vaguely recall seeing the notification for. I can't even bring myself to read the caption because I'm stunned by the photos he shared.

They are photos of us being *un-cousinly,* as his mom had called it. Photos where we look like a couple. Selfies of us laying together, sometimes under blankets, sometimes obvious one or both of us is not dressed. Pictures with our arms around each other, ones where he is placing kisses on my cheeks. The pictures are the truth we have lived since we left home for college. They are the truth that we just told our family about mere days ago.

My hands shake as I scroll through the photos. Then I go back to the post, seeing a mixture of reactions: likes, loves, laughs, and wows. There are fifty-four comments under the post.

River uses the name Riv Mac on social media and gaming platforms for two reasons. The first being that it's a play on the name his dad is known as, Wes Mac. And second, he thinks it gives him some anonymity and prevents him from being identified as his father's son if some political radicals decide to come after him because of some bullshit his dad does. Nothing on his page is public and his profile picture is something that has to do with gaming, not an actual photo of himself. It's rare that he even posts anything. But now there is an entire photo spread of our life, or secret, for all one thousand plus of his closest friends to see.

Our fate was written in the stars twenty-four years ago today when we were born only eight hours and twelve minutes apart. There is no one else I want to share every moment of forever with. You are my twin flame and the loml Emma Novak. Happy birthday.

Holy. Fucking. Shit.

I'm going to throw up.

Against my better judgement, I open the comments. Much of what's there is from people back home saying things like:

April Fool's Day was last month with laughing emojis.

Wait, you guys are cousins!

This is a prank, right? More laughing emojis.

I knew you guys moved to the south, but I didn't think you'd gone that far...

Am I the only one NOT surprised by this at all? Eyeroll emoji.

Bruh that's your cousin lmaoooo

This is sick if it's true.

I swallow and take a deep breath. It's over an hour before River gets his lunch break, but I text him anyway. *Take down that post NOW.*

Next, I check who reacted to the post, surprised to see Jordyn left a love reaction, but not at all shocked that Kyler responded with a laugh.

They were the only two family members to react, which I suppose is for the best. Everyone needed time to get used to this change without it being all over Facebook.

I needed time to get used to this change without it being all over Facebook.

Don't get me wrong. It's not that I wasn't thrilled that this was happening, and that River was taking this as seriously as he was by publicly professing me as the love of his life. Because I was. I was ecstatic.

But also mortified.

CHAPTER EIGHTEEN

River

Work is a clusterfuck on my birthday. But then again, it usually is no matter what the day is. Today however, there is a big ass fight that breaks out right at the start of my shift. Once we go on lockdown and get that all situated, we don't even have time to start the paperwork before an inmate is found unresponsive in his cell. It appears to be an overdose, so then we have to toss every cell on the block, which puts everyone in shitty moods—inmates and officers. All this chaos causes my lunch to be ninety minutes late.

When I get my phone from my locker, I ignore every notification I have except the text from Emma telling me to delete my Facebook post. With the way my shift is going, I really don't want to deal with whatever her issue is. Now that we've told our family, I don't give a shit what anyone else thinks.

Without replying to her text, I open Facebook and check the comments on the post. They're exactly what I expected. As I'm reading through them, Jack comes into the breakroom and pulls out the chair across from me, dropping his lunchbox onto the table with a thud.

"Screw this day," he says.

I scoff. "It's my birthday. Emma's too."

"Oh, yeah," he says as he unzips the top of his lunchbox. "Saw that on Facebook."

I glance at him. "Did you see the post I made?"

He nods. "With the pics? Yeah."

"She wants me to take it down."

"Why? See, that's what I don't get. Makenna would love some shit like that. Women don't make sense."

Setting my phone on the table, I turn it to face him. "Check the comments."

Jack looks at my phone as he pulls a sandwich from a baggie. "Damn. I didn't even think about the whole—" He pauses and looks around the breakroom before leaning forward toward me. "Well," he says in a low voice. "You know."

"Yeah, well, looks like you're the only one." I pick my phone up and scan the comments again, noticing one of them is from Makenna. *You guys are so cute* with two heart eyes emojis *Love you both.* "Why did you tell Makenna, anyway? Not that it matters now."

He shrugs. "Didn't think it was a big deal."

It's not, honestly, and I tell him that. "It's just that we had agreed not to tell anyone."

"You realize anyone who sees that post knows now, right? Not just your friends, but hers too since you tagged her." He takes a bite of his sandwich. "Is she friends with coworkers on there?"

Probably. I let out a frustrated sigh and push my lips together in a frown. "I don't know." I start typing out a reply to the hateful comments. *Emma and I were friends long before we became STEP cousins. My aunt would have never even met Emma's dad if me and her weren't friends. We are not blood related. Y'all are making this out to be something it's not.*

I set my phone down while I opened a snack-size bag of cheese crackers. Before I'm done chewing, my phone rings. Unsurprisingly, it's Emma. Closing my eyes, I suck in a breath before answering. "Hey, babe," I say, as if I have no idea that she's about to dump twenty-four years of pent-up emotion on me.

"River." She sounds breathless.

Worry creases my brow. "You okay?"

"I don't know. I want to be, but I don't know. It was a really shitty day at work and then your Facebook post and I don't even want to talk to my parents, and it just seems like a lot."

"What happened at work?" I ask, hoping whatever it was that it's something worse than the comments from our high school friends about our relationship.

She sighs. "Just some bullshit. We can talk about it later. But can you please take down that post? Your reply is just going to make it worse."

"Emma, no. This is what you wanted. This is what we both wanted. We're not going backwards and we're not living anymore lies. I don't care what anyone thinks and neither should you." She sniffles, and for a split second I want to feel bad for being harsh, but what I'm saying is honest. "People will get over it. We aren't living our life for them anyway. We're living for us."

"I know but—"

"But nothing. And I mean that. I'm done hiding."

Jack is watching me as he eats, hanging onto every word I say, his face expressionless.

"I know, I know. Can you just let me talk?" Emma asks.

"Talk."

"It's just that now people who didn't know are going to know and they're all going to look at us different and think we're weird."

"And?"

"And I have people from work on there."

This has to be the worst birthday ever. I'm exhausted. "There is nothing wrong with what we are doing, is there?"

Her voice is tiny when she says, "No."

"Then if any of your coworkers say anything just tell them the truth. It's not as bad as you're making it out to be."

Emma draws in a tattered breath. "Wake me up when you get home so we can share that cupcake?"

"I will."

Her turmoil lays heavy in my mind. I want to believe she will get more comfortable with people learning about our familial ties, but part of me wonders if I'm trying to convince myself too. When I get off work, I check the post for new comments and discover she's deactivated her Facebook account.

I feel like I'm trapped in a sinking ship. For years, we kept this ship afloat with lies. And now, with revealing our truth, a million tiny leaks have sprung. Coming clean was supposed to be the part that set us free. This is our new beginning, the first step toward our future together. The only mountain we ever thought we needed to climb was our family. Our biggest fear for the last decade had been them finding out about us. Now that we pole-vaulted over that mountain, the grass is supposed to be greener and the sun brighter.

We had not even remotely considered the reactions of anyone beside our family.

Had I considered what old nobody's from our past would think when I made my Facebook post that morning? Vaguely. Had I considered how Emma would feel about it? No.

No, because I thought this was what we agreed we wanted. To stop living in the shadows of lies and being ashamed of something we don't need to be ashamed of.

When I get home, Emma is asleep in bed with the TV on as usual. The covers are pulled to her chest as she lies on her side facing away from me. Her hair is pulled up on top of her head and she's wearing a white camisole. I go to her, tickling my fingers over her shoulder and collarbone. She doesn't stir, so I crouch down in front of her and brush my knuckles along her cheek before kissing her forehead.

Her eyes flutter open into mine as her lips smack together. "Hey."

"Hello, beautiful." That earns me a smile. "Cupcake time."

She rolls to her back, pulling her arms from under the covers. "It's so pretty I don't even want to eat it."

I stand. "Pretty things are meant to be eaten," I tell her. "Just look at you."

Her smile grows as she flips her eyes upward dramatically. "Haha."

"Let me go get changed and I'll bring it in here."

In my bedroom, I meticulously take off my uniform and rehang it. We're only provided with three, so I typically wear each one twice before washing it. Which goes out the window some days. The number of times I've ended up with someone else's bodily fluid on me is staggering and I've only been doing this for a year. After hanging my uniform, leaving on a ribbed, white tank top and my boxers, I go to the kitchen and find the cupcake in the refrigerator and place it on a plate before grabbing two forks.

"Do you want anything to drink?" I call out to Emma.

"I have my water," she replies.

I help myself to a soda and go back to her bedroom. She is sitting up in bed; the lamp on her nightstand is turned on, giving the room a soft yellow glow. The TV is on its home screen now.

"What do you think about making my bedroom kinda like an office?" I ask. "I can set up my gaming stuff in there instead of the living room." Sitting beside her on the bed, I move to rest my back on the headboard to be comfortable, then set the soda on my nightstand. "It's not like I ever sleep in there."

Her eyes are on the cupcake. "Let me light the candles." Throwing the covers back, she jumps up to go in search of a lighter, and I'm pleased to see she isn't wearing anything but underwear on her lower half. When she returns to the bedroom, her nipples are poking through the thin fabric of her top, her round areola's visible as well.

I can't deny the twitch I feel in my boxers at the sight.

She kneels on the bed beside me as she flicks the lighter. My free hand automatically reaches out to her, running along the back of her thigh and ass cheek. Once the candles are lit, our eyes meet, and the way the flickering light hits her eyes is so beautiful I feel a lump forming in my throat.

"Happy birthday, babe," I say quietly.

"Happy birthday," she parrots. "Blow them out on three. And don't forget to make a wish." She lowers her butt, resting it on the backs of her calves under her. Her eyes fall to the twin flames on the cupcake.

"I have nothing left to wish for," I tell her.

Looking up at me, she says, "I do." She smashes her lips together briefly before saying, "One, two, three."

Together we blow a puff of air at the candles, effectively extinguishing the twin flames. I wish for forever with her, and it's not that different than any other wish I've ever made in that it still has to do with Emma.

We discover that the rose on top of the cupcake is crafted from some type of frosting that looks way better than it tastes. Emma pokes at it with her fork. "Now I kinda feel bad for trying to eat it. We could have just left it alone and saved it."

I sink my fork into the cupcake. "Maybe we can plant it and see if a real rose sprouts."

She shoots an amused look at me. "Right. Like a potato or something."

I shrug. "You never know."

The rest of the cupcake is delectable, and we finish it off. I set the plate on my nightstand and neither of us gets up to brush our teeth before we snuggle together, our heads on the pillows.

"So, what do you think about me moving my gaming stuff into the other bedroom?" I ask again.

Emma closes her eyes. "It's fine I guess, but I also want to talk about moving. Like, to a new state or something."

"Why?"

"Because this is our life. We're young. This is the time we should be doing fun things and exploring the world. Figuring out where we want to settle down and build our future."

My heart sings at her words. Anything with her is all I want, but I also feel like her idea is her trying to outrun who we are.

"A city maybe. Definitely a more urban area." She looks over at me. "I did all that research regarding having sex in your teens, and I just really want to find a job where I can share my knowledge. Like, my job is fine and what I'm doing has meaning and purpose, but it's more like a Band-Aid for a problem that could have been prevented with earlier education. And, yet it's not even in the plans for me to share the tests and stuff with high schools." Frowning, she looks away. "But then again, I feel like there are ample resources and whatnot available and accessible in urban areas and the rural areas need this, but it's not actually me that they need."

Emma has always been passionate about her field of study. When she landed her job, she had been thrilled at the opportunity. She anticipated having an impact on the lives of teens, not realizing they wouldn't be the focus of her work.

"Today was the co-op meeting and they're talking about having our health department bid on the grants for other counties that we don't currently cover. Ones that are further south." She shakes her head. "I'm just not sure this is what I want to be doing."

"What about just looking for something else that's still local. Even St. Louis wouldn't be too far."

She rolls to face me. "Wouldn't it be cool to move to somewhere like Denver? Or even California? It's so beautiful in both of those places. So much to explore. We could go hiking and stuff."

There's hope in her eyes. It's contagious and gives me my own vision of what she dreams. The work she wanted to do is needed everywhere, but there were definitely more opportunities for her to live her purpose in an urban area. I could find a job in law enforcement or corrections anywhere. It doesn't matter that we both know she wants to run from the truth, trying to start again like we had when we moved here to go to college. We'd grown since then. Grown up and grown together. We made mistakes and learned from them.

"Don't you think it would be cool to live somewhere completely different than what we've ever known?" she asks with stars in her eyes. "Mountains and oceans and no cornfields."

I move my neck, lifting my face to kiss her shoulder, breathing in her soft, flowery scent. "Is that what you wished for?"

The corners of her mouth tick up in a smile. "I can't tell you what I wished for otherwise it won't come true."

By her theory, I can never tell her I want her forever. Or maybe I just can't tell her that's what I wished for. "I'll follow you wherever you want to go, Emma."

Her eyes widen. "Really?"

I nod. "But in the meantime, I'm making the other bedroom my gaming room."

CHAPTER NINETEEN

Emma

Sometimes I wonder if I'm an idiot. There has to be a reason River isn't telling me what happened between him and Lillian. And I can't help but think it's the same reason he won't tell me why Jack was at Lillian's apartment. When I called Makenna, she never even mentioned anything about her and Lillian hanging out, so now I really don't know what to think.

My mind runs away with the possibility that all four of them are lying to me.

But when River gives me his mega-watt smile, all my wayward fears fall away.

We go out for dinner on Friday night to celebrate our birthday together. After eating, we visit a cider house that recently opened. River tells me cider beer isn't actually beer.

"It's apple juice with a little alcohol," he says. "Not beer."

"Don't be mad because what I'm drinking tastes good." I glare at his glass of dark beer topped with foamy head. "I can smell that from here and it doesn't smell good."

"Then don't drink it."

"I won't. And you don't have to drink mine."

But he does. He tries each flavor from my flight, agreeing with me that they all taste good. "The peach is my favorite by far."

"Wow." I clutch my non-existent pearls. "Riv Mac enjoying a fruity drink?"

He frowns and leans toward me, his brows creased, and his mouth set in a flat line. "Look, this is between you and me."

Knowing he's joking, I bust up laughing at how serious he looks. He lets out a chuckle and picks up his mahogany-colored drink as my phone vibrates on the bar. We both look at it to see a text from Makenna. I pick up my phone, the face ID activating to show the message.

What are you doing tonight?

Out with River for our bday

Oh yeah. Okay. Well... do you want to meet up somewhere?

I look at River. He's reading our texts. Our eyes meet. "Up to you," he tells me.

Who will be with you? I ask Makenna.

She doesn't answer immediately, and I'm reminded of how I feel like I'm being kept in the dark about something. "What's going on with her and Jack?" I ask River.

He looks away.

My stomach sinks. He's definitely keeping something from me. "What is going on that you're not telling me?"

The way his shoulders stiffen isn't missed by me. "Nothing." His gaze falls to his beer. "We haven't talked much this week. Work has been a shitshow."

Makenna replies. *Jack.* And then a second text. *Lillian might catch up with us later.*

I glance at River to see if he's reading Makenna's texts and if he has a reaction to them. Keeping my eyes on him, I type my reply on my phone without looking. When he says nothing, I look at the screen to be sure that I correctly typed out my message. *For sure.*

Ninety minutes later, we're at Club W and I am too many fruity drinks in, standing between River's legs while he sits on a barstool behind me, his hands fixed possessively on my hips. Makenna and I are talking shit about a couple of muscled up guys who keep circling the dance floor like mighty lions looking for something small and weak to prey on when I spot the dude that I hooked up with a few weeks ago. He's about ten yards away from us, his eyes narrowed as he stares at us.

I meet his stare with my own, recalling River telling me he beat up my one-night stand, or something like that. It's probably the reason for the death glare. Leaning back against River, he runs his hands up my sides, sending chills down my arms. I shake off the feeling and pick up my drink, my eyes still locked on one-night dude, daring him to do something.

Lillian bounces up to the table in a tiny pair of denim shorts and a tangerine-colored tube top. She's wearing white cowboy boots and too much makeup and jewelry, looking like she stepped out of the pages of an early 2000s gossip magazine. Her bleach blonde hair is pinned back with gaudy barrettes that match her shirt. "Heyyyyy," she says, dragging out the word.

Without acknowledging her, I look back at one-night guy to see he's shifted his eyes to Lillian.

"There's my girl," Makenna says with way too much excitement.

"Miss me?" Lillian turns her face away, pulling her shoulder up to her cheek, pretending to be bashful.

And then they kiss. Not just a peck on the cheek but a full on make out session like one of them just returned from the war or something.

Rolling my eyes, I face River. He's smirking, obviously amused by what's happening behind me. Jack stands beside him watching Makenna and Lillian. "I can't believe both of you stuck your dicks in her."

River bites his bottom lip, one eyebrow raised. "Didn't say I enjoyed it."

"Didn't say you didn't either." I spin back around and look for one-night guy as I lean forward, resting my elbows on the table in front of me. He's still nearby but no longer looking in my direction. Probably because Makenna and Lillian stopped kissing. Jack moves to stand beside Makenna.

Lillian leans toward me. "Have you had any trouble with the washers eating your clothes?"

I'm not sure I heard her correctly. "What?"

"Like, half my underwear were destroyed in the laundry."

I bite my lower lip, recalling my scissor session earlier this week. "Uh, not that I've noticed."

She shrugs one shoulder and turns back to Makenna.

River moves closer to me, his hands circling around the front of my upper thighs underneath my sage-colored sundress, his lips tickling across my shoulder. I close my eyes, reveling in his touch. "You never have to worry about her again," he says so only I can hear. "Just like I don't have to worry about that dude over there who can't stop staring."

My eyelids pop open to see one-night watching us, his eyes narrowed again as he sips from a cup.

The fingers of River's right hand brush lightly along my center. Instinctively, my thighs spread for him and my breath catches.

"What if I pulled these little sexy panties to the side, unzipped my pants, and fucked you right here in front of everyone?" He tugs the crotch of my underwear to the side and runs his index finger along my sensitive area. "Would you stop me?"

My mouth hangs open; I'm rendered speechless, as he dips his finger inside me quickly, pushing it a little deeper with each thrust. Would I stop him? Would I?

I'm not entirely sure.

"Or I can just make you come right now while he's staring at us, wishing he was me." He removes his finger from inside me and begins rubbing circles over my clit.

In a matter of seconds, my breathing picks up and I drop my head forward knowing my face will show what's happening to my body.

"Come for me, Em," he whispers. "Right here in front of everyone." He spreads his other hand across my chest, his thumb and forefinger applying pressure to the jugular veins on either side of my neck.

The sounds of the crowded club, the bone rattling bass of the music, the drunken laughter, the bottles clinking behind the bar, all of it fades into the background. All I can hear is the sound of my heart beating in my ears and River's voice telling me, "You're mine and I want everyone to know it."

The creek rises inside me, angry waters ready to spill over and sweep me away. I want to hate myself for being so weak, but the fact of the matter is that River knows me better than he knows himself. He knows how to distract me, forcing me to look away from the crumbling façade of our lives.

He also knows how to break my fucking dam in the middle of a bar packed with a few hundred people.

My orgasm shoots through me like a tsunami, causing my knees to wobble. River presses against my backside, holding me up like a crutch. I hold my lips between my teeth, biting them to fight the urge to vocalize my pleasure.

"Oh, my God, Emma." His voice is scratchy in my ear. "I fucking need you. Like, right now."

I straighten my posture, nodding, refusing to look at anyone. I don't want to know if they know. Turning, I bring my hands to River's face, nipping at his lip when I kiss him. "C'mon."

"My dick..." He looks down.

I follow his gaze to see the more than obvious hard-on in his pants. "You're mine and I want everyone to know it," I say, echoing what he said to me minutes ago.

It doesn't take much to tug him into a standing position, his erection pointing the way through the crowd as we weave in between people all the way to the exit. The air is cooler when we step outside, and I feel like I can breathe better without the stench of sweat and booze surrounding me. River's erection is barely visible now.

"I can't believe you just did that," I say as we make our way to where we parked.

He chuckles. "I can't believe you let me."

I look up at him beside me. "Do you think anyone knows?"

His cheeks flush as he fights his grin. "They know."

Oddly, there is no embarrassment. It was one of the hottest things River has ever done. "Next time maybe we can take it a step further."

"Oh, really?"

"Really."

We reach his Jeep. There is nothing discreet about where we parked, but it is in a parking lot across the street from the club so there isn't much traffic. We go around the back of the vehicle; River opens the hatch and lifts the glass while I pull off my underwear and toss them inside. He begins to unbuckle his pants, and I help him along, my lips lazily moving across his as I take his semi-erect length in my hand and begin stroking. In a matter of minutes, he's ready, pushing me forward into the back of the Jeep as he lifts my dress over my ass. His hand smacks hard on my right cheek and I envision his red handprint on my ass. I swear the image my mind conjures causes a faucet to turn on between my legs.

"Fuck, babe, you're so wet," he breathes out behind me.

The sound of our bodies slapping together drowns out the hum of cars on the nearby road and the crunch of gravel as people walk through the parking lot.

River's fingers dig into my hips as he lets out a low growl. "This is too good, babe. You're too good."

I reach between my legs and find my clit, ready for another wave of pleasure in time with his. "C'mon, baby. C'mon. Just like that," I tell him, lost in the feel of him inside me, filling me with his unbridled need.

"Fuck yes," he calls out, his pace quickening.

My back arches and my toes curl against my sandals as River hammers into me. I lose touch with the world for the second time in an hour, groaning as pleasure surges up my spine, exploding into my limbs.

Everything between my legs feels warm. I can feel our combined juices on my inner thighs. River is barely moving but still inside me. As the world returns around us, I can hear his heavy breathing above me.

"We're not done." He speaks quickly. "Wait until we get home." Pulling away from me, he grabs a handful of my ass and squeezes. "You're not sleeping tonight."

A breathy laugh escapes me as I straighten and face him. "Let's go then."

He shakes his head. "Not yet. Let's go back in for a while. I wanna watch you dance without any underwear on."

I reach for my underwear, but he beats me to them, holding them to his nose and breathing in. My jaw falls in mock amusement. "Damn," he mutters with his blue eyes locked on mine. "Nothing to catch all that cum. Gonna have to let it drip down your legs." He tucks my underwear into his front jeans pocket. Holding one hand out for me, he places the other on the glass above his head, preparing to close up the back of his Jeep.

Standing beside him, I wrap my arms around his waist, resting my chin on his chest. He lowers his face and kisses my forehead. As we walk back to the club, I realized that I had left my phone and purse inside. I tell River, and add, "I hope they didn't just leave it sitting there."

"I'm sure Jack's still sitting right where we left him."

As we near the entrance, I can feel River's thick, sticky semen running down my thighs. "I'm gonna go to the bathroom and clean up a little. I really don't want a UTI."

He chuckles but nods, letting go of my hand as we walk inside.

I go down the long hallway to the bathroom. In the few times I'd been to Club W, I had learned the bathrooms by the entrance were considerably less busy than the ones by the dance floor. I wet down some paper towels before going into a stall and locking the door. As I gently blot my nether regions, I hear the person in the stall next to me vomiting as someone else comes into the bathroom. The sound of her retching makes me queasy, so I hurry to get myself as clean as I can with paper towels in a public bathroom. I shove the trash into the tiny can beside the toilet and then sit down to relieve myself. After wiping again, I flush and open the stall door just as the vomiting girl lets out what sounds like an entire four-course meal being regurgitated into the toilet.

As I step out of the stall, I am hit in the face with a force so substantial that everything goes black.

CHAPTER TWENTY

River

After Emma cut me off the last time, telling me there would be no more sex, I wanted to take it with a grain of salt. She had said things like that before and then would cave as soon as my fingers tickled her sensitive little nub. There was something different that time, though. More conviction in her voice, in the way her face contorted as if she was being forced into a situation that she wanted nothing to do with.

Emma left for work that Monday morning and I tried unsuccessfully to go back to sleep for about an hour before I got up and logged onto my computer to get in a few games before I needed to get ready for work. Somewhere around noon, I was getting hungry and planned to stop after my current game to eat and then shower.

But then there was a knock on our apartment door. "Who is it?" I called out, not wanting to get up mid-game.

"It's me. Lillian."

I rolled my eyes. Lillian seemed to know my schedule and was regularly outside or in the hallway when I was leaving for work. She said cringy things about how sexy men in uniform are and shit. "Give me a minute."

There was no telling what she wanted. Could need to borrow some laundry soap, could need to say some asinine shit without shame.

A minute passes before I get to a point where I realize I'm gonna die in my game, so I leave it active so someone can get the kill and go answer the door. "What's up?"

She shrugged. "Just bored and know that you're home during the day so thought I'd come see what you do while you're all alone."

I hadn't encountered a girl as needy as Lillian in a few years. She had no shame. "Don't you have a job?"

"I work from home." She spun back and forth on her heel, and I noticed she was barefoot.

"I see." My eyes traveled the short length of her. She wasn't wearing anything special. Some biker shorts and a T-shirt from a local car dealership. It occurred to me that I could be wrong about her intentions. "I'm just playing Fortnite."

"Fortnite?" She balked. "Paxton plays that."

I snickered. "Lots of people play." Turning away, I left the door open and returned to my desk.

She followed me inside, shutting the door behind her. "Or maybe it's Roblox. I can't keep those two games straight."

"Roblox seems more his speed." I sat down on my desk chair and looked at my screens. I was dead, so I left the game and debated starting a new one. Seemed rude with Lillian there but then again, I didn't invite her over. "What's your job that you get to work from home?"

Falling onto the couch like she belonged there, she held one of her manicured hands out in front of her face. "I'm an influencer."

My eyebrows lifted. "An influencer. Really?" She nodded, glancing at me briefly. "And you make enough money from that to just not work?"

"It is work," she said defensively. "And yes."

"What platforms are you on?"

"A couple," she replied quickly. "What does Emma do?"

At the time, I didn't even notice how she breezed right over my question with her own. "She works at the health department."

"Did you always want to work at the prison?"

I shook my head. "I don't even want to work there now. I want to be a detective, but we just graduated a year ago and you gotta start somewhere." She didn't say anything for a moment, and I faced my computer screens and started closing out of the open apps. It was almost 12:30 p.m. "I need to start getting ready for work, so unless you're gonna suck my dick or something, you should probably go."

It was a joke, for the most part, and I never expected her to rise from the couch, cross the room, and get on her knees in front of me.

When she came back a few days later, we didn't even waste time with small talk. She gave me some head before riding my cock on the living room floor. Sex with Lillian was like fucking a half-dead fish. It was warm and wet but there wasn't enough oxygen to flop. When I came, it was equivalent to the relief I felt when I popped my back after sitting in my desk chair too long.

After that, I ignored the next few times she knocked on our door. I left for work earlier to avoid her. But then after nearly two weeks of rejection from Emma, I found myself watching old videos of us fucking and my dick was semi-hard. I decided that Lillian's lifeless pussy was better than no pussy at all and grabbed a condom and went downstairs.

She opened the door in a matching underwear and bra set with some cartoonish looking cats on them. Her hair was in pigtails, and her face was fully done up with makeup. I didn't question it. I held up the condom like it was a winning hand in poker. She smiled and led me to her bedroom.

The sight of her room gave me pause. At least for a moment. It looked like it belonged to a little girl with frilly pink bedding and curtains to match. There were stuffed animals on the bed and shelves, along with Barbie dolls and other toys. For a moment, I thought she'd taken me to her kid's room, but then remembered her kid was a boy and let the thought go.

She called me 'Daddy' while we were going at it and begged me to punish her for being a bad girl. I tried to ignore her; closing my eyes and pretending her narrow hips were Emma's curvy ones bent over in front of me, but it was so far from the real thing that it started to feel like a bad dream.

A sorry excuse for an orgasm built in me and I pulled out of her, tugged one of her pigtails, turning her and bringing her face to my cock as I peeled the condom off. She took it in, milking it for a minute before I jerked my hips back right as my sticky white essence shot her in the eye, hanging from her fake eyelashes. It didn't stop her from gazing up at me like I just handed her a pot of gold, and I think that was the only part that made it worth it.

She licked the last of my ejaculate from the tip. "Thank you, Daddy."

I rubbed my dick on her lips because why not. "Stop saying that. It's cringy as hell."

Shrugging, she stood. "It's my kink. You don't have any kinks?"

I thought about tying Emma up. About fucking her ass while there's a vibrator in her other sweet hole. About the first time she asked me to choke her, and then the time she told me not to let go until I thought she lost consciousness. How she likes for me to treat her like she means nothing, that she is just a body for me to use when she is actually the only body I will ever worship.

Lillian, however, was a body to use.

But also, those kinks are all Emma's. I like them and willingly partake in them, but they're not my kinks.

"No, I don't."

Lillian harumphed. "You guys are not having plain ole vanilla sex up there, River."

I grinned at her, amused that she could hear us from her apartment.

After that, I fucked her a few more times before I realized Emma meant what she said about us being done. Then my goal was to prove my loyalty and devotion to her at any cost even if it meant I was celibate for the rest of my life.

And then we introduced Lillian to Jack and Makenna. They had their fun with her, and it was a little too enjoyable for Makenna. When Emma and I saw Jack leaving Lillian's apartment, I assumed he was sleeping with her. He was not.

When the three of them hooked up at Jack and Makenna's place, they all had been involved, and from what Jack told me, it was pretty damn steamy. She and Makenna hit it off and hung out a few times that week. So, when they went out the following weekend, Jack had hoped for a repeat of the time before.

Instead, he found out that Lillian's kinks run much deeper than calling someone 'Daddy' and asking to be punished. Lillian, with her tiny body and high-pitched voice, bright colored clothes, and small frame, had an OnlyFans. And on OnlyFans she portrayed herself as a little girl.

Learning this, the way she and her bedroom looked made more sense. And I was thinking it was a pretty creative way to make some money because plenty of guys definitely had that kink.

"They wanted me to pretend I was their stepdad while she recorded it," Jack told me quietly at work that night while we walked the blocks. "Like, they had this whole scenario where they were going to play with

Barbie dolls, and I was supposed to bust in and catch them using the dolls for... not the way they're supposed to be used." He shuddered. "It's fucked up, River."

"That is fucked up," I agreed, my mind wandering over the details of the trysts I'd had with Lillian.

But Jack wasn't done. "To try to convince me, they showed me videos they made together when I thought they were just chilling over some glasses of wine or some shit."

"What?"

Jack nodded. "Makenna pretends to be Lillian's evil stepsister and *forces*," he used finger quotations when he said the word 'forces,' "Lillian to eat her out." Slowly, he shakes his head. "I don't know, man. And Makenna was all hyped about it and really thought I'd be down with that shit, but hell no. That's not for me."

I'm baffled but intrigued at the same time. "So, what did you do?"

"Passed out in the living room while my girlfriend pegged your neighbor, bro." He shifted his weight, and I realized we stopped walking. "And I don't know what's worse. The fact that it happened or the fact that I can't stop thinking about it."

"Is that why you went over there today?"

He nodded. "I offered her a thousand bucks to not put that shit out there and she laughed at me. Told me she would earn that in the first hour it was up."

"A thousand dollars in an hour?"

Jack shrugged, looking defeated. "It's literal porn. I'm sure she's putting that shit more places than OnlyFans if she's making that much."

I looked around the area we were supposed to be monitoring. "She told me she was an influencer but that is definitely not what I had in mind."

"Yeah, influencing my girlfriend to being a porn star."

"Holy hell," I muttered.

After learning these fun new facts about my neighbor, I decided it would be wise to speak with Lillian to make sure she didn't record anything we did. After the first two times in my apartment, all the rest had been in her apartment with her calling me 'Daddy' while she asked to be spanked for being bad. And my dumbass went right along with her stupid little kink hoping it would make the sex better.

It didn't.

The day after Jack told me everything, I knocked on Lillian's apartment door. She opened it wearing a one-piece bright floral shorts romper that tied on the shoulders and barely fit her. Her hair hung loose and there were two barrettes with flowers to match her romper in her hair.

"Did I interrupt your workday?" I asked her.

She cocked her head and smiled. "Actually, yes, but come on in."

I stepped inside and closed the door as she headed towards her bedroom. "I'm not here for sex."

"Well, I'm kinda in the middle of something."

"I just have a quick question."

Frowning, she held her hand out, indicating for me to ask my question.

"Did you record us having sex?"

Her grin spread ear to ear. "So, you heard about what me, Makenna, and Jack have been up to." She nodded. "Jealous?"

I let out a hoot of laughter, absolutely floored that she thinks I would be jealous. "Hell, no, I'm not jealous, Lillian. I just need to know."

She twirled a lock of hair with her finger. "Worried Emma will get mad?"

That actually wasn't my biggest concern, but I went with it. "She will beat your ass, you know. I'm actually surprised she hasn't yet."

Lillian rolled her eyes. "She doesn't scare me."

Unless Lillian had some secret powers, she should've been scared. "So did you, or didn't you?"

"I did."

"You recorded us doing it?"

"I recorded us doing it."

My cheeks flush and I feel lightheaded. "Why?"

"You came in when I was mid recording, and it just happened."

"Which time?"

"Every time."

"You recorded every time we had sex?"

She nodded. "When we were down here, yes."

I backed up, leaning against the door behind me. "Why?"

Shrugging, she walked toward me. "Why not? You're hot. It was good footage."

"Delete it. Please, Lillian."

"Why?"

"You didn't have my permission to record me. That's illegal."

Her lips quirked up into a satisfied look. "Actually, there's a notice on the door when you walk in here that says you're being recorded so I am completely within my rights, Officer McIntyre."

I pointed a finger at her. "No. C'mon, Lillian. You can't be serious."

She lifted one shoulder and dropped it as if what I said meant nothing.

"Let me buy them off you."

A maniacal laugh slips between her lips. "Oh, River, don't worry. I blurred your face."

My stomach lurched into my throat. "You what?"

"No one can see who you are. They don't care who my Daddy is. They just want to see a little girl getting fucked and cum dripping from her face. They only want to see me."

I get that people have fetishes. I know there are tons of people who are into the whole Daddy Dom/Little Girl thing, but it's just not for me. My head spun with so many questions I'm not sure I want the answers to.

"Relax. I know who you are, which is why your face is blurred."

My throat was dry when I asked, "What?"

"I know your dad is a senator or whatever. And that Emma is your cousin by marriage. So don't act like you don't get the whole incest thing."

I shook my head. "There's no incest."

"You know what one of my highest grossing videos has been lately?" she asked, laughing. "I hooked up a mic to the ceiling so they could hear you guys going at it but only see me lying in bed." She started batting her eye lashes and put a finger to her lips like she was deep in thought. When she spoke again, her voice was childlike. "Mommy and Daddy are doing it again. It makes me wish," she paused and ran her hand down the length of her body, "makes me wish Daddy would come down here and make me feel so good I scream just like he does for Mommy. But I guess I just have to wait my turn like a good little girl." She straightened her posture, slipping right back out of character. "And then I fuck myself with a big ass dildo while you guys are screwing each other's brains out in the background."

I turned around, opened the door, and left, tearing down the tiny sign that warns people who enter that they are being recorded.

Now it's the Friday after I found out that there are videos circulating on who knows what porn circuits that show me fucking some grown woman pretending to be a little girl. I haven't told Emma yet because I wanted to celebrate our birthday without the chance of her getting arrested for battery to Lillian. My plan is to tell her next weekend when I'm off work again, so we have ample time to work through it together.

As soon as I walked up to the table after coming back inside from mine and Emma's little tryst behind my Jeep, Jack starts laughing. "Did you really get Emma off right here in front of everyone?"

I couldn't have hidden my grin if I wanted to. "Was it that obvious?"

"Bro, people all around were staring."

I saw them. But I had been more focused on achieving what I did than who was watching. Jack and I bantered for a while and finished off our drinks before I surveyed the dance floor for Emma. Lillian and Makenna are easy to spot at the center of the crowd with their hands all over each other. I don't see Emma anywhere near them, so I start looking around the perimeter of the dance floor, not finding her.

"Emma went to the bathroom when we came back inside," I yell over the music to Jack. "And I haven't seen her since."

Jack scans the crowd too. I spot the guy Emma hooked up with a few weeks ago standing alone at the edge of the dance floor. It's like he can feel my eyes on him because he looks over at me while I'm eyeing him.

"I don't see her," Jack says.

"I'm gonna go check the bathroom."

Pushing my way through the thick crowd of bodies takes me way longer than it did earlier and it occurs to me that I could definitely get away with fucking Emma with so many people around. Even if she just sat on my lap with my dick buried all the way inside her while we talked with our friends, I would be in heaven.

Maybe I do have my own fetish. Just the thought of it makes my dick twitch in my shorts. If she's up for it, I'm making it happen tonight.

When I reach the women's bathroom, I pause, unsure what to do. I have no idea how many women are in there or what their reaction would be if I entered. After a full minute, two girls approach. They're engrossed in a conversation but one of them, the brunette wearing a faux fur jacket, is eyeing me.

I turn on my politician's son's smile and make eye contact with her. "Hey."

She smiles back, her interest obvious. "Hey." Stealing a glance at her friend, she asks me, "What's your name?"

I fake that I'm nervous for her benefit. My eyes fall briefly, and I close my mouth. Then I glance at her friend before smiling again and reply. "River."

The brunette flips her hair over her shoulder. "Hi, River."

She expects me to ask her name, but I couldn't care less. "Hey, so my girlfriend went in the bathroom a while ago and hasn't come out. Can you check on her for me?" The brunette looks taken aback, so I glance at her friend. "Please. Her name is Emma. She's wearing a green sundress."

Her friend, a darker skinned girl with braids in her hair, nods and takes the brunette by the hand. "Yeah, no problem." She pushes the bathroom door open and scans quickly. "Emma? Are you in here?"

I can hear that no one replies.

"Do you know what kind of shoes she has on?" the brunette asks.

"Uh, sandals. They were black I think."

The brunette enters the bathroom while her friend holds the door open. "She's not in here."

I move forward, sticking my head in the door. "You sure?" There are a few women standing in front of the sinks and they all glance at me in unison. "Sorry," I offer. "Emma?" I look at the bottoms of the stalls and don't find any shoes that look familiar. I glance at the brunette and then her friend. "Thanks."

My feet move faster as I head out of the club. I jog across the parking lot, wait for cars to pass on the road, then jog some more to where I parked across the street. My Jeep is locked, and she is nowhere near it. I can't call her because her phone and purse are still at the table. She couldn't have gotten an Uber without her phone, and even if she did, she can't get into the apartment without her keys.

Maybe she went into the other bathroom. I run, not jog, back into Club W. I push people out of the way until I reach the table. Jack's talking but I'm not listening. I unzip Emma's little purse and pull out her phone, keys, and wallet.

My vision tunnels and all the sounds around me, the music, the people, fade into the background. I look at Jack. "I can't find her."

CHAPTER TWENTY-ONE

River

After I pull Makenna and Lillian off the dance floor and make them search in both women's bathrooms while Jack scours every inch of the club, I feel panic settle into my bones. Swallowing a huge ass mountain of pride, I seek out the guy whose ass I beat a few weeks back.

He starts walking away when he sees me approaching. "No, wait." He doesn't wait, so I grab his arm. "Hey, I'm just looking for Emma. Have you seen her?"

His eyes narrow as he looks at my hand on his arm. Dropping my hand, I wait for his reply. He looks at me from under hooded lids briefly before turning away again.

"C'mon, man. All bullshit aside, I haven't seen her in, like, two hours. I'm really worried."

"Haven't seen her since the two of you walked out of here earlier." This time when he turns away, I let him go.

Makenna and Lillian approach, shaking their heads. I don't even wait for them to reach me before I head toward the entrance. The bouncers manning the door are ogling a group of half-naked women who just came in, taking extra time to study them and their lack of clothes compared to the identification cards handed to them. I shifted my weight, clearing my throat several times, impatiently waiting to get their attention.

"What do you need, bud?" one of them finally asks without looking at me.

"I can't find my girlfriend. I was hoping you could check the security cameras or something."

"We can't do that."

"Please. She wouldn't just leave. She left her purse and phone at the table and went to the bathroom about two hours ago and no one has seen her since."

"Sorry, man. I hope you find her."

I want to scream. Punch something. Punch them. Flip their table over and bash their heads in with it.

Instead, I step outside and text Jack to bring Emma's purse to me. After he replies, I call the police. By this time, it's one in the morning and it takes the police almost thirty more minutes to arrive. And I don't know what I expected but it definitely wasn't for them to stand there uninterested while I tell them what's going on.

"She probably just ran into some friends and took off with them," one of the cops says. "I'm sure she's fine."

I point my thumb at Makenna and Lillian. "These are her friends and they're here. She wouldn't take off without her phone and purse."

The other cop pulls out his notepad. "What's her name?"

I give them Emma's information, and then mine, explaining again what happened. I mention *Schmiz 1* inside knowing if they talk to him, he may tell them I jumped him, but I don't care.

"We'll enter her in the system and if anyone comes in contact with her, we'll let her know she's been reported missing."

"Sir," I say more firmly. "Something bad has happened. You don't understand. Can't you watch the surveillance cameras from here?"

He chuckles, clicking his pen shut and tucking it into his breast pocket. "I think you need to watch a little less *Law & Order.*"

My jaw tightens and I look at Jack. It's true, I do watch a lot of crime TV, but this is not my overactive imagination. "I mean no disrespect, sir, but my friend and I are both officers out at the prison, and I have a criminal justice degree with a minor in forensics. I know my girlfriend well. We have been together for ten years and have known each other since we were four. Can you just trust my gut on this?"

They look at each other, and for a moment I think I might have reached them. "Give us a call if she doesn't come home tonight." They turn to walk away, dismissing me, dismissing Emma as someone who is irrelevant.

I don't want to do this, because I do not like being this person, but feel I have no choice. "I know I gave you my name, and I understand that McIntyre is a somewhat common last name, and maybe you don't really follow politics, but my dad is Senator Wes McIntyre. And I really don't want to have to call him and alert our families when I have so little information."

The two cops look at each other again. "Anyone with that last name can try to claim something like that."

I nod, acknowledging that fact. "Google me. Or Wes McIntyre's family. You'll find what you need." I know damn well that my dad's website has a photo of me, him, and my mom on the main page. And if they search my name, they will find the article from this time last year that ran in several newspapers around the state about my college graduation.

The officer pulls his cell phone from its holder, opens it and types something. A moment later, he eyes me and then looks back at his phone before showing it to his partner.

I hate that I had to pull clout but am thankful for my asshole father and his shitty viewpoints at that moment. "So, am I calling my dad or are you going to help me find Emma?"

One of the officers enters Emma into the system as someone to be on the lookout for. A third officer goes to our apartment to confirm that her car is still there and that she is not at home. The other officer starts talking with the bouncers at Club W, but I am not privy to that conversation.

"It's gonna be okay," Makenna tells me, but there is no conviction in her voice.

A man in a suit joins the officer and the bouncers. After a moment, they all look over at me. The officer turns away and speaks into his radio.

My palms feel clammy, and my breath seems to be caught inside me as my vision gets hazy with speckled stars flashing. Cement encases my legs making it impossible for me to move and I need Emma. I need Emma right now, but I can't find her. And it hits me then, as the second cop comes back inside and the two of them along with the man in the suit start to walk away, that something bad happened to Emma.

I don't know life without Emma.

"Sir," I say, my voice inaudible.

"Sir," Jack says more loudly for me.

The officers look our way. "We're going to check the camera footage."

Jack and I stared at each other for a moment. "I don't know what to do."

"Do you want some water or something?" Lillian asks.

I nodded because I think that's what you're supposed to do, and they walk toward the bar. At what point do I call her parents? Should I do it now? Do I wait until the police tell me to? The thought of going home to an empty apartment and an empty bed makes me sick to my stomach. Even worse is the thought of it forever being that way.

"Closing Time" by Semisonic fills the club as the lights flip on, telling me it's now three in the morning. One of the bouncers tells us to, "Watch for your friend," as people make their way to the exit. But I know she is not among the drunken patrons spilling into the parking lot, though I would easily give up my left and right nut to see her mixed in with the nameless faces. She would smile and say, "Oh, my God, River. I was looking everywhere for you." But it's been four hours, and this club isn't so big that we could lose each other for four damn hours.

I spot *Schmiz 1* coming toward the exit, his eyes on me. He has a girl beside him who appears to be completely wasted. "You find her?" he asks, pausing in front of me.

Shaking my head, I tell him, "No, man. Cops are here now."

His eyebrows arch in surprise. "No offense, but are you sure she didn't just leave with some random guy?"

"Her phone and everything are still here." I look past him for a moment. "That's not something she normally does."

Schmiz looks skeptical. "Hope it all works out, man."

"Hey," I call out as he starts to walk away, recalling how he'd been watching us earlier, and consider that he could be a suspect. "What's your name?"

He faces me again. "Drew." Jabbing his hand in my direction, he says, "Drew Schmidt."

I take his hand. "River McIntyre. No hard feelings man."

His eyes twitch a little before he offers a quick nod and drops my hand. "Good luck finding her."

The way he said it seemed like a challenge. 'Good luck finding her.' Like it would be impossible. Like there wasn't a chance in hell Emma would ever be found.

I'm trying to stay calm and feel like I'm in control, but I've never felt so alone before. Makenna and Lillian are talking quietly to each other. Jack is standing beside me, hands in his pockets, looking as lost as I feel. I'm about to ask him if he thinks I should call Emma's parents when two more cops walk in followed by a plain clothes cop wearing his badge on his hip.

They don't even glance in our direction. One of the bouncers leads them wherever the other cops went.

"This is not good," I say.

From that point on, time seems to either speed up or stand still. I'm not sure. It's like nothing is happening and I'm frozen in time and then suddenly everything is jumbled and crazy. They allow us to sit at a table in the bar and offer us drinks, but I decline, aware that I need to keep my head clear.

A uniformed cop appears, looking us over. "McIntyre?"

I stand so quickly my chair tips over behind me. "Yes, sir?"

He jerks his head for me to follow him. "Come with me."

Jack stands too. "What's going on?"

"Just some questions," the officer says.

"Do you want a lawyer, Riv?" Jack asks.

I pause and look at him. "For what?"

He shrugs. I shake my head and follow the officer. He leads me down the hallway where I last saw Emma and up a staircase to a room with several monitors showing the interior and exterior of the club. Some of the screens are active, others are not.

The plain clothes officer stands and faces me, blocking my view of the screens. "Mr. McIntyre," he says. "Detective Morgan." The pen in his hand clicks over and over, like he has a nervous tick. My eyes are drawn to it. Detective Morgan. Detective. They called a detective.

Darkness creeps into my vision again but I have to focus. I have to listen.

I need Emma.

They show me a zoomed in face of a man I don't recognize and tell them as much. They show me the same man a few times in different shots from different angles. The image etches into my mind but like the toy from my childhood, someone shakes it, and the image vanishes. Every time they show me the man's face, it's like I'm seeing it again for the first time.

But when the images change, what they show me next will be burned into my core memories forever.

A still shot of Emma and I walking back into the club after being outside appears. She's smiling at me. I'm grinning, my hand outstretched like maybe it had been on her back, but I started to pull it away. My eyes aren't on her, and I know this was the moment I let her go. I didn't even watch her walk away.

I suck in my breath and close my eyes. Why didn't I just wait for her to come out of the bathroom?

"Is this Emma beside you?" Detective Morgan asks gently.

Nodding, I open my eyes. "Yeah. I should've waited for her to come out of the bathroom."

Morgan doesn't immediately reply. "River," he says, "the next images I show you might be difficult to see. But I need for you to confirm it is her."

Looking away, I'm forced to swallow down the bile rising in my esophagus. This is bad. This is so, so bad. I can feel it in my bones. Something is very wrong, and I can't fix it. I can't grin and make her come home. I can't make promises to her when she's gone. I can't do sweet things for her and ensure her love is still mine.

"River?"

Closing my eyes, I nod before lowering my head to my hands. I draw in a quick, deep breath, straighten my posture, and open my eyes to see a still shot of Emma being carried over the shoulder of the man they'd showed me before. Her long honey locks are hanging down the backside of the man I don't know; her arms limp, hanging on either side of her hair. I'm shown another still image from the other side of the man. He's smiling, talking with the bouncers at the front entrance, Emma's black sandals in one hand. His other arm is holding her in place on his shoulder. But it's his hand placement that sends me over the edge.

It's inside her dress.

When we were outside, I breathed in the feral scent of her arousal on her underwear and then shoved them into my pocket. She never put them back on.

"She's not wearing underwear," I say without thinking, as if it makes a difference in the grand scheme of things. "She's not wearing underwear."

Morgan nods. "How do you know that?"

"We had sex outside. That's what we were doing. She didn't put them back on. And his hand..." I lean closer to the screen.

Morgan places his hand on my shoulder, pulling me back. "Okay, River. We're going to find her. One of these officers is going to meet you and your friends at the station for some official interviews. We have plenty to go on. I feel confident that we're gonna find Emma quickly."

"Did he drug her?" I ask, thinking of her limp body.

"We're gonna figure all that out in time."

"What were him and the bouncers talking about?"

Morgan stares at me for a moment, like he's trying to decide if I'm a child or a man. I straighten my posture. "They asked if she was okay. He told them she drank too much."

I am both dumbfounded and livid at the same time. "And they just let him leave with her like that?"

"They did."

Jack drives my Jeep to the police station. When I got in, I immediately pull her underwear from my pocket. This time, though, I don't smell them. I just hold them in my fist like they're all that's left of her. I didn't understand what was going on. What parallel universe I had been transported to.

After a few minutes, I looked over at Jack. "I think I should call her parents."

CHAPTER TWENTY-TWO

Emma

The unfamiliar sound of someone grunting pulls me into consciousness. At least I think I'm awake. It's a struggle to open my eyes, like they're stuck or something. I think they're open. There's barely a sliver of light. I turn my head to see pale, paperwhite skin covered in a light layer of dark hair. I blink, trying to force my eyes open more. I can see light behind the body beside me, a lamp maybe.

"You woke up just in time," the voice attached to the skin says, grunting through the words.

Pain radiated through my face and head, centered between my eyes. Pushing to keep my eyes open is making it worse, but it's nothing compared to the pain that suddenly descends on my left nipple. It feels like someone has attached pliers to it, pulling on it in hopes of detaching it. I scream out, grabbing at my breast, just as the pain stops.

The calloused palm of the man's hand covers my mouth. "Shut the fuck up! Fucking whore." The stench of cigarettes and dirt permeate my senses, transferring onto my tongue and lips from his rough skin. It makes me want to gag. "Don't act like you don't like it rough."

I have no idea where I am, who this man is, or how he knows the way I like sex. I'm freezing. Running my hand over my body confirms that I have no clothes on. Gingerly, I touch my face, feeling my swollen browbone and there is something crusted on my skin.

I start to get up.

He flattens his hand over my chest, pushing me down onto the ground. "You're not going anywhere."

"Where am I?"

He doesn't answer me. I try to make sense of what is happening. There is a lamp somewhere in this room. I can't see it and consider that it is behind this man. I'm naked. Lying on a blanket or some type of fabric on the hard floor. I can't see the man's face because I can't look upward, but I can see that he is pasty white and hairy. He smells disgusting. It's a mix of odors. Besides cigarettes and dirt, there's the smells of unwashed, sweaty body parts, and something damp. Like clothes that are left in the washer too long.

He's cupping my breast. The only sounds I can hear are his breathing, occasional grunts, and... and... skin on skin friction.

I lift my head again, trying to see if what I think I'm hearing is what I'm actually hearing. But as soon as my head rises, he pushes my skull back to the floor forcefully. The pressure of his hand on my brow and then the back of my head hitting the dense ground behind me sends reverberating waves of pain and flashes of light into my brain.

It's even harder to keep my eyes open now, but when I hear movement, I force them to stay open. His body shifts and then I feel the pressure of him as he straddles his weight over my chest. My arms are held in place beside my body by his legs. There's a putrid new smell now and it makes me turn my head and fight the urge to gag.

"Get off," I whisper. I can't breathe between the stench coming from his body and the pressure of his weight on my chest. "Please," I say a little louder. "I can't breathe."

The back of his knuckles hit my lips with force. "Shut the fuck up and open your mouth."

I squeeze my eyes shut and try to hold my breath, the taste of blood filling my mouth. He's jacking off inches from my face.

My fear seems like it's on hold, waiting for someone to acknowledge it. I'm not even sure what I'm supposed to fear at this point because I have no idea what's happening, where I am, or who this man is.

His backhand pummels into my face again, on my left cheek this time. Pain sears through the bones in my face. My brain throbs. "I said open your fucking mouth." Rough, calloused fingers pry my mouth open, pushing into the back of my throat causing me to gag. "There you go. Oh, yeah," he groans. I move my head back and forth quickly, trying to loosen his grip on my jaw but he is undeterred. "Here it comes." Pulling on my bottom teeth, he holds my jaw open despite my resistance. My legs come up, kicking at the air and unable to make contact with his body.

I scream out in hopes that someone will hear me without having a clue if there is anyone else around but holy-what-the-fuck-is-happening-to-me-right-now?

You're being assaulted, Emma, I tell myself. *This is sexual assault.*

Hot, sticky ropes of his nasty cum hit my face. I didn't think anything could smell worse than the stench of trash I was already surrounded by. Very little goes into my mouth, thank the fucking stars. Not that it matters because he almost immediately rubs it into my face and lips like moisturizer and then sticks his fingers back into my mouth.

"Next time, I'm fucking this mouth," he tells me, pulling on my lips, as if that is something for me to look forward to. "Your face is jacked up, but I still wanna see these gorgeous lips wrapped around my cock."

"What the hell is happening?" I ask, somewhat rhetorically, not expecting an answer.

"Couldn't tell you, sweetheart," he says as he heaves himself off me. "You've been marked. Forget everything you ever knew 'cause that life is gone."

With him off me, I sit up. He doesn't stop me. The lamp I saw before turns out to be a flashlight. It's lying on the floor a few feet away. The man is husky. He has dark hair on top of his head, covering his chest, and on his legs. I can't really see his face because of the light behind him and my eyes not being able to open completely. I don't see a window, but it's probably still dark out. Maybe. It was dark when I was at Club W with River.

"What do you mean I've been marked?"

"Hand-picked."

I don't understand. "What does that mean? Marked for what? And by who?"

"Couldn't tell you, sweetheart. Just know what you're worth."

"What I'm worth?"

He chuckles. "What you're worth to me. The money I'm gonna make once you're delivered."

"Delivered?" Things were starting to click in my mind, but I wanted to hear him say it. "What does that mean?"

He pulls a black shirt over his head. "It means someone wants you. I don't know who and I don't know why. I can guess that you're probably about to become someone's personal whore because you're far too pretty to be in a brothel or some shit."

I suck in a deep breath, not entirely convinced I can't get out of this. "Wow. Okay."

He chuckles as he stands and pulls on his pants. "You're pretty calm," he notes.

I look up, trying to see his face. "What good would it do to freak out?"

"None, unless you want me to knock you out again."

Honestly, that might be better. "Where are my clothes?"

"You'll get new clothes when it's time to go. Clothes are evidence. They're long gone." He pauses as he picks up the flashlight. "Not that you had much on." The bright tunnel of light shines in my face. "One fuck out there in the back of a Jeep wasn't enough? You had to leave your underwear off so you could get more inside?" He crouches down in front of me and uses the head of the flashlight to spread my legs. I push against it, twisting my body to fight what he's doing.

The flashlight cracks against the side of my face with a skull crushing blow. Cries of pain escape me. I lower myself to the floor and curl into a ball, my arms covering my head as I brace for another blow. He grabs my hair and pulls me toward him, but I keep my legs tucked in tight.

The room goes dark, the only thing I hear is my own pleas for him to stop as he presses the flashlight between my legs, rubbing the length of it along my center.

"Scream all you want, sweetheart. No one is gonna hear you." He nudges the edge of the flat end of the flashlight against my clit. The plastic moves painfully over my dry folds. "You like having dick inside you, don't you, Emma?"

I'm stunned to hear my name. My cries cease.

"You want me to fill you up, don't you?" He pulls the flashlight away and replaces it with his rugged, dry fingers. "You want me, Emma?"

I lay frozen in a ball, unable to think or move. He knows my name. He saw River fucking me outside. How long was he watching me?

I left my body then. I'm sitting in the corner of this pitch-black room, watching this strange man stick his fingers in both of my holes alternately, and all I can think about is the UTI and other possible infections I'm going to get. I want to tell him about the risks of what he's doing and share the benefits of safe sex with him. It's probably knowledge he could benefit from.

He grows bored or something. I'm not sure. Maybe he can't get hard again. His words fall on deaf ears because I'm not here anymore. I'm not sure where I am.

The only thing I am sure of is that he did not have intercourse with me and for that I am grateful.

I lay there for a long time after he leaves. It seemed like hours, but it may have been minutes. When I sit up, I reach between my legs for the flashlight but it's not there. I crawl around on my hands and knees looking for it, finding only an empty bucket and the blanket I was lying on. I wrap it around my shoulders, pulling it closed in front of me and walking the perimeter of the room, running my hands along the wall for a window or door.

I find the door easily. The doorknob is locked and there is a deadbolt. Neither one has a lock on my side. The deadbolt only has a keyhole on it. The walls are smooth, like the drywall in my apartment, and I consider where I could possibly be. It's a small room, maybe even a closet. Drywall tells me I'm unlikely to be in a basement, but it's not impossible. The floor was hard, but I couldn't really identify the material. I didn't feel any divots or seams in the walls that would suggest a window had been covered up. There weren't any air vents on the floor or walls, which meant they were on the ceiling or that the only air flow was under the door.

After exploring all there was to explore, I sat back down on the un-forgiving floor with the blanket wrapped around me. There was nothing else to do but let the time tick by.

I have no idea how much of my life passes by while I sit there, drifting in and out of consciousness, wondering if I have a concussion and if this is really how my life will end. I think about River and my dad. Christy and Cora. I tell myself I'll see them again. This isn't the end. I'm not going to be someone's personal whore. I'm just not sure how to get out of this.

The door opens and I'm startled to alertness. I lift my head, my eyes more open than before. The light feeding my hope from outside this prison burns my retinas.

I don't look at the man, I look past him, trying to take in what's beyond the door. The odor accompanying him assures me it's the same guy from before and I wonder how long I've been here. For all I know I've been here for a week.

"Getting hungry?" he asks, his voice rough.

Could I have survived a week without food?

Probably not. But I am hungry. And thirsty. Really thirsty. But before I can open my mouth to request sustenance, the door slams shut and the flashlight shines in my face, making me flitch.

I did not hear the door lock.

I nod eagerly, but my thoughts weren't on food. They were on the fact that he didn't lock the door.

"Open your mouth."

There's not a bone in my body that believes he's actually going to feed me. He's going to shove his nasty dick in there. At least he warned me by telling me he planned to do it.

I lick my lips, barely wetting them, and open wide.

He grabs the hair on the top of my head and slides his dick between my lips. The only movements are his because I'm frozen again, outside my body, somewhere in this dark room with the unlocked door.

I don't hear him groaning and muttering words of encouragement because the wheels are spinning in my head.

The door is unlocked.

I don't feel his prickly balls hitting my chin.

The door is unlocked.

I don't smell the rotting death aroma that comes from him.

The door is unlocked.

One of his hands is on my head, the other hangs at his side, the flashlight shining at the floor, held loosely in his fingers.

The door is unlocked.

I don't know what's out there, but it can't be worse than what's in here.

My fingers circle the cylinder shaft of light as I rise onto my knees. I pull my mouth back as I take the flashlight from him, surprised he did not resist. I hold the flashlight below my chin and shine it at my face.

He makes a growling sound as he looks down at me, both hands gripping my hair now as he pushes into my mouth with more force. His eyes flutter some before rolling back in his head. "Oh, fuck, yes." Streams of praise continue, but I am gone again, gathering strength and courage.

I keep the flashlight shining upward from under my chin so I can see him, and he can see me. When he comes, shooting his load of rotten, coagulated milk into my mouth, I lift one of my legs so that my bare foot is on the floor. As he finishes, I act especially interested in sucking every last drop from him until he shudders and his head falls back.

And then, because it's the only way I can possibly think of to defend myself, I sink my teeth into the softening flesh of his penis as hard as I can. He tries to pull away, a high-pitched scream sounding from his lungs. He pulls my hair, trying to jerk my head away from him until he realizes my jaw is stronger than he expected. I don't let go, suddenly afraid he will still be able to go after me. I need to be sure he hurts so bad that he can't move while I go out that door.

I ignore the fact that I could be completely wrong about it being unlocked and that I have no clue what's on the other side. What I do know is that I am not going to be someone's personal whore and I'm not dying in this dungeon.

The metallic taste of blood fills my mouth, and I let go of him. He doubles over with pain, gasping and crying as I back away, the flashlight pointed at him. Falling to his knees, he's not even looking at me. I debate hitting him in the head with the flashlight as I spit his cum and blood onto the floor, but I don't.

I walked out of the room without interference and shut the door behind me. The deadbolt key is still in the lock, so I turn it, locking him into the dark room, and take the key. I lock the doorknob too just in case he happens to have a key on him. He is screaming still, begging for help, which kinda makes me want to laugh.

Well, unless there's someone here who's going to come to his aid and potentially my demise.

It should feel like a victory, what I just did, but it doesn't. Because while I may have escaped that room and that man, I have no idea what or who is waiting for me out here.

I stand at the end of a hallway. There are three open doors, dark empti-
ness beyond their thresholds, just like the room I came out of, on either
side for a total of four rooms. Well aware that I am buck naked and just
escaped from a room I had been placed in because I had been marked for
trafficking, I move quietly down the hallway with the flashlight drawn
and ready to bludgeon anyone I see. The key is tucked into the palm of
my other hand. A commercial for a well-known insurance company plays
on a TV in a room wherever the hall leads. I have no choice but to go in
that direction.

My heart pounds so hard that if there is another soul within two
hundred miles, they can probably hear it. My body shakes from a combi-
nation of cold, fear, and adrenaline, but the only thing I can think about
is getting out of here and finding River.

CHAPTER TWENTY-THREE

River

The sun is shining by the time mine and Emma's parents arrive. After Jack, Makenna, Lillian and I gave our statements to the police, we were told to go home. Detective Morgan assured me he would call with any updates.

Going home without Emma wasn't natural. We left our apartment together, sharing a meal and drinks, thinking we would be home in a few hours. We were supposed to go to bed together, wake up together. Seeing her car in the parking lot made it seem like she would be upstairs waiting for me even though I knew it wasn't true.

From my spot on the couch, I watch Jack introduce himself to our parents. Lillian went to her apartment shortly after we got here, and Makenna was asleep in my bedroom. Jack nodded off on the couch beside me while I paced a groove into our living room floor, alternating between looking out the front window and checking both of our phones for updates.

My mom sits beside me, pulling me to her tightly while my dad, Chris, and Christy survey the holes in the walls and the busted TV. They don't ask questions which I'm grateful for because I don't have the energy to answer them.

Emma's parents walk around the apartment slowly, holding hands. Makenna made sure everything was in order in Emma's room, so I knew they weren't inspecting stains on the sheets or checking out our collection of sex toys. Though after last weekend, it's safe to say they know we're sleeping together.

"Did you have the sense to get a lawyer?" my dad asks.

I'm honestly surprised he's even here after the way he left things last weekend. "I don't need a lawyer, Dad."

"You always need a lawyer when talking to the cops. I'd think you would've learned that in college."

I made a face at him. "I learned how to *be* a cop, not how to lie to one and make their job harder."

"And yet you're not a cop." He holds his hands up in front of himself. "This is not the time." He looks at Chris. "I apologize."

I swallow and close my eyes. The next thing I know, my mom is gently shaking my shoulder. I'm still sitting on the couch but covered with a blanket now, evidently having dozed off. Jack and my mom stand over me with sympathetic gazes.

"I'm gonna head out," Jack tells me. "Don't think I'll be excused from work."

Sitting up, I nod, realizing I should probably call to let them know I won't be there. Makenna is standing near the door, a hoodie over her dress from the night before.

"I can stay if you need me to," she says quietly.

"No, no. Go home and get some rest." I waved my hand in the direction of my family. "They're here." Lifting from the couch, the blanket falls to my feet. I raise an arm to hug Jack. He comes in, squeezing me tight as he pats my back.

"She'll be back soon," he tells me, as if he has some sort of sixth sense.

But in all honesty, Emma could be dead right now.

I shake off the thought as I cross the room to Makenna. She hugs me tightly too, but not like Jack. Her hug is softer, and maybe that's because she's softer. Her smile is forced, and she offers no false platitudes.

After they leave, I go into the kitchen, knowing I should eat something but not really feeling hunger. My dad sits at the kitchen table with his laptop open, his eyes focused on his phone. When he sees me, he sets it face down on the table.

"Have a good nap?" he asks.

I grunt, which is basically how I've communicated with him most of my life.

There used to be a family that lived next door to us when I was younger. They had three boys who were all older than me. When I was about ten, their youngest was thirteen or fourteen. No matter the season, they were playing a sport. Football, basketball, soccer, baseball. Their parents would always be outside with them, offering pointers, throwing balls, doing what they could to make their sons into the best athletes they could be. Sometimes I would sit in my yard and watch them, envious. A few times, they invited me to come play too, but I never would. I didn't know how.

Sports meant nothing to my dad, and I meant nothing to my mom. One year, I convinced them to let me join the soccer team. My mom rarely took me to practice. My dad never attended a single game.

Noni and Aunt Christy came to every game, Emma with them. They would stand on the sidelines and cheer even though I sucked, while my mom sat in a chair beside them nursing whatever cup she'd hidden her booze in, uninterested in the game and me in general.

Academics were what impressed my dad. Unfortunately, I never excelled in that area either. There was no hiding the repeated looks of disappointment on his face time and again when he scanned my average report cards, followed by whooping my ass. At some point, I was put on medication for ADHD, and Mom told me, "Your grades are going to skyrocket, and your dad is going to be so proud of you."

They didn't and he wasn't.

I'm not stupid. I know that now. I didn't then. But when I was at home, I felt dumb and worthless. Useless. Unwanted. My mom had cycles when she tried to care, but I'm not sure she ever really did. I'd hear Dad yelling at her, calling her names while she sobbed and promised to do better. They would send me to my bedroom when they argued, even as a teen. Behind closed doors, I would hear the sound of physical struggles and smacks followed by my mom crying. On the rare occasion I would walk in while they were mid-fight, my dad would frown and leave the room while my mom would compose herself the best she could in an attempt to fool me into believing our life was as perfect as everyone thought it was.

My dad clears his throat while I stare into the refrigerator without seeing anything in it. "I, uh... River." I close the fridge and face my dad. "I realize I overreacted last weekend when you were home."

I wait for him to continue, anticipating an apology. Some sort of expression of regret. Appearance is important to my dad. Which I can understand given his job. Sometimes I think that's the only thing I've managed to do right since I was born. Look pretty. Have a nice smile. Grow tall. But none of that was in my control. It was simply the cards genetics dealt me. The rest of me and my underachiever spirit, well, my dad could do without it. All he expected from me anymore was to play the part of his son. Naturally, he sees me being with Emma as a threat to his image. Any journalist worth the weight of the paper they wrote on will easily find out she's part of our family.

"As your father, I should want you to be happy. But too often, I find myself thinking only of myself and not of you and your mother." His phone vibrated and he picked it up, pulling his attention away from me. Sliding a finger up the length of the screen, he frowned while his eyes scanned the screen.

As seconds ticked by, it became apparent that our conversation was over. That was probably the closest I've ever gotten to an apology.

I returned to the living room, taking in the solemn faces of my mom, Christy, and Chris lined up on the couch in a row. For the first time, it occurs to me that we don't have enough furniture in our apartment for everyone who's here. Plus, Jack and Makenna were here.

"Sorry we don't have more furniture." I walk to my desk and spin my chair so I can face them when I sit. "No one ever comes over here, really."

"It's okay, River," Chris says.

The worry lines around his eyes look more pronounced today, understandably. Emma is his too. But the difference is that she is all I have. He has Christy and three other kids.

I swallow and look away from him, feeling bad for thinking that way. But it's true. Everyone has something else, someone else. All I have is Emma. She's all I've ever had even when I didn't have her.

The summer after we turned sixteen, my parents took us on a cruise. When they told me I could bring a friend, they assumed I would ask Bryan Rayburn, my best male friend back then. But I'd asked Emma without even considering Bryan. No one objected. No one batted an eye at us sharing a room and then we barely even saw my parents during the whole cruise.

There was a teen club on the ship. During the day, it was a cool hangout spot. At night it transformed into a nightclub of sorts. On the final night of the cruise, I convinced Emma to go to the club in only her bikini top and denim shorts. She looked sexy as hell but kept her arms crossed over her stomach for the first hour we were there and refused to dance.

While Emma was busy being a wallflower, I noticed some girl who had also noticed me. We started talking, and the next thing I knew, Emma was nowhere around.

I figured she would come back eventually, and I'm not sure how long had passed when I realized she hadn't. When I mentioned that my 'friend' had left, the girl I was talking to scrunched up her face and asked, "The fat girl you were with earlier?"

Her judgmental assessment of Emma made me sick. Emma called herself fat all the time, but I didn't see it. She had curves in all the right places and was gorgeous. I never once thought of her as fat. And the fact that this girl we didn't even know wanted to discount Emma based on something so shallow made her suddenly unattractive to me. "I need to go find her."

"Ugh, seriously? You can do so much better than her."

At sixteen, I didn't have a comeback. All I did was walk away with the knowledge that Emma meant more to me than some random cruise girl from North Carolina that I would never see again.

I went back to our room to discover she had been there, having left a note that said 'Fuck you' on the bed that was supposed to be mine—not that we had used it. But she wasn't there.

Frustrated, I went to the restaurants she liked, checked in the shops that were still open. Even scanned the pools knowing she wouldn't go swimming alone.

Panic grew inside me with each place that I checked where she wasn't. I started to think of worst-case scenarios, and each one I thought of was worse than the one before it.

After checking everywhere I could think of, I decided to go back to our room and check there one more time. When I didn't find her there, I felt I had no choice but to tell my parents.

I went to my parents' suite a few decks up, knocking on the door several times before they answered. "I can't find Emma," I told them.

"What do you mean you can't find her?" my dad asked.

"I mean that she was with me and then she was gone. I've been looking for her for, like, an hour already."

They exchanged glances. "Okay, let us get dressed."

My parents walked with me everywhere I had already looked, then, just after midnight, they determined that we needed to contact guest services.

The panic inside me was like a pot of water about to boil over, except somehow it all stayed at the exact right heat and water level, building and burning inside me. My organs were eroding with every second that ticked by where I didn't know where Emma was.

We passed through a breezeway where I could see out into the night, into the infinite blackness of the ocean under an ominous, dark sky. The sight of the never-ending nothingness grabbed me. It took my mind and my sense, and I was overcome with the urge to run and jump off the ship. Because if that's where Emma was, then that was where I needed to be too.

I realized that Emma and I weren't inseparable. We were not one and could possibly part in some way that meant we were not daily fixtures in one another's lives. And at sixteen, I was keenly aware that was not how I wanted to live. I would have rather died than return to shore without her.

Emma was found quickly once we contacted guest services.

When I spotted her being brought to us, her arms crossed over her middle, with a blanket draped over her shoulders, her face was red and splotchy. Black streaks of mascara trailed down her cheeks. I walked quickly to her, notably feeling my heart return to its place in my chest.

"You scared the shit out of me." I wrapped my arms around her.

"Surprised you even noticed I was gone," she whispered as my parents approached.

I'd been so caught up in finding her, I hadn't even considered the reason I hadn't been able to find her was because she was rightly mad at me. And apparently, she hadn't been gone long enough to forget what I'd done.

My parents walked us back to our room, my mom and Emma a few steps ahead of me and my dad. Emma leaned into my mom's one-armed embrace as they walked.

Once we were alone, she went to change in the bathroom. While she changed, I pulled off my shirt and looked for a pair of shorts to sleep in. Emma reappeared in a crewneck sweatshirt and leggings; her face washed clean. She got into bed without saying a word.

"Where'd you go?" I asked gently, hoping to cut a hole in the tension surrounding us.

"Fuck off."

"What did I do?" I asked, even though I knew.

"What did you do?" she shrieked, sitting up, her eyes narrowed at me. "What did you do? Are you serious right now, River?"

Frowning, I swallowed, not sure what to say. Storms raged in her eyes. It was the first time she ever looked at me that way. Like she was disgusted by me. As if the sheer audacity of my existence made her violently ill.

It was the way my dad looked at me.

"You made me wear that fucking bikini top, first of all, despite me not wanting to wear it. You lied to me, told me it looked good, and then spent the night talking to some skinny hot girl, leaving me all alone for people to stare and laugh at."

"Emma—" I was going to tell her she did look good and that no one was staring and laughing.

"Fuck you, River." Her face scrunched up and I knew she was about to cry again. "You did all that after we had sex. Which is the only reason you wanted to bring me and not Bryan."

"I'm sorry." I went to her and started to sit beside her, the need to hold her overwhelming.

"Sit on your own bed. I'm fucking done with you." She laid down and rolled away from me. "When we get off this ship, you're nothing to me. Not even my cousin."

My bond with Emma ran deep; I realized this. I also realized I didn't want anything to ever sever that bond. I acknowledged, at least in my mind, that we would never have a normal relationship. That I would always put her on a pedestal above everyone else.

And that I never wanted her to look at me the way my dad did again.

Over the years, I would pretend I could push her off the throne she sat on in my mind, but that's all it ever was. Pretending. Other girls would enter my realm and other guys entered hers, but they would come and go.

I made so many more mistakes after this, but my heart was never not hers.

Now, years later, I can't find Emma again. But this time, the possible places she could be weren't confined to a ship. This time, Emma could be anywhere.

My mom gave me a sleeping pill after we had food delivered for lunch. I went into Emma's bedroom, shut the door, and climbed into her bed without even moving the throw pillows. After making sure the ringers on both phones were on and as loud as they could go, I pulled the covers up to my neck and cried in private, where no one could see me. Eventually, I drifted to sleep.

When my phone rang hours later, I sprang upright and answered it before I was even awake. "Hello?"

"River? Detective Morgan here."

CHAPTER TWENTY-FOUR

Emma

I stare at the reflection of the monster in the mirror, not even seeing myself. My left cheek is distended almost to the point it looks like a tumor has grown on my face. There's a two-inch gash and dried blood across my cheek. Purplish bruises underline both of my puffy eyes. The space between them and part of my forehead is swollen and red.

It's my mouth that pulls my attention. My chapped lips are bulging, a deep shade of pink. On the edges of them and my chin are speckles of blood and probably cum.

I look feral.

Turning on the faucet, I cup my hands under it, filling them with water before splashing it on my face, wiping gently over my cheek to get the blood off, and then clean off my mouth and chin. I fill my hands again, this time sucking the water into my mouth, rinsing it, spitting, and then taking a drink.

When I swallow, I realize that I just washed away the evidence of what that man did to me. With all the crime shows I've watched with River, I should know better.

It's irrelevant. What matters is that I get out of here.

No one else is here besides me and that man who I can still hear calling for help. I found a grocery sack on the floor beside a chair near the TV that had black leggings and a long-sleeved royal blue T-shirt with the logo for some team I'd never heard of on the back. Wondering if these were the clothes the man said he had for me when we left, I put them on. They were tight but would work. Definitely a better option than going outside naked.

I find my own sandals laying on the floor, recalling the man saying something about getting rid of the evidence. If they intended for me to wear them when they took me wherever I was supposed to go next, they wouldn't be left behind as evidence and would be destroyed at a later point.

I desperately want to wash my vagina to get rid of the cross contamination from my asshole but restrain myself. Risking infection against my better judgement in the name of evidence preservation.

Although, biting dudes dick was poetic justice if I'd ever seen it.

Armed with the flashlight and key, I left the bathroom. I grab a small, unopened bag of potato chips from the table and shove them into the grocery sack I'd gotten the clothes from, along with the flashlight and key. I scan the small sitting area once more for anything that could be helpful to me, deciding to take a cell phone charger with an extra-long braided fabric cord, realizing the man whose dick I just took a chomp out of probably has his cell phone on him since I didn't find it anywhere.

Fuck.

It's pitch black when I step outside of the warehouse type building that I'd been in. There are other similar looking buildings around where I'm at, but no open businesses or houses. The lights of a town glitter in the far-off distance. Once my eyes adjust to the darkness, I start walking, not really having a clue which way I should go.

There's a streetlight down the road to the right. It may signal that there's an intersection there. An intersection would have street names. Street names may tell me where I am.

For all I know I could be hundreds of miles away from home. I was knocked out with one punch in the women's bathroom at Club W and have no idea how far I was driven or how much time passed between then and now.

The night air is chilly and I'm grateful for the long sleeves, but I'm still cold. Hugging myself for warmth, I walked quickly toward the streetlight with the grocery sack hanging from my arm. My mind is jumbled with wondering how safe I truly am and River and whether or not he's called my parents. It clicks that it couldn't be that long since I was taken from the club because the bruising and swelling on my face didn't look very old. For all I know, it's only been a few hours. Maybe he's just now realizing I'm gone.

I reached the intersection. The green street signs say 1350W and 2900N. Not helpful whatsoever. Many rural Illinois counties have re-named their county roads with actual words, but many have not, including most in my area. If anything, the numbered roads tell what counties I'm *not* in, leaving it to be so many others.

I go left toward the glow of a town in the distance. After about a mile, I consider opening the bag of chips but decide against it when I spot headlights coming toward me. I stopped walking, debating if I should dip into the cornfield along the road and hide among the stalks, or if I should try to flag the car down and ask for help.

I decided to try for help.

I set down my bag and start waving my arms as the car approaches. It slows, coming to a stop beside me. When I see it's a man, I'm uneasy, but he's older, maybe fifty, wearing a baseball cap, and driving an SUV.

He rolls down his window and rakes his eyes over me. "What are you doing out here?"

Something strikes a nerve then. Maybe it was the sound of his voice. Or the way he looked at me. Or the smell coming from his car. Cigarettes and the stench of an un-showered man.

"My car broke down," I lie. "Can I use your phone to call someone? Mine is dead."

He looks down the road. "Where's your car?"

I look in the direction I came from. "Quite a ways at this point. Up a few miles and to the left."

His eyes take me in again. "What happened to your face?"

I touch my obtuse left cheek gingerly. "I just need to call someone to come get me."

"There's no service out here," he tells me. "Hop in and we can go down the road where I can pick up a few bars."

My stomach is tight at the thought of getting into a random stranger's car, but my only other choice is to keep walking.

He pushes the unlock button and nods his head in the direction of the passenger door.

Against my better judgment and without consulting my common sense, I pick up my grocery sack from the ground and get into the car.

"I'm Scott," he tells me as he pulls a five-point turn in the road to take us in the direction of the town. "What's your name?"

"Emma," I say, wondering if I should have lied.

He repeats my name, looking at me. "Nice to meet you, Emma." Licking his lips, he shifts his hands on the steering wheel. "I can just take you into town if that's where you're headed.

Scott's cell phone is connected to the car, Apple CarPlay in use. I can see that it's 10:52 p.m. and that he has full bars of service and I'm pretty sure I just made a big fucking mistake. "Okay."

What I don't understand is why he would lie about having cell service but then offer to take me into town. Based on the time, I know that it's been at least twenty-four hours since I was at Club W, but possibly more.

"You live around here?"

It depends where we are, I think. "Uh, no. I was visiting my boyfriend."

He smirks. "Is he the one who fucked up your face?"

Pulling my grocery sack tighter, I nodded. "Yeah."

"Sometimes, women just need put in their place, you know, Emma?" Scott asks, agitation littering his voice.

I look over at him. The car is traveling about fifty miles per hour. If I jump out, I will be injured and unable to get away, so that's not an option. I don't answer him because if I were to agree with him that women deserve to be 'put in their place' by being hit, even if it's just to keep the peace, I feel like I would be betraying all women everywhere.

"I asked you a question, Emma." His voice has an edge to it that sends shivers down my spine.

"Yeah," I agree, betraying every female on the planet. "Sometimes."

"What did you do?"

"Cheated," I say instantly. It's the first thing I think of.

Scott's quiet for a moment. "So was the guy you were fucking in the back of a Jeep your boyfriend or the one you were cheating with?"

The blood drains from my head. I feel like I'm going to pass out. I don't move; just keep my eyes peeled on the road as I try to figure out what to do.

He pulls his hand back and then lets it fly into my face. Pain shoots through my jaw and over my scalp. I cry out, shirking down in the seat and putting an arm up to block any more blows.

"Wait until they find out you bit Ben's dick. They're probably going to pull all your teeth out, so you don't do it again."

This is way worse than I thought. There are still several miles until we reach whatever town is ahead, but I feel like that's not really our destination. I feel like there will not be any stopping.

I am not free.

Should've hidden in the fucking cornfield.

If death was guaranteed by jumping out of this vehicle, I would gladly do it.

His hand grips my left thigh. "That pretty little mouth is gonna make someone a whole lot of money, but I suggest you keep it shut for now before I have to knock you the fuck out again." He glances at me. "Can't keep hitting you in the face or it'll never heal in time."

So, Scott is the one who hit me at Club W and not the dude who I locked in that room with a bloody cock. My head spins, thoughts rapidly firing, but for the life of me I cannot come up with any way to get out of this at the moment.

"Maybe I like it like that," I say quietly. It's true. I do like it when River is rough and forceful. Sometimes I think there's something wrong with me that I like fighting River off so he can make me submit to him and take everything he wants from me. It's possibly one of my most favorite forms of foreplay.

But I don't want Scott and this isn't foreplay. This is my attempt to soften him up and make him believe I won't slit his throat if I get the chance.

Slit his throat.

Throat.

Phone charger.

I also like being choked. Hands, belts, cords. And I just so happen to have a phone charger in my grocery sack.

"I'm starving," I say. "Is it okay if I eat these chips?" I pull them from the bag, holding them up for Scott to see.

His thumb and forefinger graze over my left breast, pinching gently on my pebbled nipple that pushes against the fabric of the too small shirt. "Go ahead."

I keep one hand in the grocery sack, unplugging the charging cord from the box that plugs into the wall. I'm able to cover up the noise the bag is making with the crinkling of the chip bag at the same time. "Did you fuck me when I was knocked out?"

"Nah," he says, his hand back on my thigh now. He's moving it aggressively along the length of it, like he thinks it's going to turn me on. "It's technically not allowed but some of you whores I just can't let go without dipping into the goods, ya know?"

I finish chewing and swallow the chips. "You been doing this a while?"

"Couple years."

"So, you fucked a lot of women then?" Of course, I'm considering what STIs this asshole probably has and how many unsuspecting women he's passed them on to. "Do you use condoms?"

He gives me the side eye. "Depends."

"On what?"

"The girl."

"What does that mean?"

He shrugs, his hand resting at the apex of my thighs, rubbing me, and not in a good way. "Depends on if she seems like she would be clean or not."

"Are you gonna use a rubber with me?"

"What's it matter to you? You're probably gonna die in a year or so anyway."

His words strike me, the full gravity of the situation coming down on me like an anvil. "I'm just trying to understand," I say quietly.

"If I fuck a whore, I use a condom. Someone who seems like they've been around. But sometimes we get young ones. I don't use condoms with them."

"Young ones?" My stomach twists. "Am I a young one?"

"Nah. You're older than most girls we pick up." He pulls the waistband of my leggings away from my body, his eager fingers sliding over the fluff of my belly. "And thicker. It's been a long time since I fucked a body like yours." He grips the extra skin on my stomach.

Great. I suppose I should feel honored. But I'm still stuck on his 'young ones' comment. "So, how old is young then? Because I'm only twenty-four."

"Eh," he says like he's considering what he wants for lunch. "Probably the youngest I've grabbed was five or six. But that's too young to fuck. For me at least," he adds, like that catapults him into sainthood. "I've heard too many stories about girls that age dying from..." He trails off, leaving my imagination to assume the worst.

I stopped chewing and stared at him.

"Your pussy is fat. And wet." He looks over at me. "What?"

It doesn't even register that his hand is rubbing between my legs. "Five or six?"

"It's not for me to judge." His voice is low, and I wonder if he has a moral compass at all.

I am sick to my stomach and want to spit out the chips in my mouth. "What's the youngest you've fucked?"

"Don't worry about it."

Yeah, okay. Does he really think he can tell me some fucked up shit like that and I'm just going to not worry about it? What the hell is wrong with people that they want to have sex with little kids? Like, one day they're learning to read and then some sick fucker coughs up a fat stack of cash and next thing they know their life is over.

And this man, Scott, sitting beside me, driving me to my own death, plays a part in it. I can't just sit here and do nothing. There's not even a second thought when I decide I will die before I let myself become a statistic. I will die before I let Scott live to steal the life of another innocent child for someone's sick pleasure.

And I thought my sexual fetishes were depraved.

We've finally reached whatever town this is. I didn't see any sign, but in all fairness, I've been distracted.

I close my eyes and count to five. Then in one swift movement, I sit up, look at Scott just as he turns to me, and spit my mouthful of chips into his face.

"What the—" he starts but doesn't finish.

The grocery sack and bag of chips fall to the floorboard, the phone charging cord in one of my hands, flashlight in the other, as I lift myself up into a position that twists his arm so that he cannot immediately pull his hand from between my legs. I bludgeon him upside the head with the flashlight, his baseball cap falling to his lap, revealing a receding hairline with a few sad strands reaching across the crown of his head to the other side. I hit him again, this time on the stretched skin on the top of his head, before dropping the flashlight to the floorboard.

Scott is fighting to pull his hand free from between my legs while trying not to stop driving. I clench my thighs together. He probably thinks I will try to run if he stops, but honestly, that's not even my goal at this point.

I wrap the cord around his neck like a scarf, circling his sagging skin twice before he realizes what's happening. As I pull the wire tight, he takes his hand off the steering wheel and tries to stick his fingers between his skin and the braided cord. I am pulling it as tight as I can, watching his eyes bulge and his skin flush a scarlet color, and I forget about his other hand when I shift my position to get better leverage.

Before Scott can do anything with his newly freed hand, the sound of tires squealing and crunching metal catches me off guard as I'm throttled against the passenger door. Glass shatters and the SUV flies through the air. Everything goes silent for a moment before I hear more crunching metal combined with the sound of the SUV scraping on its roof across the asphalt.

My body is easily tossed around like the ball in a pinball game, slamming against the confines of this vehicle. When it stops moving, I hear nothing except the engine. I have no idea what we hit. I'm lying on my back on the ceiling of the car. When I turn my head, I see Scott held in place by his seatbelt, the charger cord still hanging from his neck, blood coming from a gash across his forehead. He's not moving.

I try to move, knowing I need to get out of the car, but I can't. Blood drips from Scott's head and I wonder, no, I *hope* that he's dead. When I try to suck in a deep breath, there's a stabbing pain in my chest.

"Hello?" I call out as loud as I can. "Is anyone out there?"

I have never felt more alone than I do at this moment. I don't want to die. Not here. Not now. Not this way. Not in a year from now. I need to tell someone about the children. I need to save the children.

I definitely don't want to die in the car next to this sick, vile piece of shit.

And then, I have an epiphany. "Hey, Siri," I say, waiting to hear her reply, letting me know I've activated the feature on Scott's iPhone. "Call 911."

Chapter Twenty-Five

River

When I come out of the bedroom after Detective Morgan calls, I find my mom passed out on the couch, her phone resting on her chest. No one else is here and I assume they went to a hotel. A nearly empty glass sits on the coffee table in front of the couch. The clear liquid and lingering condensation on the lower half of the glass tells me it's probably melted ice. We don't even keep alcohol in our apartment, so she must've brought it with her or bought it since arriving.

"Mom," I say loudly. She doesn't flinch. I pull a T-shirt over my head, feeling that time is of the essence currently. "Mom!" I yell her name this time.

Her eyes flutter open in confusion, darting around her surroundings before landing on me. Frowning, she pulls her brows downward. "What?" Her tone is tentative, unsure whether I've woken her to share good news or bad.

"They found Emma." Saying it aloud makes my throat tighten. I should feel relief but I'm not sure I do.

She sits up, her phone falling onto her lap. "They did?"

Her words are slurred, and my jaw tightens with familiar agitation. "Yeah."

"Where was she?" My mom tries to stand, her knees wobbling, and I wonder how much she had to drink.

"I don't know. I didn't think to ask. They're taking her to a hospital over in St. Louis."

She stands, barely catching her phone before it falls to the floor. "Why? Is she hurt?" Without waiting for a reply, she holds her phone inches from her face to unlock the screen. "I need to call your dad."

"I'm going to the hospital. Hopefully I'll get there before she does."

My mom's blue eyes squint at her phone screen. "I'll go with you."

As drunk as she is, no thank you. I had woken her thinking she understood the gravity of the situation and would not be drunk for once. I regret having false hopes. "Mom—"

She cuts me off. "I'm fine, River. I am not so drunk I can't go to the hospital to see my niece."

I turn away from her, not wanting to see the frown lines around her mouth while she lies to me. Maybe she doesn't even realize she's lying. "Please don't call her that anymore."

"What am I supposed to call her?"

"I mean, you can just call her Emma."

"I'm just not sure I'll ever get used to... whatever this is."

I want to be mad. I really do. But I spent so many years being mad at my mom that I can't let it take up my headspace anymore. Leaving home for college put much needed distance between us. My dad was rarely around even before he was elected to office. His work and local political aspirations took precedence over family always. It's been years since I realized I had been a mistake. They never wanted me. I'm not even sure they ever wanted each other.

"What me and Emma have is real despite what anyone says or thinks." I glance back at her as I open the door to leave the apartment. "I'm sorry you can't recognize what a real relationship is."

My hands shake as I pull out of the parking lot onto the road. There shouldn't be much traffic at this time of night, so it should take less than an hour to get across the river and to the hospital. I can't quite grasp what it is I feel. It seems like a year has passed in the last twenty-four hours. "I'm gonna call Christy," I say. I glanced at my mom in the passenger seat. There are tears running down her cheeks.

I know what I said was harsh, but it's true. And when it comes down to it, if it weren't for Emma, Aunt Christy, and Noni being constant in my life, I don't know where I'd be. They gave me the consistency and stability that my mom never could.

In second grade, on the night of our school's winter program where kids sang songs and families gathered to sip hot cocoa and chat with Santa, my mom dropped me off at the elementary school I attended. The problem was that the program was being held at the high school, nearly two miles away. She pulled up like she was dropping me off for school at the front entrance. I got out and she pulled away. I walked to the door of the school in my khaki slacks and red and green sweater with my hair combed back away from my face and pulled on the door.

The door didn't open. I tried all six doors at the main entrance and every single one was locked. I ran down the sidewalk looking at the taillights of my mom's car as she drove away. It was mid-December, and the sky was an inky black canopy overhead while my breath hung in front of my face. I wasn't even sure I knew the way to the high school. Not to mention I'd chosen not to wear my stocking cap because I didn't want to mess up my hair.

I walked back to the school entrance and looked inside as hot tears ran down my cheeks. My seven-year-old brain didn't know what else to do, so I looked for a rock big enough to break the glass door. If I could get inside, then I could use the phone in the office to call Christy or Noni. I spotted one about the size of my hand in the landscaped area under a classroom window. After retrieving it, I went back to the door and started to beat on the glass with the rock. And then, like a true Christmas miracle, the school janitor, Sam, appeared in the hallway. His eyes went wide when he saw me.

Sam drove me to the high school and walked me inside. I missed singing with my class but got to have some hot chocolate and tell Santa what I wanted for Christmas, and those were the best parts. The parts I'd been afraid of missing.

When everyone started to leave, I couldn't find my mom. I ended up at the police station and Noni came to get me. I didn't understand it then, but now I do. And I'm not sure if anyone ever told me, or it's just that I got older and started adding things up. My mom had been too drunk to realize there was no one at the school when she dropped me off. When the police went to the house, she was passed out in the car with it still running. That was her first DUI and the first time she went to rehab. It was the first big letdown from my mom that I remember. I stayed with Noni while she was gone; my dad was too busy to be bothered with being a father.

Not much has changed.

Christy answers on the first ring. "Hello?" Hope powers her voice.

"They found her."

She lets out a sound that is loud and full of emotions. It makes my heart feel like it's being squeezed. I give her the information I know, listening as she repeats it to Chris. They say they'll see me at the hospital and the call ends.

"I'll call your dad," my mom tells me. "He's probably asleep, though."

I say nothing. I can't imagine my dad will leave whatever bed he's sleeping in to come see Emma at the hospital.

Fair to say I'm surprised when he does. My dad shows up wearing grey joggers and a henley, definitely not his usual public attire, and I can tell everyone is just as surprised as me.

"How is she?" my dad asks, the last to arrive.

"She's not here yet," my mom explains.

I imagine the way I feel is similar to what a father waiting for their child to be born feels like. It's a mix of anxiety, excitement, and fear all rolled into a flaming ball setting your brain on fire. Chris has seemed calm since he arrived, barely speaking, asking few questions of me. Never shedding a tear or breaking away from his cool demeanor. Christy is trying to be strong, probably for my sake.

The truth of the matter is that this is fucking scary. All of it. The image of Emma's limp body hanging over the shoulder of a stranger as he stole her from me, from us, will forever be tattooed in my mind.

My dad sits beside me and puts his arm around my shoulders. "It's going to be alright, son."

I cannot remember the last time my dad touched me, let alone touched me affectionately. I lift my eyes to my mom sitting across from me. She's taking in the scene before her. Her mouth is open slightly, a V stitched between her brows. Maybe in the wake of this... whatever it is... a near tragedy? Maybe it has my dad realizing how life can change on a dime.

Nodding, I look at my dad. "Yeah. I hope you're right."

The softness in his eyes tells me this could be the fresh start we need.

It seems like hours pass before we're told Emma is there. The medical staff let us know that she was involved in a motor vehicle accident and is injured but stable. Aside from the medical staff treating her, the police need to speak with her.

I'm pacing back and forth across the waiting room floor, ignoring everything that's being said. It's an internal battle not to push open the double doors into the exam area and find her. I need to see her more than I need to breathe. She's right here in the same building as me, injured, and I'm being kept from her.

The bluish light of morning peeks through the windows when a nurse dressed in minty green scrubs finally tells us, "Two people can see her at a time."

I approach the nurse, not even questioning whether I'm one of the two people, and glance at Chris and Christy.

"Go ahead," Christy says to her husband.

I feel a twinge of guilt for blatantly insisting that I see Emma before Christy, but it fades quickly.

Chris nods. "Okay."

Together, we follow the nurse down the hallway to where Emma is. I spotted Detective Morgan as we approached. There's a uniformed officer beside him. When he sees us, he holds up his hand to the officer, indicating for their conversation to halt. "River," he says to me, holding his hand out.

I nodded, shaking his hand firmly. "How is she?" The detective glances at Chris beside me as the nurse walks back the way she came. "This is her dad, Chris Novak."

"Mr. Novak," he says. "Glad you're here. I'm Detective Morgan."

Chris shakes the man's hand. "Thank you for finding my daughter." There's a waver in his voice that catches me off guard, and I'm surprised to see his eyes misted over.

"I'm afraid that I didn't have a whole lot to do with it." Detective Morgan glances behind him. "She made sure she was found." He places his hands on his hips, pushing the front of his grey suit jacket behind them. "The FBI is on their way. I can't say too much, but what I can tell you is that she went through something pretty traumatic and that it could've been a whole lot worse."

Chris's forehead is creased. "What can you tell us?"

Detective Morgan clears his throat. "They were attempting to traffic her. And it seems like it's part of a bigger picture than just her based on the rap sheet of the man she was with."

The man she was with. The man carrying her out of Club W. Was he the one trying to traffic her? Had he touched her? Because if he did, then my work is about to become my home. I will rot in prison for the satisfaction of ending someone who hurt Emma.

"Was she..." I can't bring myself to say any words that would mean someone did something to Emma against her will.

"There's a lot of moving parts," Detective Morgan explains. "Right now, she just needs the support of the people who love her." The nurse in the green scrubs skirts around us to go into the room. The urge to push past the detective and go to Emma is overwhelming. "Excuse me," he says to the passing nurse.

She faces him, shooting a glance at us. Her smile is tight and forced.

"This is Emma's father and boyfriend. Can you give them an overview of her injuries?"

"She's pretty banged up," the nurse tells us. "A few broken ribs and a facial fracture are the major injuries. She'll be sore for a while, but overall, she'll be fine."

"What are the broken bones from?" Chris asks before I can.

Detective Morgan replies. "The car accident. The car flipped when they were T-boned in an intersection."

"Where?" I ask.

"Little town about two hours west of here. Mayville, I think."

"So, they brought her into Missouri? Across state lines?" I know this detail makes whatever crimes the man committed have higher consequences. Seems like such a small detail to cross an invisible line and your potential punishment gets worse.

I would cross all fifty state lines to unalive the man who did this to Emma. He was planning to traffic her. He wasn't planning on getting caught.

"You have him in custody, right?" I ask.

The detective nods. "I've taken enough of your time. Go see Emma."

I enter the room in front of Chris and my stomach drops clear to the basement of the hospital. Emma is barely recognizable. The left side of her face is grotesquely swollen in an obtuse way, red and purple bruising shading her normally fair skin. Her eyes are swollen to the degree I can barely see her irises between the narrowed lids. Her honey-colored hair is disheveled and pushed away from her injured face. An IV of fluid runs into her arm at the crook of her elbow.

Chris exhales beside me but the sound of it is drowned out by the noise that escapes Emma's lips. It's desperate, like she's gasping for air, a short, staccato grunt. She lifts one hand, beckoning to us with her fingers.

Her dad is beside her before I can even make my legs move. I am stunned by how she looks, realizing I must not have ever seen a facial fracture before. Anger tries bubbling to the surface at the thought of someone intentionally doing this to Emma, but the recollection that she had also been in a car accident keeps it in check.

"Daddy," Emma says as Chris takes her hand. He leans down and kisses her forehead gently.

"You're okay," he tells her. "You're safe now."

She looks in my direction, sniveling. "Why are you..."

I close the distance between us, standing on the opposite side of the bed from her, and take her other hand with mine. It's cold to the touch, so I wrap it with both of mine. My eyes burn with tears, but I don't care. Chris isn't going to tell my dad. "I was so scared," I whispered, knowing she had to be a zillion times more scared than I was. My fear was of losing her. Of having to figure out how to live without her.

Her fear would have been completely different. A legit fear of what was happening to her, what *could* happen to her. Of physical harm. Of death. Of being violated.

Emma nods. "Me too."

The three of us stand there for several minutes in silence. There wasn't anything to say. In time, questions would be answered. Right now, we were all just grateful to be here.

Chapter Twenty-Six

Emma

I've been home from the hospital for a week. River had to go back to work, but my dad is staying in a hotel. When River leaves, he comes over to stay with me. I'm not sleeping well, if at all. Sometimes I just lie there in a semi-conscious state, never really falling asleep.

I haven't gone back to work. Not sure I will, honestly. Detective Morgan is working with the FBI, and I know there have been several arrests related to my kidnapping as they were tied to a rather large human trafficking ring. I wish Ben, the man who assaulted me at the warehouse where I was being held for transport, had never told me I had been 'marked' because what that meant was that someone hand-picked me to be abducted and sold into sex slavery.

There were several possibilities being considered, one of which being someone who was opposed to the work that I did, promoting safe sex and family planning, including a woman's authority over her own body. Which made sense. What better punishment for someone like me than to give me no control over whether I'm having safe sex and ensuring I have no say-so regarding what happens to my own body.

Another possibility is some disgruntled prisoner who didn't like River had set me as a target to get back at him for whatever.

While I wanted answers, what I needed was to find those innocent children who fell prey to the depraved men who saw them as commodities to use and throw away. I want to comfort them and hold them and give them back their innocence.

Sometimes I am suddenly jarred to full alertness with thoughts of the terror the children must have felt. Not what I went through, what *they* went through. The nameless, faceless children whose families will never stop questioning why it had to be their child. Second guessing their own choices that may have put their sweet, innocent babies in harm's way.

I want to tell River everything, but he has been handling me like I'm fragile, and I just don't think he's ready to know. He knows the bullet points of what happened. He knows I was sexually assaulted. He knows I fought back by biting a man's penis and that I tried to choke the driver of the vehicle with a phone charger that I didn't even have a phone for.

What happened had made the news because I'm the niece of a senator. I was told that Wes's office never made any type of statement, but I doubted that he would have said that I was his son's girlfriend instead of niece after the way he had reacted to our news. River told me his dad apologized for his reaction and that they shared some type of moment that left River feeling better than ever about his relationship, but it still didn't take away the years of narcissistic abuse he had to deal with from his father.

"Ready to start the movie?" My dad sits on the opposite side of the couch. He replaced our broken TV for us without being asked. He'd also patched the holes in the walls.

We'd been working our way through the Harry Potter movies. Tonight, we were watching the fourth one, *Harry Potter and the Goblet of Fire.* I haven't seen the movies since I was in middle school after a short stint of obsession with the franchise. We even went to Universal Studios in Orlando just so I could experience The Wizarding World of Harry Potter over Thanksgiving break during ninth grade. I'd been a true fangirl wearing my Gryffindor gear, drinking butterbeer, and begging for everything in sight.

"Yeah," I replied, pulling my fleece blanket up a little bit. The swelling to my face had gone down considerably though I still looked battered. Other than going to the doctor and police station, I hadn't left the house.

It was nice spending time with my dad. Aside from watching movies together, we talked about anything and everything except what happened and my relationship with River. Each night, he would make dinner with the groceries he brought over or have something delivered. Christy would call and he would talk to her, Cora, and Wyatt. Cora would ask to talk to me, but Dad would tell her I was napping or showering, somehow knowing I didn't have it in me to deal with my younger sister.

We were about an hour into the movie when Christy called tonight. Almost immediately, I could tell something bad happened.

"What's wrong?" my dad says into his phone, alarm registering in his voice. My stomach tightens with fear. I can't hear Christy's response, but then he looks at me. He's blinking quickly. "Oh, God. Okay."

I raise my eyebrows, desperate to know what has my dad's face looking like someone died. "What's going on?"

Dad lets out an exhale and pulls his brows together. "Noni's gone."

Something clicks in my brain. I hear it. It's an audible *click.* Like the sound a camera makes when taking a photo.

It's all my fault. These bad things are happening to me because I did a bad thing. I fell in love with someone forbidden. Someone completely off limits. Now we were trying to make something that had always been clandestine into something public, and the universe wasn't having it.

Someone marked me because I'm immoral. And now they took Noni.

Okay, the two have nothing to do with one another, but the feeling sticks. These bad things are happening because me and River are committing major sins.

Later, after River is home and my dad has gone back to his hotel, we lie in bed, my head on his shoulder, his arm around my back. He's holding me but I can feel the distance between us. Since I came home from the hospital, he's barely kissed me. I know I look repulsive with my fading bruises and swelling. They said it could be months before the fracture in my cheek healed completely.

"Do you ever think…" I start, unsure what I'm trying to say. "Like, because we did something bad, now bad things are happening to us?"

He doesn't answer immediately. "What did we do that was bad?"

I lift my chin to see his face illuminated by the light of the bedroom TV. "You know."

"I *don't* know, Emma." The agitation in his tone tells me he *does* know what I'm talking about but disagrees.

The first time we had sex happened on a whim. I had thought about it plenty and figured we'd do it eventually. Since our first kiss, our adventures steadily progressed. It seems like yesterday when he hovered over me, panting, asking if I'm sure I wanted to do it, to cross this line, because it was wrong. I nodded because I didn't care if it was wrong. Together we made the choice to be wrong. To go against the norms and expectations of society and our family. We made the choice to love each other, not only with our bodies, but our hearts, souls, and minds too.

This was what we wanted.

"Like, maybe it was one thing to be doing this and keeping it a secret, but now that we let it out to the world, bad things just keep happening."

River rolls to face me. I absorb the vulnerability in his red-rimmed eyes. "There is nothing wrong with what we are doing now or ever. Our fate was written in the stars the day we were born. Your dad and Christy getting married was a trial for us to overcome. It wasn't the end of the road." He pauses, pushes the hair from my face. "And us being honest has nothing to do with what happened to you. And Noni, well, she's old. It's sad, but we all knew it was going to happen eventually."

When River looks at me the way he's looking at me now, with softness and love, I know there is nowhere I ever want to call home without him. But the affectionate way he's always looked at me is tainted with something new. Worry. Concern. Questions.

My heart is a mess. My mind is fragmented. There's before and there's now. There's also whatever is to come. Physically, I will heal. But my mental healing will take much longer. Sticks and stones can break your bones, but words do way more harm.

It all could have been so much worse. I'm well aware of this but refuse to think about where I would be right now had we not been hit by that other car.

"What are you thinking about?" River asks.

"Do you still want to move away from here?"

He winces, but it's barely noticeable. "As long as it's not back home, yeah." His tongue darts out, wetting his lips. "Is that really what you're thinking about?"

I nod. "Yeah."

His lungs fill as he studies me. "At some point, you're going to need to address the mental toll this has taken on you."

We lay in silence for several minutes. Being around River makes the weight of it all seem lighter. His presence alone brings things into perspective. "There was something..." I want to tell him about the children. The ones I never saw but know exist. They have families searching for them, praying endlessly for their return. I run the tips of my fingers along the soft blond stubble on his jaw. "There are kids too."

His face shows no emotion. If he doesn't understand, I'm not sure I have the words to explain it to him. I already know I can't repeat the depraved details that will forever live rent free inside my head.

Finally, he says, "I know." His hand runs softly down the length of my arm.

My face scrunches up, my internal turmoil showing. "It's not fair. Like, why me but not them?"

He pulls me to him, resting his chin on the top of my head. "I don't know, Em."

The following morning, we leave to go be with our families. My dad left way earlier than us. Last night, he was torn between leaving as soon as River got back or waiting until morning. I tried to tell him he could leave me alone, but he wouldn't and I'm glad. I didn't mind being treated like a child right now. The thought of being alone terrified me.

We drove River's Jeep this time, and Aunt Megan... err, Megan, said we could stay together at their house. I hope they realize we'll be in the same room and the same bed too. Typically, we visit home a handful of times a year and the occasions are spread out. It's been less than a month since we were last in our hometown. So much has happened in that short period of time, but it still feels like just a few days ago.

When we arrive, everyone is gathered at River's family home. The mood is notably somber with photo albums spread out across the formal living room and dining room. People talk quietly with gentle smiles as they reminisce over Noni's life. Megan isn't wearing any makeup, which is unusual, but the half-full glass is in her right hand like normal. It's honestly the most normal thing in the whole room.

Cora is in the backyard with Wyatt and a couple of Uncle Jake's kids while Eli, Kyler, and Jordyn sit at the dining room table. The adults, and by adults, I mean our parents, aunts and uncles, are assembled in the living room with Grammy. After forlorn greetings are exchanged and generic inquiries about my well-being given what recently happened, River and I take our bags upstairs to his bedroom. No one mentioned my still swollen face or the yellowed bruises sitting below my eyes like added punctuation to a sentence.

I groan loudly as I plop down onto River's bed. "This brings back memories." Falling back on the mattress, I grab a pillow and hold it to my chest. "Can we just stay in here?"

My legs hang over the side of the bed. River stands between them and leans over me, resting his forearms on either side of my body. Our faces are so close I feel the breath from his nostrils. His body hovers above me, not touching mine. "And do what?"

Pulse quickening, I lift both hands and rest them gently on his hips. There's hunger in his eyes, and normally it would drive me wild, but I have zero interest in sex right now. Or at all, honestly. "Nap?"

He grins and lets out a chuckle as he straightens. "C'mon." His hand extends toward me, and I take it, allowing him to pull me to my feet.

We walk hand in hand downstairs, letting go when we reach the first floor. Together we join Jordyn, Kyler, and Eli in the dining room. The three of them stare at me for a moment and I wonder why, then realize that I felt normal until then. As if there wasn't a reminder of what happened to me on my face.

"Do you want to talk about it?" Jordyn asks slowly, her eyes darting between me and River.

I grab one of the photo albums on the table and bring it close to me. "Talk about what?" Inside the album there are a myriad of sepia photos. Grammy looks to be in her late teens, early twenties. Noni looks like she's about the age Christy is now.

"She doesn't," River answers Jordyn.

Looking over at him, I point at a picture. "Is that your grandpa?"

He looks down at the photo and nods. "Yeah."

"You look like him, don't you think?"

The doorbell rings as River answers me. "Actually, yeah." He squints his eyes at the photo. "It's uncanny." Pushing the photo album toward the center of the table for the others to see, he says, "I need to find pictures from when he was my age. Or as a kid."

I think about River looking like his grandpa does in the photos as he ages. The strong jawline. The easy smile. Broad shoulders. "Did he have blue eyes too?"

He shakes his head. "I don't know."

"Megan," Uncle Wes calls out. "Can you come here?"

There's something unsettling in his voice and we all exchange glances before standing in unison. Wes never needs Megan for anything. And on the same ticket, if someone came to the door for Megan today, on the day we are all together as a family mourning the loss of Noni, even Wes would have sent them away.

The five of us reach the foyer just as Megan does, drink in hand with Christy on her heels.

A man in a black suit stands beside Wes. He glances at us before looking at Megan and Christy. And then, like his mind is catching up with his eyes, he looks back at me. My skin crawls with the way his eyes dance over me. Instinct makes me want to take River's hand but, despite everyone knowing our truth, I'm still not ready to be affectionate in front of them.

Wes chuckles nervously. "I didn't need everyone." He looks at his wife. "I'm going to step outside."

Megan turns away, uninterested in the visitor. "Okay."

Wes and the mystery man step outside. As the door closes behind him, I catch a whiff of something familiar that drifted in from the outside. I can't quite place it.

Christy follows Megan back into the living room. "Who was that?"

"I thought it was going to be the catering," Megan says. "I think that's one of his advisors or something."

River, Jordyn, and I follow them into the living room. "Catering?" River asks.

"For after the services." Christy glances at the clock. "They should be here any time."

I realize I know nothing about when the services are. "What day are the services?"

"Friday." She sits beside my dad on the couch. "I hope you guys can stay until then and don't have to leave and come back, but we understand if you can't."

River nods. "I have three bereavement days. Today is my regular day off so I'm using them for tomorrow, Thursday, and Friday. I don't have to go back to work until Monday."

I love Noni and I love my family, but I really don't want to be in this house for the next four days. There's no way I can tell River that. Noni was more of a mom to him than Megan was. Honestly, I'm surprised he's not more upset than he is. His eyes have misted over but I haven't seen him cry. Being here, with Wes lingering around, River will hide all his emotions.

"Oh, that's good," Megan says. "It'll be nice to have you home."

River sits on his dad's overstuffed armchair. He looks over at me. "Feel like I need some time off anyway with everything that's been happening."

Silence hangs in the room, no one sure what to say. Jordyn sits on a folding chair, leaving me standing in the arched doorway alone, all eyes on me. Because I'm the one something happened to.

I swallow and clear my throat, debating sitting on the other side of Christy, between her and Aunt Kelly, but decide I'd rather be close to River, and sit on the arm of the recliner.

He reaches over and rests his hand on my thigh. Thinking nothing of it, my hand covers his and squeezes. People shift uncomfortably in their seats but fuck them.

CHAPTER TWENTY-SEVEN

River

By Wednesday afternoon, I've decided I will never again stay at my parents' house with Emma. Not that I had ever been super comfortable there since moving out five years ago. But now, with the way things have changed in the last month, it's even worse.

The almost apology that my dad gave me when he visited our apartment was a farce. It might be a leap to think this, but I don't think he believed Emma would be back. That would make it easy for him to pretend he could have been okay with it. Like, *oh, River, I'm so sorry you lost the love of your life, but I'm sure you'll find someone else who's not related.*

My mom isn't a whole lot better, which, considering she admitted to catching us fucking years ago, surprised me. When my dad tossed out snide comments about us touching or holding hands, sleeping in the same bed, looking at each other with affection, my mom kept silent.

It was like they decided we were incestuous deviants who weren't worthy of them. But when I thought enough about it, when had I ever felt worthy? They made me. They raised me. Yet for years, all I ever felt was unwanted. Jealous of everyone else and their normal seeming families. Even Emma's. The number of times I had wished Christy was my mom instead of Megan was staggering.

From the outside, we looked like the perfect family. I was scared to open up to anyone about how I was treated at home, learning from my mom how to lie away the bruises. But Emma always knew. She was the only one who did. Because she was family, I could trust her.

Maybe it's because I almost lost her, but my heart was a raging blaze of fire with how much I felt for her. The feelings were way more intense than they'd been before, cementing into my very soul that I had undoubtedly made the right choice.

Emma is my forever. Nothing will change that.

I'm lying in bed Wednesday night watching Emma pull the towel off her head, her wet hair falling like tentacles onto her shoulders. "When we have kids, I'm going to figure out how to be a good father."

She stands statuesque, her eyes unfocused.

"I can't imagine creating a life just to make them feel like you wish you hadn't."

Emma pushes her lips together, swallowing as she drops the towel onto the foot of the bed. "When we have kids?"

"I don't mean anytime soon."

Her eyes find mine. "Right, yeah." Her mouth twitches, letting me know she has more to say. "I've been thinking about the future too."

I sit up, excited to talk about something less depressing for a change. "Yeah?"

She nods, getting onto the bed. Crossing her legs under her, she sits in the middle facing me. "I think I want to go back to school. For social work or something."

That wasn't what I expected her to say. "A graduate program?"

"Yeah." Her brows pull together as she frowns. "I don't want to go back to work. I want to move away."

Moving away we had mentioned before. Not going back to work though, that could be tricky financially. Moving away, going back to school, those things cost money. And my salary isn't especially great. I guess I could pick up some overtime or maybe find a second job. But, wait, if we move away, then I need a new job. "Oh."

She senses my hesitation. "I'll get a loan for school. And I have money in savings that we could use to move. We'll have to get a smaller place probably, but..." Her eyes fall away.

But what? I want the end of her sentence but recognize that she needs a moment.

"All this... it's like, I don't know. It's a wake-up call. A sign that we need to stop doing what's expected of us and do what we want to do. And I feel like if we keep trying to do what they want, then we're never going to be who we want to be. But, like, River, I always knew I wanted to do more to help people. And yeah, sure, in a way I'm helping by making sure they have access to free condoms and shit, but I want to do more. My dad really wanted me to go into the health field, preached about how there's no money in helping professions, but I don't give a shit about money. I would rather be broke and homeless with you than stuck in a job that I don't absolutely love. And we can't be who we want to be living under your dad's shadow." She takes a breath. "I'm tired. I'm so tired of pretending to be someone I'm not and I think you telling everyone has made me realize that I can really only be my true self when I'm around you and you alone. Everyone else just gets these distorted versions of me. But you, you know me. All of me. We don't have secrets. And if we go somewhere new, somewhere no one knows us, then we can just be us. And it sounds like a dream, but you said someday when we have kids, but how the fuck can we have kids without everyone finding out my dad married your aunt? Like, maybe our kids will have a fighting chance if we go somewhere else and... and—"

"And I'll change my last name," I tell her. It's the first thing that comes to mind.

Her face goes rigid. "You would do that?"

Nodding as the idea solidifies in my mind, I say, "Yeah, I think I would."

"You'd give up being Riv Mac?"

I chuckle, a smile creeping onto my cheeks. "I would give up anything and everything as long as I still have you."

She shakes her head. "You can't do something like that because of me."

"I wouldn't do it because of you or even *for* you. I would do it for *us*. For those future kids. For our life together that we are going to build." I sit up, reaching for her hands. "I love you, Emma. We knew this wasn't going to be easy. We're going to have to deal with things normal couples don't and make decisions that seem unfair. But none of it matters. It really doesn't."

Her fingers intertwine with mine. I look past the remnants of injury on her face and into her eyes that have been my home for years. The words I don't say—that I will never say—is that someone tried to break her, to take her from me, from her family, from her entire life, and it sparked something in me. Something that will not rest until I know who was behind it. She wasn't chosen randomly. She was marked. Someone wanted her. I'm not even sure I care what their reason was. Emma is mine. Emma will always be mine and no one is going to take her from me.

I haven't told her how badly I need answers so I can avenge what happened to her. And make no mistake, I will get answers, and I will get revenge. I don't care if it takes the rest of my life. It will happen.

Fuck the justice system. The only justice for what they've done is death.

"I love you," Emma tells me, her voice heavy with emotion.

I lean forward for a kiss. She meets me halfway, letting her lips linger longer than she has lately. When she doesn't pull away, neither do I, and the tickle of her fingers on my upper thigh wakes me up. I push my fingers into her damp hair, pulling her face to mine, hungry for her.

Emma's tongue slips past my lips. I pull away to see her eyes open. I'm unsure of what's happening. Other than quick pecks on the lips… well, nothing for weeks. She can't possibly think she's ready for anything more.

Her head moves side to side just slightly before she leans back in, her lips finding their way back to mine. We make out atop my childhood bed for an everlasting moment. Like we're fourteen again and just discovered how good it feels to be desired. Emma's hands trace over my forearms and then back to my legs, tucking themselves inside the legs of my athletic shorts.

I'm afraid to touch her. I'm afraid of reminding her that she was violated by a stranger. The details of what happened those hours she was gone are unknown to me, and that's okay. I don't need to know the specifics. I just need to know how not to hurt her.

As if she can read my mind, she stops kissing me and brushes her thumb just below my lower lip. "I know you won't hurt me."

We gaze at each other for a moment, thoughts firing left and right in my brain. "I don't know what you want," I finally say.

The corners of her mouth quip up slightly. "You. Forever."

Well, she has that. It doesn't answer my question. With a swallow, I frown.

"I'll tell you if I need you to stop."

Now, that was the answer I needed. "You're sure?"

"I am." She leans back and grabs the hem of her shirt, lifting it over her head to reveal her ample, bare chest to me. Tipping her head to the side, she waits for me to look back up at her face. Then, like she can once again read my mind, she lifts onto her knees, placing her hands on either of my shoulders, giving a gentle push for me to lie back.

I do as I'm instructed, my skin tingling in anticipation. While I'm not expecting to go all the way, I'm willing to go however far she's ready for. Her mouth crashes onto mine, hot and hungry with need. The feel of her bare breasts on my skin causes heat to build in the pit of my stomach. I reach around her, grabbing her curvy backside, longing to feel friction below my waist.

Her body stiffens, but I don't let go, thinking *this is what she wants.* She initiated it. She said she would tell me if she needed to stop, but she's still kissing me. Her legs move, one on each side of me so she's straddling my body. I grip each of her ass cheeks and move my hands up her sides, our mouths still locked onto one another.

I angle my hips slightly, my groin making contact with the apex of her thighs as my fingers tease over her bare skin. When I cup her engorged breasts with my palms, her mouth stops moving over mine briefly. This time, I freeze.

"Babe," I whisper against her lips. "You okay?"

Her hesitation doesn't go unmissed. But then she nods.

"You sure?"

She pushes her center against my groin in response. I meet her motion with my own, my cock ready for action. I groan against her mouth, my hands slipping into the backside of her pajama pants, pleased to find she is sans underwear. As I start to push the fleece pants over her voluptuous hips, I feel her body shake against mine.

Emma pulls her mouth from mine and drops her head to my shoulder. "I can't, I can't. I'm sorry." She collapses beside me, her hands shielding her face.

I wrap my arms around her, sex the furthest thing from my mind now. "It's okay," I promise her. "You have nothing to be sorry for."

The only other funeral I ever attended was for Grandpa Gary. My mom's father died when I was eight. I don't remember much about it other than I had to wear a suit. However, I am certain it didn't have the turn out that Noni's does. There has to be a few hundred people here easily. Noni was well known and well liked in our neck of the woods. My mom's family was from Adamsville, the next town over from Thomas City. Noni's grandmother's maiden name was Thomas and was a descendant from the founders of Thomas City. Their family had been instrumental in the early days of growth and development in this part of the state; the county even being named for them. Noni was one of those people that knew everyone and everyone knew her.

Aunt Christy asked if I wanted to say a few words at the service, share a favorite memory of mine. I declined, as did Emma. My mind could not accept that Noni was gone. Even seeing her still body lying in the baby pink satin-lined casket wearing a studious gray skirt suit, didn't make it seem real. Her greyed hair was arranged in a bob around her make-up caked face. I hated the way she looked.

The memories I had of Noni loving and accepting me for who I was were mine. I didn't need to stand before a room of mostly strangers and try to convince everyone how great she had been. They already knew.

Emma and I sat beside each other in the row behind our parents. I was closest to the aisle while Cora was on Emma's other side. When Jordyn stood before everyone and started talking, I felt a twinge of guilt for not wanting to do as she was doing. It was strange, because I knew Noni wouldn't care either way.

"Do what you feel you need to do," she would say.

I leaned forward and pinched the bridge of my nose while sucking in a sharp breath as Jordyn droned on about how Noni was a pillar in our family. Emma placed her hand on my thigh. When I lowered my hand, I rested it on hers and shared a sad smile with her.

My dad turned around, his glare falling straight to our hands. His face contorts with disgust, his beady eyes darting between us.

I tighten my grip on Emma's hand and stare at my dad until he looks away. Emma squeezes my fingers, a smile tugging at the corners of her lips when she glances my way.

Fuck my dad. I'm allowed to have emotions over Noni's passing, and I'm allowed to be with Emma. Over the last few days, he has been on edge over everything. Maybe it's because he's home and not in Washington. Maybe it's because my mom's drinking seems to be at an all-time high. Maybe it's because I'm around, or even because I exist. I don't care about the reason.

Emma and I are leaving in the morning. Since our talk the other night, she has found several cities actively hiring police officers. I've looked at the links she's sent but haven't applied for any. For every city she's explored job opportunities, she's also looked into colleges where she could earn a graduate degree.

It's pretty much all we talk about when we're alone. Emma doesn't want to return to work next week, but we agreed that until we know exactly what our next steps are, she needs to. She's uneasy about traveling, and rightly so. We've had some contact with Detective Morgan but since we left home to come to Noni's funeral, we haven't heard anything. Maybe I'll give him a call on the way to the cemetery. Something to keep my mind off the fact that we're about to put Noni's frail waif of a body into the ground.

After the services, my dad says, "You're riding with me and your mother to the cemetery. Emma can ride with her family."

I scoff, turning to walk away. "Nah, I'm good." My Jeep is already in the procession line with a magnetic funeral flag secured to the hood.

"That wasn't a request, son."

White heat boils inside me. I can't blow up at him here. My body twists so I can see him. "This isn't the time or the place." My hand reaches out for Emma's. "I'm not riding with you."

Emma grips my hand tightly as my dad steps up to me. His face is so close I can smell his morning coffee and stale aftershave. "Let go of your cousin's hand right fucking now, River. I will not have you out here in public embarrassing our family this way."

There is nothing more I would love to do than spit in his face right now. Or maybe head butt him. He's worried about me embarrassing the family by holding Emma's hand when he should really be worried about me beating his old ass. He's banking on the assumption that I won't. That I value his image, and maybe my own, more than I value my relationship with Emma.

Considering I spent years of back and forth, screwing with both of our emotions, and then once I claimed her as mine and almost lost her, I have zero plans to ever let Emma doubt my love and commitment to her. To our future together.

And if my dad doesn't like it, tough fucking shit.

I narrow my eyes and lift my chin slightly, letting him know I'm not backing down. "What are you gonna do about it?" My voice is low when I speak so that only he and Emma can hear me. "Gonna hit me right here in front of everyone?"

Uncle Gary suddenly appears on my left, pushing his body between me and my dad. "What are you guys doing?" he hisses. "This is a funeral. Not a fight club." He looks back and forth between us. "Whatever this is, deal with it later."

I smirk at my father's red face as I walk away, mentally preparing how to get back to the house, pack our stuff and get the hell out of there before he comes home. Part of me feels bad for bailing on my mom so quickly after the services, but I don't think I can deal with my father for another night.

When we're in my Jeep, waiting for the funeral procession to start, I tell Emma my plans to leave ASAP.

"What about the reception or whatever it's called?" she asks.

"We'll still go. Just leave early."

She's quiet as we start to pull forward with the other vehicles. "Can we just go to my... my parents' house?"

I study her, seeing worry creased across her face. "Yeah, if you want to."

Her eyes find mine. "Don't you think they all need time to get used to this? To get used to us?"

"Get used to it, yes." I look at the road in front of me. "But I feel like my dad has made it clear that he has no interest in accepting it and instead it's like he just wants to break us up." I let out a sigh. "I'm just done with them, Emma. I can't stand either of them, and I don't want to be around them. They're not good people and I would rather hang myself with barbed wire than turn out like either of them. We don't need their toxicity in our life. Especially not now when we're just getting started."

Emma leans back in her seat. I know she agrees with my take on my parents. She's watched me deal with them my entire life. Once, she told me that I was like a book with a really pretty cover that had a completely twisted story on the inside. I wasn't the golden child the world saw me as. I didn't have a charmed life. In the press photos where my parents put their arms around me, those were the only times they touched me.

Well, unless it was my dad hitting me.

"I spent so many years hating myself. Thinking I was nothing but a disappointment and a letdown to them," I tell her. "You know this. I hate how I feel when I'm around them and I don't want them to be a part of my life anymore. It's not worth our energy to wait around for them to come to some type of understanding that what we have is real." I shake my head. "I'm not doing it. End of story."

Chapter Twenty-Eight

Emma

River has been in bad headspace since we arrived at his parents' house on Tuesday. I'm not sure what to pin it on exactly because there are so many things. Noni's death, his mother's constant drinking and slurred words, his dad's disgusted glares, or the lack of sex we've had.

They told me it might take a while before I would feel comfortable having sex again. Which was dumb because those assholes didn't have sex with me. It was off limits. I thought that maybe if we just skipped me giving oral sex, I would be okay.

I wasn't.

I panicked despite knowing I wanted it. Knowing it was River touching me, wanting me, being as gentle as he could, didn't matter.

I just want everything to feel normal again.

To make matters worse, I was turned on virtually around the clock. I thought about the feeling of River's cock filling me, stretching me, hitting all the best spots inside me. About my skull hitting the headboard as he plowed into me from behind. Our groans, the sounds of his hand smacking my sweaty bare skin. His face buried between my legs while his fingers gripped my thighs so tightly there were bruises when he was done. The phantom feeling of his hand on my throat made my clit come to life. Visions of my arms tied behind my back while he blew his hot, sticky come on my face had me on edge.

Masturbating helped. I got myself off in the shower a few times, but it's nothing compared to having a body pressed against me working for the same euphoria. I considered getting shit-faced drunk so I wouldn't care anymore, and that pissed me off. I shouldn't have to do that. This is my body, and I know I want sex, however, something in my mind won't let me. Try as I might to not be mad at myself, it didn't work. It's only been a few weeks since it happened and maybe I'm just not ready yet.

Even as we rode to the cemetery to watch as Noni was lowered into the ground, all I could think about was putting River's hand between my legs. I would slide my underwear to the side, letting him dip two fingers into my wet center. I'd spread my legs wide, lowering the seat a little so I could thrust against his hand, desperate for him to hit my G-spot while my clit rubs on his palm. Then he would be turned on too, pull over to lick and suck me until I came on his face. After that, if I was lucky, we'd get out and he would take me on the side of the road. My back pressed against the side of the Jeep, legs around his hips while he slammed into me with one hand on my throat. I'd see stars as I came again while he filled me up with his own climax. When he pulled out, I would feel his sweet leftovers dripping down my inner thighs. Maybe swipe my fingers between my legs to gather the goodness and take a taste of it.

I shuddered, trying to pull myself back to the present as River parked the Jeep at the cemetery.

"You okay?" he asks before opening his door to get out.

I nod. "Yeah." Reaching over, I open my door and hop out onto the ground. River is there taking my hand almost instantly.

We walk hand in hand to where a small group gathers near a tent to shield the sun. There are a handful of chairs surrounding a hole in the ground. The place where we leave Noni behind and keep on living life without her.

It doesn't seem right, nor real. "I'm glad we told everyone while she was still here," I say to River quietly. "It means a lot to me that we got her approval."

"Me too," he agrees. "But we don't need anyone's approval."

"I know." I look at River to gauge where his emotions are at that moment, but I don't see him. Past him, near the parked cars, I spot a man in a suit lighting a cigarette. He looks vaguely familiar. "Who's that?"

River looks where my gaze has landed. "I think he works for my dad. He was at the house the other day."

"Oh, that's right. I knew he looked familiar." I watch as my dad and Christy sit in the chairs beside Uncle Gary and Aunt Kelly. There are only eight chairs. Wes and Megan, along with Grammy and Uncle Jake take up the rest of them. "I guess we're standing."

Jordyn comes up beside us, Brody with her. She's not wearing any makeup. When I first saw her earlier, it was like being transported back in time to our childhood when we would have sleepovers at Noni's house. It would be me, her, River, and Kyler. We'd play board games and eat junk food all night. Then, after Noni went to bed, we would play hide and seek. River and I would try to hide together unless one of us was 'it.' One time, when River was 'it,' Kyler tried to hide with me in the front coat closet. I didn't want him to and kept trying to close the door to keep him out and ended up smashing his fingers. His crying woke Noni up, and all I remember was him and Jordyn saying that River and I only like to hide together so we can kiss.

I remember feeling repulsed by the notion that I would kiss River at eleven years old.

Now all I can think about is being impaled by his dick.

What the fuck is wrong with me?

It surely doesn't help that his slate grey button-down shirt is tight across his broad shoulders and chest, showing me the outline of his defined muscles that I love to run my fingers across. The warm temperatures and bright sun have caused him to sweat some, making dark spots on his shirt. The black slacks he's wearing hug his ass so well I want to pull them down and lick his perfect, firm ass.

The pulse between my legs is throbbing. I'm not sure I can wait but I'm also not sure I can do it. Even worse, I'm not sure how kindly River will take to me proposing sex at the cemetery.

Good Lord. What if Noni literally rolls over in her grave?

Okay, that's enough to pull my mind back to the here and now. So much so that I find myself listening to the words of the officiant. His words about salvation and everlasting peace, and I picture Noni up in the clouds of heaven watching over us as we get older. I wonder if she will meet my mom in heaven and tell her all about me. I wonder what my mom would think of River, if she would approve. I feel like she would, not that I have any reference point. My perception of my mom is that she was just this wonderful, super sweet and kind woman who was a friend to all. One of those live, laugh, love types. She would be very giving when it comes to affection and excited for the little things in life, like getting a pickle jar open by yourself.

River puts his arm around my shoulders and nuzzles his face into my ear, and I realize I'm crying. Not for Noni, but for my mom. The mom who was taken away from me, who I never really got to have. But besides that, the knowledge that if she would've lived, I would never have met

River. My dad wouldn't have dropped out of medical school or moved back to his hometown to care for me.

I pull away from River, stepping out of the crowd gathered at the grave, searching for somewhere to hide. In the distance, I spot a building and wonder if there's a bathroom in there. It's quite a distance. I would hate to walk all the way there just to discover there isn't a bathroom.

River follows me. "You okay?"

I cross my arms over my chest and shake my head, letting the tears fall from my eyes. He pulls me to him, pressing my face to his shoulder. His hands rub small circles on my back, a sob escaping me. I want to burrow myself into River, let him care for me, believe him when he tells me everything will be okay.

When the graveside service is over, everyone is supposed to return to the church for the reception. River whispers to me, "We're gonna go get our stuff from my parents' house before we go to the church."

He doesn't need to explain why. I get it. "Let me just tell my dad so he doesn't worry."

As I make my way to where my dad is walking with Christy and the kids, I pass Wes talking with his advisor or whoever he is, and a familiar scent catches my attention. I glance at the man to see him staring at me again, like he knows me. When I look at Wes beside him, he's watching me too.

Chills run down my spine.

I shake them off as I reach my dad. Cora comes up and hugs me. I hug her back with one arm as I say, "We're going to stop by Wes and Megan's and get our stuff. River doesn't want to stay there another night. They keep butting heads." My dad nods with understanding. "Just didn't want you to worry."

"Thanks, hon," he says, leaning in to kiss my cheek. "I appreciate that." He backs away. "You doing okay?"

I nod, making a mental note to talk with him about my mom later. It's been so long since we talked about her. "Yeah, I guess."

River turns up his grunge music loudly as we drive back into town. He gets into it, singing along and moving his hands with the beat of the music. It makes me smile watching him be so animated, and for a moment, everything feels normal again.

When the song ends, I sit up and look at him. He glances at me with a smile, his cheeks flushing with embarrassment, like maybe he forgot I was in the passenger seat. "I wanna fuck," I tell him.

His eyes dart back and forth between me and the road as the next song starts. He lowers the volume. "Come again?"

A smile spread painfully across my cheeks like it's been years since I've used those muscles. "And again, and again hopefully."

"Are you serious right now, Emma?"

I nod. "Very. I need it. I need it so fucking bad. Not that sweet, make-love-to-me bullshit we tried the other day. I need you to take it. Make me forget the last several weeks ever happened even if it's just for a moment."

He sets his jaw for a moment and then licks his lips, nodding. "Okay, bet." Leaning on his elbow on the center console, he places his other hand on the top of the steering wheel. "Safe word?"

I consider this. What if I'm wrong? What if I'm not ready? It could be too soon. But on the other hand, this is River, and he knows what I like and how to give it to me. I shake my head. "No safe word."

His beautiful grin makes my heart swell and my pussy wet. "You're sure?"

"I'm sure." I reach under the bottom of my dress, lift my hips, and pull off my underwear, flipping off my sandals as I do. The black cotton underwear is nothing fancy or sexy, but it doesn't matter, I dangle them from my forefinger in front of him anyway. When he reaches for them, I snatch them away and loop the leg hole around the Jeep's gear shifter.

River runs his fingers along the fabric, feeling the moisture collected on them. "Fuck, yeah." He presses harder on the gas pedal.

I giggle as he moves his hand to my thigh, pushing my black dress out of the way so he's touching my heated flesh.

"My fucking dick is hard already." His fingers inch close to the crease of my hip.

I spread my legs a little more, inviting him to touch me and ease my desire momentarily. "Good, because it'll still have to be quick."

His reply comes in the form of his fingers dancing over my throbbing nub as we pull onto his parents' street. I draw in a sharp breath at his touch, a hollowness inside me begging to be filled.

River parks in front of the house and we walk as casually as we can to the front entrance. He unlocks the door and quickly enters the alarm code when we go inside. No sooner than he shut the door does he grab me forcefully by my hair, making my scalp burn in the best way. I let out a yelp as he drags me by my sandy locks into his dad's office while unbuttoning his shirt with the other hand. He shoves the door open with so much force that it hits the wall and bounces back, latching behind us.

My body is shoved against a bookshelf, causing it to rattle. Something falls to the floor, but I don't see what it is because River's mouth crashes hungrily into mine, hot with desperate need. He bites my lower lip as he rubs his fingers along my wetness, singling out my clit and flicking it gently. I moan against his mouth.

"No safe word? 'Cause I'm about to fuck you up."

"Fuck me up," I beg. "Please."

His hand comes up around my throat, barely applying pressure. "Say it again."

"Please, River. Please fuck me. Please." I start unfastening his belt and pants. "I need you inside me."

He licks his lips. "I fucking love it when you beg."

"I love when you fuck me."

The pressure on my throat increases as he pulls me away from the shelves, digging his fingers into the tender flesh of my upper arm. When he lets go, he grabs my hair again, whipping my body around so I'm facing away from him. He presses against me, his hard cock throbbing against my ass through his gaping pants. Instinctively, I push back against him, wishing I could absorb his cock inside me.

But River is the one in control, just the way I like it. Using his arm, he shoves things off his father's desk to the floor. I imagine the papers are important government documents being pushed away, falling to the floor like useless fodder. A half-full coffee mug. Keyboard and mouse. Pens and sticky notes. All discarded to the floor so that River can shove me face first onto his dad's desk.

He takes both my wrists in one hand as he pulls his belt through the loops on his pants. The ache inside me grows tenfold and I let out a breathy sigh. My body relaxes as he wraps the leather around my wrists and tugs it tight. My dress lifts and almost immediately my ass cheeks are met with a hard slap.

I cry out, a mixture of pleasure and pain. Pleasure from the pain.

"Tell me what you want, Em," River growls.

"Fuck me, please. I need you inside me. Hard. Deep as you can go. Make it hurt so fucking good." I can't see him from the angle I'm bent but I can tell he's kneeling, spreading my legs. He tugs my hips toward him, his fingers kneading into my supple skin.

River's tongue takes one swipe along the length of my vagina before locking his mouth onto my most sensitive spot. I moan, letting out a constant steady sound as he slips his fingers inside my heat, thrusting them deep. My body is reacting instantly, an orgasm building in my center, rising up like a volcano that's been dormant for a decade, exploding, spreading ecstasy throughout my body, stretching to my limbs.

I don't think I have ever come so quickly in my life.

"Oh, God, don't stop. Please. Please. Don't." I'm muttering nonsense but that's what he does to me.

"Shut the fuck up," he says, pulling his mouth from my clit. He tugs on the belt holding my arms in place. "You want me to fuck you or not?"

I whimper, my orgasm fading away while my body still longs for more. "Yes, please."

River leans over my back so he can see my face. "What?"

I can feel his rock-hard shaft resting between my ass cheeks. "Fuck me, please. Fuck me hard, babe."

He kisses the tip of my nose. "Keep begging like a whore."

"Please, please, please," I say as he straightens, lining his dick up with my entrance. He runs the head between my wet lower lips, pressing it against my sensitive clit. "Please put it in," I beg. "Please, I need it."

He lets out a low growl and smacks my ass again. I know he wants to be inside me as much, if not more, than I want it. "What do you need, Emma?" He rubs the sting of his slap away.

"I need you inside me."

I barely have the words out of my mouth before he plunges deep inside me, hitting the deepest point he can with one thrust.

I yell out, guttural and animalistic and laced with oh-so-much fucking ecstasy. He hammers into me, deep, hard, and fast just like I requested. My body surrenders to him, eager to let him take me in any way he wants.

The tension in my body releases. All fear and worry are washed away in a sea of sublime sensations that I only experience when I am getting fucked by River. He's stretching my body to make room for him, owning me, taking me for himself. And I love it. I love listening to his grunts and the sounds of our heated, slick skin slapping together. I love the way his strong hands grip onto my body like if he lets go, I might fade away. I love the way he's the only one who can make me feel this good. I don't ever want it to end, and I never want to be apart from him.

He's fucking me into oblivion. My mouth can only form two phrases: "Don't stop," and "So good," which entirely sum up the way I feel when his dick is inside me. I keep repeating the same things over and over, my way of praising and thanking him for doing what he does to me.

I'm so fucking high on dick right now and I never want to come down.

But like all good things, this too must end.

I'm suddenly empty and his hand rips into my hair pulling me off the desk. The blood drains from my head from the quick motion as I struggle to stand. River doesn't help. He's already let go of me while he continues to jack his cock, not even looking at me as I fall to the floor. Initially, I land on my ass, but the momentum forces me back and I end up on my still secured arms.

Looking up, I watch River grunt as he blows his load onto his dad's desk.

He drops his semi-erect dick, finished. "Fuck!" He screams the word, startling me. "Wish I could be here to see his face when he comes in here."

Chuckling, he looks down at me. "Sorry." He helps me up, turns me around and starts loosening the belt from around my wrists. "You okay?"

"For now."

"For now?"

I face him, a teasing grin on my face. "You said you were gonna fuck me up but all you did was fuck me."

He laughs, his head falling back. "Who said I was done?" His hands come around my waist, pulling me close to him. "We're just pausing for now." Our lips meet in a soft kiss.

Chapter Twenty-Nine

Emma

River starts throwing our clothes into the suitcase we brought with us from home while I go into the bathroom attached to his bedroom to clean myself up. While I wait for the water to warm up in the sink, I pull back the shower curtain and gather our hygiene supplies and set them on the counter. After wetting a clean washcloth, I press it between my legs, reveling in the warm feeling it puts on my freshly abused skin. That may not have been the hottest fuck session we've ever had, but he definitely put it in the top ten when he jacked off on his dad's desk. I feel like we'll be talking about that for the rest of our lives.

After washing my face, I quickly reapply my moisturizer before opening the bathroom door. I place my shampoo, conditioner, body wash, and River's three-in-one bottle of man soap into my arms and step into the bedroom. "These are still a little wet from this morning. Maybe we need a grocery sack—"

I stop talking because Wes's suit wearing assistant is standing in River's bedroom. "Why are you in here?"

He grins at me. "Because it seems no one else could handle the simple assignment they were given. So, now, it's up to me to take care of the problem."

Ice replaces the blood in my veins. I feel lightheaded. My mouth is dry. "River!" I yell, but my voice sounds like it's coming from another room.

The brooding man looks down to the floor. "Him?"

I lean forward a hair, discovering River lying on the floor beside the bed. He's on his stomach, shirtless. His eyes are open and unfocused. I don't see blood. I watch for the rise and fall of his breaths.

"You're welcome for letting you guys finish fucking for the last time." The man chuckles. I notice there's nothing in his hands, leaving me to conclude he hit River in some way, and that he is likely not dead. "Kinda cool I get a two for one deal for my trouble. We'll get top dollar for his tight, virgin asshole."

I'm not understanding what he's talking about. I'm really not even listening. My mind has turned off the external and is considering my fight or flight options.

There are few in either category, especially since he is standing between me and the bedroom door.

In one swift motion, I throw the shampoo bottles at him and go back into the bathroom, shutting and locking it behind me. I quickly glance around the bathroom to see what I can use for a weapon since the window is about six feet above the floor and only opens about three inches to let the steam out. Not to mention I'm on the second floor. I grab the first thing I see when I hear the man beating on the bathroom door.

It doesn't even take him a minute to kick the door in. His size fills the frame and he's unimpressed by me holding the shower curtain rod with the curtain still attached. "What are you gonna do, Emma?"

I have no idea, but I'm not giving in that easily. Using all of the strength I have, I lunge at him, hitting him in the chest with the end of the shower curtain rod.

He lets out an *oof* sound, grabbing the pole in one hand and jerking it away from me. Chuckling, he shakes his head. "Just stop. There's no point in fighting this. It could've just been you, but now it's your cousin too. That's how badly he wants you out of the picture. He's willing to sell his son too." He shrugs as he tosses the shower curtain rod onto the bed behind him. "C'mon. I'll even let you guys be in the same room for the first few days."

My back is to the wall as I absorb what this man is saying. *He* wants me out of the picture. *He* is willing to sell his son.

What in the actual fuck?

In all the years of Wes spewing bullshit about family values and the importance of upholding traditional marriage between a man and woman, I never expected that he would be so threatened by *me* that he would want me kidnapped and sold into sex slavery just to protect his image. And now River too? Was it some sort of publicity stunt? Is it an election year? Boohoo, vote for me, my son and niece have been kidnapped.

My hand covers my mouth as tears blur my vision. "River's alive?"

"Just a taser, buttercup. Followed up with an injectable cocktail. Which I'll use on you if you try to fight me again."

I shake my head. "Please, no. Whatever he's paying you, we will pay you more. And you can take him. Take Wes." If I can just keep him talking long enough until River wakes up, I'm sure together we can come up with something to get out of this.

He lets out a haughty belly laugh. "Oh, sweet Jesus. No one wants that. They want young, pretty, tight things."

"You don't know that."

"I do know that. I've been in this business long enough to know what I'm talking about."

I nod. "Right. The younger the better."

He cocks his head. "Exactly. Now, should we stop and pick up Cora on our way, or are you just gonna come with me without any more bullshit?"

His words are like a punch in the soul. "No," I say quickly. "She didn't do anything. Leave her out of this."

"She's pretty like you," he says. "Starting to fill out in the chest. Hips getting a little curve to them. That's the high dollar shit right there."

My head and hands shake violently. Never in a million years. "Okay, okay. I won't fight. Just leave her alone."

He steps into the bathroom, closing the distance between us in two wide steps. When he's close enough, I can smell him. It's the smell from that room I was in. Musty, dirty, laced with cigarette smoke. It's the same smell as the car I got into when I escaped. It's the scent that wafted through the door when he came to the house the other day, when I walked past him and Wes after the funeral.

Never in my life have I regretted anything more than not realizing what that smell was. If I had made the connection sooner, maybe I wouldn't be giving up my life right now so that Cora could stay untouched.

He tucks a lock of my hair behind my ear. "Do we have an understanding?"

It's over. Even if Wes and Megan walked in right now, it would still be over. This was all Wes's doing and even if she tried, Megan couldn't stop him.

I nod, feeling myself slipping away like I did when I was in that room.

He takes my arm, gently leading me from the bathroom. River hasn't moved, but this time I can see his back rise with breath and, I don't know why, but it's like a spring of hope comes alive in me.

The sound of metal clanging together pulls me back to reality as the man pulls my hands in front of me. He secures my wrists with metal handcuffs, muttering something about, "This isn't going down like it did last time."

River blinks.

I'm not sure what that means. I'm not sure if he's faking being incapacitated or if he's still able to blink with whatever he was given. But he's breathing and he blinked. It's the only hope I have left.

The man grabs my arm again, tugging me toward the hallway. "C'mon."

"What about him?" I ask.

"I'm gonna come back in. He's not going anywhere."

I look over my shoulder at River, not trusting this man whatsoever. I wholly believe it's the last time I will ever see him.

He blinks again.

And I just know he's telling me it's okay. That he's okay. That he's going to do something to save us both. I believe with every fiber of my being that River has a plan.

Tears burn my eyes again as I step into the hallway, the man leading me toward the stairs.

"We'll go slow so you don't fall. Your balance will be off with being handcuffed."

I'm thinking sarcastically how gentlemanly of him to warn me as I glance back one last time, hoping to see River coming toward us with a baseball bat or something. Then I hear a crack of lightning, a firework, an atomic bomb. Something bone shatteringly loud.

The man beside me gasps and before I can look at him, he's falling down the stairs and taking me with him. The fall seems to go on and on and my body is crushed by him as we tumble. When we finally hit the bottom of the stairs, he lands face down on top of me with his torso horizontal across my supine body. My arms hurt, gut wrenching pain ripping through them, but my mind is focused elsewhere.

My eyes immediately lift to the top of the stairs, expecting to see River there, my savior. Our savior. But he isn't there.

"Are you okay?" Jordyn stands over me looking down. "Get this man off her, Brody. He's bleeding all over."

Brody appears and pulls the man off me, turning him on his back. The release of the pressure of him on top of me causes new pain to radiate from my handcuffed arms that lay at an odd angle on top of me. I don't care about me right now. I'm okay. River needs help.

"He did something to River," I say. "He's unconscious or something upstairs. I don't know." When Brody helps me sit up, I realize I can't move my arms at all. I look down to see my midsection covered with blood and my dress lifted, making it obvious I'm not wearing underwear. "Did you shoot him?" I stare at the lump of evil on the floor beside me while trying to move to cover myself up some. "Is he dead?"

Jordyn lifts the gun in her hand as she kneels to pull down my dress, careful not to touch the blood. "He will be if he moves."

"I'll go check on River," Brody says, darting up the stairs two at a time.

"Yeah, babe," Jordyn says. "I got this."

I stare at my thin, fragile-looking younger cousin. "I didn't know you had a gun."

She nods. "We always have a gun. Concealed carry. Best investment we ever made."

I hear sirens in the distance, the pain in my arms registering again. "Did you call the police?"

For a moment, Jordyn looks lost. "We were hoping they would get here before..."

Before she had to use her gun. "It was Uncle Wes."

She sucks in her lips. "I wish I was surprised."

"Why are you here?"

Jordyn's face contorts with emotion, her eyes glued to the man on the floor. "When we got to the church, I heard your dad saying that you guys came here. And on the way back from the cemetery, we were behind that guy who Uncle Wes kept talking to and saw him turn off this way and I just had a really bad feeling." She meets my eyes. "I think I killed him."

I look over at the man in the suit, blood spilling from his gut. Together, Jordyn and I watch for him to breathe like I watched River minutes ago, but this time there's no movement.

Brody appears at the top of the stairs. He's holding River up, helping him to walk.

"Emma," River says.

A dam inside me breaks and I start crying, sobbing really. I can't move. I can't get up from the floor. I can't cover my face. I can't wipe my leaking nose. All I can do is sit on the floor in hysterics while Brody slowly brings River to me.

"Help her," River says. His voice is barely audible, his eyes heavy. He leans against the wall when he reaches the bottom of the stairs and closes his eyes, like he is utterly exhausted and can't continue.

Brody steps behind me to help me stand, grabbing my biceps on each arm. Blinding, white hot pain surges through me and everything goes dark for a moment. "Okay, okay," he says. "We'll just leave you here."

"River," Jordyn says. "Sit down before you fall over." His eyes flutter open but it's like he doesn't see us. Jordyn goes to him, holding the gun out toward Brody. "Take this."

Brody steps back, his arms extended on either side of him. "I'm not touching that thing." He nods his head to the side. "Go set it down somewhere. I'll help him."

"What's wrong with him?" I'm unable to take my eyes off River.

"Must've gave him something." Brody helps River to the floor, and I recall the man saying something about an injectable cocktail.

River's head flops forward, causing me to choke up a new sob. "He said he was going to take Cora too."

Jordyn walks past me to the front door. When she opens it, I remember arriving not that long ago. River hadn't locked the door or reset the alarm. But I doubt that would've even made a difference. Wes had probably given the man a key and the alarm code and was probably sitting at Noni's reception right now thinking all his problems were being handled while he enjoys some mostaccioli and fried chicken.

CHAPTER THIRTY

River

When I decided to fuck Emma on my dad's desk, I definitely wasn't anticipating the entire house turning into a crime scene and having to explain to the police several times that it was my ejaculate on my dad's desk and had nothing to do with what happened.

And as if that alone wasn't embarrassing enough, I disregarded the fact that there are cameras in the house. Including in my dad's office. So now that everything had unfolded like it had, I was questioned about "fornicating with my cousin in the senator's office" like they were trying to solve a game of Clue.

Uncle Chris and Aunt Christy came to the hospital. They went back and forth between mine and Emma's rooms. Emma has fractures in both of her arms from falling down the stairs. Other than that, she was a little banged up but physically fine. I am also fine. I'd been given just enough to incapacitate me. The paramedics reversed the effects with Narcan, but I still felt a little groggy and had to be under observation. We would both be released without needing any inpatient care.

"Where's my mom?" I asked Christy. Part of me wanted her here with me, but the majority of me knew this was outside her wheelhouse.

"Her and your dad are both being questioned." Her tone was gentle, like I often wished my mom's voice was. Christy's words were always clear, almost saccharine sounding when she spoke. I visualized her voice like a fine crystal vase.

By now, everyone knew my dad was behind everything.

I'm not surprised. I'm disappointed. I'm sad. I'm pissed. I'm especially pissed he will never get to go home and find his would be grandchildren dried and crusted all over his oversized desk.

The nurse is going over my discharge papers with me when my dad's picture on the TV screen catches my eye. I reach for the remote to unmute the sound.

"...questioned regarding the attempted kidnapping of his son and niece. This comes just weeks after the same niece was kidnapped and then later recovered after the vehicle her captor was driving was involved in a motor vehicle accident in rural Mayville, Missouri."

"I'm changing my last name and getting the hell out of Illinois," I tell the nurse with a grin.

She gives me a sympathetic smile.

"Emma's my girlfriend. She's my stepcousin too, but we're not blood. She's my girlfriend and I don't care who knows it."

"Way to own your truth," Detective Morgan says from the door. "I like it."

His presence makes me feel lighter. "I like it too."

"Do you have any questions?" the nurse asks me.

Muting the TV again, I shake my head. "Am I free to go to Emma's room now?"

"You're free to go," she says as she walks out.

I start to get out of bed, but Detective Morgan stops me.

"Let me just have a few minutes of your time, River."

Sighing, I stay put. "Okay."

"We've arrested your dad."

I feel nothing at the disclosure. It should have felt like freedom, but it doesn't because now I am left without a doubt that I never meant anything to my father.

"They're still talking with your mom." Detective Morgan places his hands on his hips. "Now, while I don't think your mom was in on this particular incident, she is going to be a key witness in some other investigations."

"Other investigations?"

He nods, saying nothing more.

When I enter Emma's room, she is asleep. Her parents sat in two hard-backed chairs along the wall. They look up at me and Chris starts to stand, offering me his chair. I shake my head and go around to the other side of the small emergency room bed. Without even glancing at her parents, I run the back of my hand along her cheek before kissing her softly on the lips. Her tongue darts out, wetting her lips as I pull away.

"They gave her something for the pain," Christy offers.

I nod. "How long will she have to wear the casts?"

"Probably about six weeks," Chris says.

I look at them, the concern on their face, and am reminded that my own parents never wore those expressions. "I always wished you guys were my parents."

Uncle Chris smiles. "I would have loved to have had you as a son, River." He clears his throat. "But that definitely would have made this a whole lot weirder."

"But not weird enough to try to have us kidnapped and sold into the sex trade," I say with a laugh, though I'm definitely not joking.

They don't say anything for a moment, and I resign that they are just as baffled by how this all unfolded as I am on some level.

Sticking with the idea that I don't give two shits what anyone thinks about me and Emma being together, I set my discharge papers on the counter behind me and sit on the bed, running the tips of my fingers along hers where they stick out of her casts.

The still silence allows the day to settle on me like an iron cloak, and I lay my head on Emma's shoulder. It's an awkward and uncomfortable position, but I need her.

"I would take a bullet for either of you kids," Chris says, his voice thick with emotion. "That's what a dad's supposed to do."

I let my emotions go, sobbing onto Emma's shoulder. Not just for what happened today or a few weeks ago, but for Noni who's gone, for my mom, for Jordyn who is going to have to live with knowing she killed a man, for Emma who will likely need therapy the rest of her life, and for myself. For the childhood I never got. For the parents who didn't care about me. For the future that would be forever warped by what my dad did.

"Hey," Emma whispers.

I lift my head to see her soft, sleepy eyes through my tears. "Hey."

I realize as I see my love reflected in her gaze that it's all going to be okay because this is what I wanted. This is what she wanted.

And now we got it.

CHAPTER THIRTY-ONE

Five Years Later

River

There's a crease of concentration between Emma's eyebrows, her tongue resting on her pouty lower lip as she slides my morning hard-on inside of her. Her sienna eyes find mine, dark lashes fluttering. She's naked, which is not how she usually sleeps, and that tells me she's probably been awake for a while. It is a big day after all.

Her rhythm is steady, grinding into my hips as she puts her hands on my shoulders. Her perfectly round breasts are inches from my face. I pull the pebbled nipple of one between my teeth and tug before wrapping my lips around her beautiful areola. Her skin is smooth and cool to the touch when I bring my hands to her hips. Groaning, she closes her eyes, her hair falling around her face. She looks erotic, like some sort of goddess.

I could stare at her forever.

Four years ago, we moved to Las Vegas. I was hired by the Las Vegas Metropolitan Police at a much better salary than what I was making at the prison in Illinois. While I am still a long way off from being a detective, I'm on the right path. With any luck, I will get a promotion in the next few months.

Emma got a part time job working at an outreach center for human trafficking awareness shortly after we arrived. It was good to see her feel like what she was doing mattered. Not that her other job hadn't, this one just meant more to her now.

"Oh, fuck," she whispers.

I grip her hips as she grinds against my pelvic bone. I can feel the walls inside her hug my cock, telling me she's about to peak. Sometimes, Emma likes having complete and total control over sex. I feel like a prop when she does this. Like I'm being used for her pleasure. And I am one hundred percent here for it. She doesn't climb on my dick when I'm still asleep for me. It's all for her.

One of her kinks for years had been being used. Being controlled by me. After what happened five years ago, we were both so traumatized from it that our sex life started to fall apart. It felt wrong to be rough and commanding with her after all that. I feared stirring up some dormant memory. But as I talked about it with my therapist, he pointed out to me that if Emma liked it before, then she probably still would. He said it would remind her of who she was before what happened.

He was right.

Emma shudders on top of me, muttering to herself as she rides out her orgasm. I take each of her nipples between my fingers and squeeze, causing her to convulse harder. When she drops her chin to her chest, I know she's spent and it's my turn.

Sitting up, I flip her onto her back and bring my face between her thighs. I run my tongue along her heated skin, licking and sucking in every sweet drop of her wetness that I can, being sure to tease her aroused nub as I do. Her back arches, my face pressing deeper against her as her thighs grip the sides of my head.

"Yes, please," she begs, wanting to come again already.

Not yet.

I rise to my knees, grabbing her legs just below the knee and jerking her closer to me. Her legs spread wide, inviting me inside her, as soon as I let go. With precise effort, I push the throbbing head of my dick against her clit and watch her eyes flutter. Fisting my length, I stroke it a few times while I contemplate what position to put her in.

Emma's hand reaches out toward my chest like she wants to touch me. I lean forward and she runs her fingers down my front while I lock my mouth on hers. Our tongues press together as she grips my hips with her hands and wraps her thighs around me, desperate for me to enter her.

"You're a needy little bitch in the morning," I hiss at her.

She whimpers as I continue to tease her. "Please, baby."

I lift one of her legs to my shoulder, seeing her back arch as I do. Smirking, I know she thinks I'm about to give her what she wants. And she's right, but first I have to twist her a little to her side and then move my legs so they're on either side of the leg that still lies on the bed. Once I have her scissored and stuck with no way out, I line my cock up with her pleading, wet pussy.

"Do you deserve this, Emma?" I ask casually, like I'm offering her an ice cream cone.

"No, but please, I need it."

My smile comes naturally. "You don't need it." I chuckle. "You want it."

"I want you to give it to me." Her voice changes. "Kinda quickly, actually. We need to start getting ready soon."

I roll my neck. "Sounds like a dilemma. Give Emma the dick or pick up my mom at the airport."

"Hurry up and we can do both."

I grab a fistful of her hair, jerking her head back as I slide inside her, savoring her warmth like it's the first time all over again. I will never tire of the way her body holds mine, the way we fit together, linked forever by our hearts.

Emma loves this position. My personal favorite is her bent over literally anything so I can smack her ass and pull her hair more easily. She likes it this way because I can get deeper, hitting her guts, as she says.

"I get completely lost in the feeling of it," she told me once. "I forget everything else except me and you."

Is it the best coping mechanism? Nah. But I like getting lost inside her; my mind is numb in the comfort zone of her body. Blowing a nut inside her is just an added perk.

After quick showers, we leave our quaint one-bedroom apartment in the Summerlin neighborhood of the city. We love it here. There are always things to do, and I don't mean gambling or strippers. Emma loves going to the farmers' market and the many festivals and fairs that we never experienced growing up in a small town. Within driving distance, there are places to hike, go for bike rides, and rent ATVs.

Plus, we can be ourselves. When people ask how we met, we tell the truth. We explain how my aunt married Emma's dad, technically making us stepcousins. For the most part, people seem pretty chill about it. Maybe that's just how they act in front of us, but we don't care.

After my dad's arrest, his bank accounts were frozen for almost a year. Luckily, for my mom's sake, my dad had kept their joint checking account clean, and eventually she got access to that back. Then a few months later, she was given back their joint savings. When she got that money, she gave us the funds to move to Vegas. We were only three months from our financial goal of being able to move. Her help made it possible to go sooner and with more cushion.

My dad is still locked up. Wes McIntyre was indicted on multiple charges over the year following his arrest. Fraud, mismanaging campaign funds, kidnapping, soliciting, wire fraud. The one that really got me though, the one that put everything into perspective, was possession of child pornography.

After that, Emma told me what she had learned about kids dying because of what was done to them, and her need to save even just one child from that horrible life sentence.

She didn't have to say it, but I know we both wondered the same thing.

Had my dad been guilty of *that* too?

Emma

Megan appears fresh faced and rested when we spot her in the airport. She smiles at us, her eyes glossed over. But now they're glossed over with tears instead of drunkenness.

It's just shy of five years since Megan went to rehab for the last time. It's the longest she's been sober since she was in her teens. It's an amazing accomplishment that no one has taken lightly. In addition to her sobriety, she has been in therapy, weeding through all the bullshit Wes bestowed on her for twenty-five years. Once a month, River joins her sessions on a video call. He gets so emotional afterward that it's the only time I wish we were still living in Illinois so they could hug each other and maybe make up for some of the time that was wasted in his youth.

She's visited us a few times a year since we moved. After selling River's childhood home and moving in with Grammy, she said she felt like a teenager just beginning her life. Eventually she got a job as a receptionist at the Thomas City Animal Hospital to fill her days. I'd been surprised when Christy told me it was the first job Megan ever had.

The three of us hugged in the airport. River's fair cheeks flushed with emotion. He was proud of his mom but at the same time he wished she'd been able to get her act together sooner. His parents were divorced now, Megan assuming her maiden name in the settlement.

"I'm so happy I get to be here this weekend!" Megan says. "So many reasons to celebrate."

Last night, my parents arrived with Cora and Wyatt. They'd rented a car and went to their hotel, so I haven't seen them yet. Eli was surprisingly in college and his finals were next week. No one had expected that would be the route he would go after high school, but when college recruiters started showing up at his football games his sophomore year, he'd shrugged and said, "Beats going to the army." Now he has hopes of being in the NFL.

"We're glad you're here too, Mom," River says as we make our way to the baggage claim.

This weekend we will celebrate several things. River and I turned twenty-nine a few weeks back, which also marked another anniversary. About a year after we moved to Vegas, we got married in a chapel on the Las Vegas strip on our twenty-sixth birthday. We didn't tell anyone beforehand, though we definitely planned it out. I researched chapels for months, choosing the one I liked the best, and that did *not* have an Elvis Presley impersonator on hand to marry us. I wore a simple white cotton sundress with a tiny veil while River looked dapper in a grey suit. We paid extra for professional photos and regretted nothing.

But the biggest cause for celebration was my latest accomplishment. I had completed my graduate degree in social work and the graduation ceremony was this afternoon. I've been working part time as an advocate with a nationwide anti-trafficking organization since we arrived in Vegas. Earning my degree was going to allow me to work directly with victims to help them process their trauma. It was exciting and overwhelming and scary all at once. But I was up for the challenge. I'd been waiting for the challenge.

My phone vibrated in my back pocket as River drove us to the restaurant to meet my family for brunch before we headed to the graduation. Reaching behind me, I tugged my phone from my back pocket and looked at the screen. "Christy says they're running a few minutes late."

Megan laughs lightly from the backseat. "What do you wanna bet Cora is having some type of outfit or hair and makeup malfunction?"

For the next several minutes, Megan tells us about how high-maintenance Cora has become, noting she is nothing like I was at that age. Hearing Megan talk about Cora like she knows her, like they are close and have a relationship, warms my heart. It's a testament to her sobriety and how she is embracing life as it is now.

We walked into the restaurant, River and I holding hands, Megan following a few steps behind. It's a traditional restaurant, nothing too fancy, decorated in vintage southwestern décor.

River steps up to the hostess stand and smiles. "We have a reservation."

The hostess looks down at the paper in front of her. "Name?"

"Novak," he says. "River Novak."

I'm not sure I'll ever get used to him having my last name, but I love it either way.

"I'm gonna use the restroom really quick," Megan says as she walks away.

River moves close to me, his hand sliding around the small of my back as he pulls me close. I lean against his sturdy form, pressing a kiss onto his collarbone.

"Who ever thought this would be our life?" he asked quietly.

It's something we reflect on from time to time. For so many years, we told ourselves we were wrong for feeling the way we do. That our family would never accept us. That the world would see us as sick and twisted, forgetting that we were just two kids whose friendship brought together a couple who formed a bond.

All the times when we pushed one another away. The times we purposely hurt each other. The times we reminded each other, "This is what you wanted," when our feelings bubbled over because *we* were impossible. Something that would never, ever work.

But we had worked. We took a chance and made our dreams come true.

It was all for something.

"This is what you wanted," I say as I spot my family coming through the door of the restaurant.

River smiles at me, squeezing me close one last time before I pull away to greet my parents. "It's all I ever wanted."

Thank You

Whew.

This book would not have been possible without the support of Carrie and Jessica. When I told them about Emma and River, they were all in. They couldn't wait to read it. When I worried that it strayed too far from what I've written before, and maybe a little too much on the dark side, they quieted my fears, assuring me people would want to read this book. And my BFF Shawna, who was the first to ever read one of my spicy scenes and gave it five red chili peppers (that scene is actually in another book!).

I also am forever grateful to my kidlings who will never ever in a million years read this book because, "Ew, Mom. Stop talking about that." Even so, they are so supportive and love to see me achieving my goals and making my dreams come true. My hard work over the years has helped them understand that no dream is impossible. My daughters sometimes help me out at events which can be stressful and crazy! I've had a few events that I would never have survived without them! So grateful to have them.

Thank you to Devin McCain with Studio 5 Twenty-Five for the gorgeous cover art! When I say she nailed it for me, she really did. Devin asked what I had in mind for the cover, and I told her, "Dark but with some bright flowers." Specific but still pretty vague. And a big, big thank you to Ramona Mihai for saving this book when the original editor was unable to complete the project. I messaged her in a moment of panic, and she was calm, which calmed me, and told me she could accommodate my timeline. Without her flexibility, this book would have been published on time.

I also can't forget to thank my ARC readers who have made my author heart soar with their reviews. This book is such a leap from what I've published previously. I have lost sleep over my reservations, but seeing this book being shared on social media by people who love it as much as I do, has cancelled all those reservations.

And thank you, my dear reader. Thank you for being a dark romance girlie (or guy!). Thank you for not turning your nose up at stepcousins to lovers. Thank you for giving my story a chance. Whether this is the first book of mine that you've read or you've read them all, I appreciate you supporting my dreams.

Much love,

Sarah

About the Author

 Sarah Dawson Powell is a multi-genre author who was born and raised in the suburbs of Chicago and currently lives in Central Illinois with her kidlings and too many cats. Her hobbies include doing laundry, washing dishes, petting cats, writing, reading, and talking to kids who have selective hearing. In her spare time, she enjoys working sixty hours a week, sleeping, and drinking lots of coffee. When she grows up, she wants to change the world.

Sarah has a bachelor's degree in sociology from the University of Illinois and has worked in social services since graduating. Her life hasn't always been peachy, but she's made the best of every situation. She hopes her readers take something away from her stories and loves to interact with them on social media.

visit my website & subscribe to my newsletter for sneak peeks at coming books and exclusive access to bonus material!
www.sarahdawsonpowell.com

 facebook.com/authorsarahdawsonpowell

 sarah_dawson_powell

 @sarahdawsonpowell